L. C. Trobr

THE ADVENTURE OF CHRISTOPHER COLUMIN

BOOKS BY SYLVIA THOMPSON

THE HOUNDS OF SPRING
THE BATTLE OF THE HORIZONS
CHARIOT WHEELS
PORTRAIT BY CAROLINE
SUMMERS NIGHT
UNFINISHED SYMPHONY
BREAKFAST IN BED
A SILVER RATTLE
THIRD ACT IN VENICE
RECAPTURE THE MOON
THE ADVENTURE OF CHRISTOPHER COLUMIN

The Adventure of Christopher Columin

By

SYLVIA THOMPSON

BOSTON
LITTLE, BROWN AND COMPANY
1939

COPYRIGHT 1939, BY LITTLE, BROWN AND COMPANY

ALL RIGHTS RESERVED, INCLUDING THE RIGHT
TO REPRODUCE THIS BOOK OR PORTIONS
THEREOF IN ANY FORM

Published February 1939
Reprinted February 1939

THE ATLANTIC MONTHLY PRESS BOOKS
ARE PUBLISHED BY
LITTLE, BROWN AND COMPANY
IN ASSOCIATION WITH
THE ATLANTIC MONTHLY COMPANY

PRINTED IN THE UNITED STATES OF AMERICA

PROLOGUE

Chapter I

Christopher Columin sat at his breakfast table at 181 Maple Street, taking his first bite of crisp bacon at exactly twenty past eight.

Christopher lifted his coffee cup.

Alice, behind the coffeepot, said: "We have an extremely interesting lecture at the Club this afternoon." As she spoke she looked up from reading her mail. "A travel lecture!"

But although she looked at him, familiarity and lack of affection prevented her really seeing him. He said: "What lecture is it, dear?" and glanced back at her with a deference that was caused by his courtesy towards all women rather than by that set of negative sentiments which lay at the bottom of his heart labeled as "his love for his wife."

"A travel lecture," said Alice lightly. "A travel lecture, and by whom do you *think?*" Alice leaned forward. She had waved, smoky-brown hair, dressed carefully and covered by an invisible net; rather fine features, and grey eyes with well-cut brows and eyelids. Yet the whole face, pale in color, dry in texture, lacked precision of outline; as if, at some time, it had been softened, slightly melted from within, and then allowed to harden again.

Christopher could n't "think at all" by whom the lecture might be; which was exactly what Alice expected. So she revealed, giving a straight mild-beaming glance into Christopher's pince-nez, that the speaker this afternoon was no other than Hamnet Peabody.

He repeated "Hamnet Peabody" in exactly the tone she'd anticipated. For even Christopher knew all about the town's famous author, Miss Mary Peabody's nephew who had sprung into fame three years ago when his novel *Young and So Fair* had sold 120,000 copies in six months. Green Plains had accepted the fact that their celebrity should let himself be swept out on the tide of his success into a wider literary world than was offered him even by Mrs. Andrew James, who "wrote herself" and knew Alexander Woollcott; or by Mrs. Nantucket Lee, who had lived for years in Grasse, France, and stayed out in Taos with the Luhans, and wrote, at intervals, for the *Atlantic Monthly*. In fact, Green Plains, which had n't bothered about Hamnet Peabody while he was a nephew, behaved like a Roman Matron relinquishing her son when it gave him to Fame; drawing itself up and giving a series of Last Teas and Cocktails to speed him to Hollywood, where he was going — on his way around the globe — to supervise M-G-M's production of *Young and So Fair*.

Alice Columin, socially prominent and already, three years ago, Secretary of the Women's Club, and organizer of the Tuesday Discussions, had of course been one of the hostesses. She had given a tea on Monday, ending up with cocktails and sherry, and a dinner on Thursday — to which she not only had Hamnet Peabody himself and eight couples from Green Plains, but invited Thornton Wilder, whom she had met once in Chicago (and had a telegram from him, which she read aloud at dinner, "regretting" that he could not come).

So that now, on Hamnet Peabody's return, Alice Columin naturally felt thrilled. And Christopher remembered that farewell dinner well enough to be able to give a note of real interest to his "Well! — Hamnet Peabody!"

"What I was going to say was, dear, that as it's Saturday, I thought maybe you'd like to come to the lecture. And even if you don't care about all his talk of literary people and — and all that, maybe you'll be interested in the photographs he's taken. I hear they're perfectly beautiful. It seems he calls them 'My Camera Eye in Europe.' . . . And now, dear, if I'm ever to get through this morning, you mustn't keep me here!"

Chapter II

The Women's Club, built in the Colonial style, in a pleasing combination of maroon-red brick and white wood, presented a dignified portico to Egremont Avenue. And up to this portico, between two-fifty and three o'clock that Saturday afternoon, were driven, by their chauffeurs, the wealthier members of the Club; while the others, including Mrs. Jabish Peckett, the President, parked their own automobiles at the side of the sweep of drive.

Mrs. Jabish Peckett was the first to arrive. She tripped softly into the Clubhouse at twenty minutes past two, when Robert and Sally (the Club's colored servant and his wife) were dusting off the back row of the two hundred chairs in the lecture hall.

When they saw Mrs. Peckett, Sally beamed and Robert's face was a flashing smile coming out of a round sepia shadow. For that was how she made them feel.

Mrs. Peckett tripped across the lecture hall into the adjoining library where the sandwiches, cookies, and pastries for the tea were laid out on a buffet. Sally followed her.

"Schmidt's is bringin' de urns and ice coffee and cocktails at half-past three, Miz Peckett."

In the middle of the buffet table was a silver epergne filled with arum lilies and pink roses.

"Miz Columin brought these just before dinner. She come in and fixed them herself."

"Very nice," said Mrs. Peckett. "They look like a wedding."

"They certainly do, Miz Peckett!" The mere idea of a wedding made Sally beam again.

Mrs. Peckett went back into the lecture hall. The sun was streaming in through the six Colonial windows and the smell of the cedarwood, with which the hall was paneled, was pleasant. She went up to the platform, saw that there was ice water ready on the lecturer's table, and laid, on one of the two chairs, a paper with notes for her own introductory speech. While she was doing this, the door at the side of the platform opened and Alice Columin came in, wearing a mauve orchid in her mink coat, and followed by her husband.

Mrs. Peckett said: "Well, Alice, you happen to be punctual."

"Well, I hope I usually am, Mrs. Peckett . . . I brought Christopher — "

"Don't apologize, Alice. How d' you do, Mr. Columin?"

" — as it happens to be Saturday," Alice went on, looking around and deciding on which chair — somewhere over at the side of a row so he could slip out at the end . . .

"We'd be just as delighted to have Mr. Columin come, even if it *wasn't* Saturday," said Mrs. Peckett. She came down off the platform and shook his hand. When she looked upward at him, her mouse-quick softness and her bird-bright impudence were so engaging that Christopher felt less stiff in his shoulders and nervous in his wrists. (This stiffness and nervousness possessed him whenever he went out with Alice.) " — If I could ever persuade Jabish to come! . . . But I wouldn't dare to. He has an idea he might be bored!"

As she spoke, several members, preceded by their voices, came in at the far end of the hall, three of them advancing down the aisle towards Alice. Christopher stiffened again, put his left hand in his trouser's pocket, took it out again, and, when that didn't make him feel any easier, put it back once more. But "Come with me, Mr. Columin," Mrs. Peckett was saying, "you don't have to sit around here until three o'clock! And I've something special I want to consult you about — " And she led him, hurrying before him, into the library next door, and through the library across a lobby into a room about eight feet square that she said was "the office" — remarking incidentally: "I happen to be the President here." To which he replied respectfully that he certainly knew that. (For hadn't he known also that Alice had wanted nothing so much for the last ten years as to have Mrs. Peckett's position? — And had never been so cheerful as when Mrs. Peckett had pneumonia in November — or so badly in need of a trip to New York as when Mrs. Peckett recovered in time for Thanksgiving!)

Mrs. Peckett went to a small closet set in the wall next to a bookshelf containing chiefly volumes connected with the identification, distinction, or disturbance of human beings — such as *Who's Who,* the *Social Register,* and several telephone directories. From the closet she produced a crystal decanter and two brandy glasses, remarking that since Mr. Columin had been so kind as to come, the least she could do was to ask him to drink to the success of the lecture. "Also," she said, in her little voice that had most musical notes in it, "I wish, as I said, to have your opinion upon this brandy, for I have heard you are something of a connoisseur in the matter of wines."

Christopher, outwardly shy, inwardly charmed, said that he could n't pretend to great knowledge in these matters; that indeed he was n't much of a drinker. The sharp little glance that Mrs. Peckett gave him meant (though he could n't know it) that anyone could tell this was true; for behind his pince-nez Christopher had clear eyes — a pair of bright hazel, brown-lashed eyes — and a figure that was unlike most of his forty-seven-year-old contemporaries, being flat-stomached and narrow-hipped and setting off his English suiting so well that though he was a hero (at this period) to no one else, he had earned an unfeigned admiration from his tailor in Boston.

"Just the same," said Mrs. Peckett, unstopping the decanter and pouring into the bottom of each big bubble-thin glass, "it is n't the drinkers that are connoisseurs. Just," she added most unexpectedly, "as it 's the lecherers who know least about love." She stoppered the bottle. Christopher made no reply. He was almost as unused to unexpected remarks as he was to this kind warm inconsequent friendliness. She handed him his glass. "Perhaps it 's because you have some French blood in you — that gives you a kind of kinship with the Grape. Lacaze was your grandfather's name, was n't it?"

"Yes, Mrs. Peckett." She seemed to know everything. He lifted his glass and sniffed. The smell was good enough — that faint pungent odor of violets. She sipped hers, and seeing her sip he sipped too.

"How is it, Mr. Columin?"

The taste was of grape: grape "to the nth," Christopher thought. A fine brandy; very fine! (In fact his grandfather Lacaze *had* taught him a little on the subject when he used to stay with them, the old Lacazes, in the brownstone house on Murray Hill.)

"It 's wonderful, Mrs. Peckett!"

She nodded; smiled; kept her glance on him a second longer than he realized. "We ought to drink a toast."

"So we should, Mrs. Peckett."

"What then —"

"Your own health, Mrs. Peckett — the President's health!" There was such a flicker of cordiality in Christopher's face that it almost became a smile. He had a pale, grave face with fine but nervous features.

"Thank you — Mr. Columin. And now —" There was a knock at the door. A flustered girl said: "Oh, Mrs. *Peckett*, the Lecturer has *arrived!*"

"Put him in charge of Mrs. Columin."

"Yes, Mrs. Peckett. But —"

"But what, dear?"

"When will you be coming?"

"What is the time, dear?"

The girl looked at her wrist watch. "Ten minutes to three, Mrs. Peckett."

"So I imagined, dear. Now go, and I'll be along in a moment. And now," Mrs. Peckett went on, "what about another toast? Why shouldn't I drink *your* health?" The brandy seemed to be bringing out the Robin in her and effacing the Mouse. She chirruped: "Your health and happiness — or shall we say your *fortune*, Christopher Columin!" She raised her glass and looked somewhat as if she were at some sort of elfin antic with a soap bubble as large as her own head. And then before he could thank her she was proposing another toast: "And now as we're on the job, what about the lecturer — the lecturer of this afternoon. What about our Celebrated Lecturer —"

"Hamnet Peabody!" said Christopher, and by this

time he had had enough sips for a tone to get into his voice that was extraordinary for Christopher — extraordinary, because the way in which he pronounced "Hamnet Peabody" made that Celebrity's name seem (however unintentionally) absurd.

And when his hostess, once more tossing up her bubble, repeated "Hamnet Peabody," it was exactly as if Christopher's own tone had been seized by one of those echoes that emphasize any special or peculiar inflection. And, if he had n't begun to be affected by the vague gayety that emanated from Mrs. Peckett, and even a little amused by his situation out here in the office "quaffing" with the President, he would have been ashamed of that tone. For it had never once occurred to him that an author — especially of a successful book — could be absurd.

"And *now*," said Mrs. Peckett, and went to a mirror and pulled her little beaver toque down, and patted the violets that were pinned on the lapel of her beaver jacket . . . Christopher gulped the rest of his brandy. And as he followed the President back across the lobby and through the library (that smelt of mayonnaise dressing) he had that agreeable sense of his bones becoming very gradually a system of central heating; and when they got into the lecture hall he was able to regard the seated ranks of women without shyness, as if they had been so many sea lions waiting for fish!

The fish was meanwhile near enough to stir their

whiskers and make them all lean forward with expectant bosoms and eager flippers.

Mrs. Peckett, having motioned Christopher to a chair at the end of a row, changed her expression and went up the hall and disappeared through a side door.

Within a minute she reëmerged, followed by Alice Columin, who looked excited, and the Lecturer. He followed Mrs. Peckett on to the platform with that air of false modesty habitually worn by celebrities to make others (as well as themselves) believe that they are not "spoiled" by their success.

Alice Columin sat down in the chair reserved for her in the middle of the front row. And Christopher, across from where he was sitting, four rows back, could observe how his wife also was lifting her head, for fish.

Mrs. Peckett meanwhile was saying in a series of musical little sentences that it was "a pleasure" and "an honor" to have Mr. Peabody with them this afternoon. She said "they had all read his book, of course." But now they were all just longing to know what Mr. Peabody had been doing *since;* because it was three years since he had "given us" *Young and So Fair* and since then, as they had read in the newspapers in a most interesting interview given by Mr. Peabody, "our author" — if she dared to call him that — had "made the world his playground." Here she paused for the clapping and rustling, turning to smile quickly at Mr. Peabody, who, without moving his head, turned his blue pale eyes and stretched the corners of his thin yet soft-lipped mouth, to smile back at her. "Mr. Peabody is going to tell us," she concluded, "about his travels, his work, and, we hope, about some of his play." Here she paused benignly while a series of flattering, faintly meaning little smiles showed among the audience and the Lecturer looked hard at the pointed tips of his shoes. "And now, Mr. Peabody—"

Mrs. Peckett sat down and the Lecturer stood up. The light from the Colonial windows fell on the fairness of his hair, the deep blueness of his suit, his tie, garnet red against the black shirt. He placed himself beside the table so that his notes that lay upon it were at his right hand. His left hung at his side and remained there during the next hour except for a recurrent gesture, when the arm would slightly swing out as if its hand, the fingers spread out downwards, prepared to catch the upward bounce of an invisible ball, then, discouraged, subsided, until the delicate prescience of another upcoming invisible bounce opened it again.

Hamnet Peabody's manner, as he began to speak, was diffident, but not unconscious of charm. He began at once by warning his audience that he wasn't going to give them any kind of "formal lecture," because he dared to assume that, back here in Green Plains, he was among friends! . . . In the murmurous pause that followed he lifted and looked at his right hand, and glanced for an intent second at the signet ring on the little finger; then in the next moment seemed to banish the hand from his sight and the signet ring from his thoughts and went on: "Not that I expect you, my — friends, to have the same strong warm recollection of me as I have of so many of you! Three years is a long time! And much water has passed under the bridge since I — " his glance fell for one second down on his notes — "sent out that exploring Dove — which was a Humble Manuscript, and saw it return to me, after many days, with — I'm going to be thoroughly vain and say it! — with a wreath of laurels in its beak!" Once more he paused. There were sounds of amusement and a faint scraping of chairs. He half turned his person towards the President, so that Christopher noticed his chin; and realized that it was the chin, rising straight up and flat without indentation, to the edge of the lower lip, which gave Peabody his haunting likeness to the Knave of Spades. (But Alice, in the front row, was noticing his brow, and the bright wave of hair that waved up and across from it, and finding the adjective "Shelleyan" in her mind.)

But now he turned again, having trustfully deposited that little smile with Mrs. Peckett. Mrs. Peckett noticed, and remembered noticing in the past, how when he smiled his upper lip had a way of clinging down softly to the lower, and then, when it did detach itself, rising timidly up his teeth, finally forming a little arch of which his nose was the — rather overwhelming — coping stone. The nose, Mrs. Peckett noted (returning his little smile), was a go-getter's nose — a strong, pointed, insensitive nose, with small nostrils. He hadn't been able to alter his nose, she thought. He might have dyed his fair eyelashes, thickened his figure, manicured his hands, and, she suspected, brightened his hair, but his nose *was Hamnet* — as surely as poor dear Christopher Columin's nose was *him;* a sweet, kind, straight nose, whose nostrils had a nice sensitive little quiver when he was secretly nervous, or when he inwardly wanted to laugh; a sweet, and rather strokable nose, classing him among those (blessedly) constituted by the Almighty for worldly failure; among those constitutionally averse to "going" and "getting," in our civilization that, alas, judged its members primarily by what they "went and got — "

Mrs. Peckett glanced toward the end of the fourth row and noticed that Christopher's expression was hidden by the gleam of his pince-nez; and that he was seated next to Miss Peabody, the Lecturer's aunt.

Miss Peabody smelled of roses. She did so because the rose was her favorite flower, and consequently a bottle of Attar of Roses was sent her every Christmas by an Austrian *Graf* whom she had "refused" when she was twenty-three. Miss Peabody was now fifty-six and the prettiness that had charmed the Austrian at Vevey thirty-three years ago was changed to a wintry but not unkindly dignity. She had a very small income, out of which she had often "helped" her nephew Hamnet, until three years ago; doing this for the sake of her dead brother, and not because she liked Hamnet himself.

Christopher knew her only slightly. She went out socially as little as he did. But he had an idea she had been at the nephew's farewell party three years ago; and he remembered seeing her once in the drugstore on the corner of Maple Street and Third, when he stopped there around six o'clock to have a sandwich (it was one August when Alice was at Bar Harbor) and Miss Peabody was just dismounting from her stool, having finished a soda. When she'd gone out, Jo, at the soda fountain, told him that Miss Peabody came there often at that hour; and Christopher had linked up this fact with an insinuation of Alice's that Mary Peabody had never had a cent to bless herself with "even *before* 1929." (Poverty *since* 1929 being in Alice's mind of the excusable sort — her own included. Her own meant Christopher going by trolley car to the office and a trip to Europe being out of the question, for her, more than once in two years.)

Now the warmth that had pervaded Christopher since his unexpected little scene with the President had been making him consider all the audience since he came in with liberated interest, Miss Peabody amongst them; while the Lecturer himself was producing in

Christopher symptoms such as inability to look long at the Lecturer without his mouth twitching, and a constriction in his throat. In an effort to dispel these symptoms, Christopher thought about his neighbor; about her pleasing fragrance, and about the fact that she had not excused herself when found supping at the soda fountain. (When he had mentioned this incident to Alice she had only said that "everybody knew that Mary Peabody was no relation at all to *the* Peabodys.")

Meanwhile Mary Peabody, who found her nephew even more unattractive as a Success than in the days when he was boastful and obscure, was listening to his description of places (these descriptions were much like colored postcards), and to his word portraits of other celebrities. But while he talked there was, evidently, rapt attention; and whenever he paused there were little exclamations and whispers expressing enjoyment and respect. And while Mary Peabody was reflecting that "swans may beget geese" (for her brother had been "a dear" and his wife, Milly, the gentlest, nicest . . .), she became aware that Mr. Columin, next to her, smelled faintly of brandy. This perception puzzled as well as pleased her. She knew Alice Columin; and could not imagine that she would let her husband drink brandy after luncheon on a day when they most certainly could not have had guests (on account of the lecture in the afternoon). And Mr. Columin would n't be likely to do anything his wife did n't like. (All Green Plains knew the story, years old now, of Christopher Columin buying himself a fishing boat and Alice going to her family in Philadelphia and refusing to come back until he sold it.) Her nephew was saying: —

"Last, and I certainly won't say it was *least*, in the European portions of my journeys, I went to Paris — " He got the titter he waited for.

Mrs. Peckett, without seeming to glance at her watch, noted that half the hour was gone. She would have no hesitation in stopping Hamnet at exactly four. She noted too that dear old Mrs. Cockspur was already asleep in the second row, that Alice Columin continued to look excited, and that her sort of look, the eyes a little glazed and prominent (the pulse probably quicker than usual), was on many faces: on Lilian Van Zoon's, on Angela Dane's. It also struck Mrs. Peckett afresh — though she had often observed it — how many of them had that doughnut look.

At this moment, at the end of the fourth row, the roses and the brandy were mingling. Mary Peabody, through her suppressed exasperation with the "Lecture," had become fidgety — so that her hands would not remain crossed in her lap but shifted and tapped and bent up, and by a series of little movements unwittingly got her handbag open (its clasp was already worn). And then the handbag, as it sloped slightly downward, began to disgorge, very gradually, while her glance was on the deep blue figure of her nephew, a thin purse of Italian leatherwork, a clean and folded pale pink linen handkerchief, a minute ivory elephant attached to a strand of purple silk, and a piece of oblong folded paper. . . . Christopher watched these things emerge, half hypnotized by their slow sliding toward the black-satin edge of Miss Peabody's knees. . . . He did n't like to interrupt her attention to the talk, so he just went on gazing down sideways; and now the handkerchief and the piece of paper had got ahead of the purse and the elephant, and, for what seemed interminable seconds, were neck and neck on that black-satin course — and then (though Christopher's money was on the handkerchief!) as they approached the turn of the knees, the oblong piece of paper seemed to take a spurt — slipped, slid, and was on the floor between Christopher's left black leather shoe and Miss Peabody's small right buckled slipper; and, lying face upward, its neat pale puce and white face returned Christopher's stare and revealed itself to be a check on the First National Bank of Boston, signed *Mary Peabody* and made out to *Hamnet Peabody*. Christopher recovered his sense of propriety before he could read the figures, and flushed the color of the check itself; and bent to pick it up while Miss Peabody, suddenly aware of her escaping possessions, grasped the handkerchief and the purse and caught the elephant in mid-air — and received the check. "Thank you *so* much . . . How foolish . . ." She flushed — gave him one of her small wintry uncertain smiles.

Christopher smiled back, equally uncertain, and intensely, chivalrously embarrassed at having seen (Mrs. Van Zoon, who was sitting directly in front of them, dressed in mink and brown velvet, turned round and said: "Ssh . . .") — having seen, Christopher was thinking, not merely into that modestly folded check, but *through* it, however inadvertently, into a quite private situation in Miss Peabody's life. For if poor Miss Peabody were, *once more,* writing checks to her nephew — ?

The nephew, up on the platform, was advancing through the final stages of his talk with an increased vitality; having thrown out the earlier anecdotes with charm, yet with the refined, slightly lackadaisical manner of a princess feeding carp, he then (since almost the time that Mrs. Peckett had secretly consulted her watch) faded out the princess — and approached the end of his lecture with the romantic and uplifted tenacity of Parsifal making for the Holy Grail. . . . The audience were responding to woodwind and brass; and took Hamnet's view of the Coronation in London ("*the little Queen*," the "*quiet-eyed young King*") with agreeably visceral emotion; and his account of "*the journey home . . . the wending westward at last,*" his visit to the *steerage,* "*where I saw the seed that would one day ripen among the golden corn of American Citizenship*" — swelling to his apostrophe of Green Plains — "*my city, your city — Our City*" — roused them to a kind of adipose ecstasy.

They were still clapping and breathing while Mrs. Peckett deftly expressed gratitude, appreciation, and interest, and then informed them that "during tea in the library Mr. Peabody would show any of them who were interested his photographs." "My Camera Eye," he murmured, his top lip lifted. His eyes shone. "Quite so. Yes," said Mrs. Peckett; and then, leaning down from the platform, asked Alice Columin if she would n't escort Mr. Peabody to tea.

In the library the warmth of the brandy had ebbed in Christopher and he had never felt more shy. He stood in a corner beside a marble bust on a pedestal and held the cup of tea handed him by the waitress from Schmidt's, and the plate on which the butler from Schmidt's had deposited a piece of cinnamon toast and a *foie gras* sandwich. On the other side of the room stood Peabody, so mobbed by all the ladies that Christopher could only see his gold-crested head, and, now and again, his black shirt, collar, and red tie. He saw Alice, too, her tricorn hat with its cock's feathers in the forefront of the scrum. But though she met his glance twice she showed no special sign of recognition. The President seemed to have vanished, and Miss Peabody, who had entered the room with him, was sitting in the embrasure of a window, chatting with another lady, and even Sally, helping behind the buffet, who had given him a friendly grin at first, was now busy with the urn.

Christopher wondered why he had come. In all his married life he'd never come inside Alice's Club; nor, in spite of one or two attempts to "make him take an interest in cultural things," had he let her involve him in her Tuesday Discussions. His resistance had n't needed to be very strong as Alice had n't supposed he would "get much" from them. Why then, for goodness' sake, had he come to-day? A kind of curiosity perhaps, to see a fellow who'd managed to make (so the boys said at the office) $50,000 out of one novel! (Christopher had once tried to read the novel; but had n't got much from it. Alice had told him it was very fine indeed.) Also — well, his curiosity had also been personal —

For Christopher was curious about people; and, behind his courteous shyness, ready to be excited, or amused or charmed, by them — his ideal would have been to keep meeting new people, but in an invisible cloak. For whenever he actually met strangers — whether at parties or in the trolley car going across town to his office — his eagerness to know more about them was counteracted by a feeling that his own personality was badly tailored, that his wits were n't polished, and that all his intellectual buttons needed sewing on.

Now he set down his cup and saucer on a low edge of the bookshelves behind him (he always found that a teacup detracted from social poise as surely as a wineglass increased it) and, cinnamon toast in hand, moved instinctively, as if for protection, towards the marble bust on its pedestal. He looked into the face; it had a domed marble brow, slightly protuberant blank eyes, a strong nose, a sweet, melancholy, carnal mouth. The self-indulgent, even weak chin was given elegance by a pointed beard. A pleasant fellow, Christopher considered; thoughtful, perhaps a bit disillusioned. But — pleasant. He wondered what he was doing in the library of the Women's Club. Christopher got a feeling that, in spite of his marble *sangfroid*, he was just as out of things here as himself. In fact the marble — which for most people stands for remoteness — did n't bother Christopher at all. (A simple and sincere attitude toward marble, whether in halls or statuary, is rare; Christopher had it; and it was later to affect his entire life.) However, unwarned of this, as he was of other and nearer influences on his future, Christopher — looking nothing more than a diffident, well-dressed, middle-aged man in pince-nez — continued to stand close to the bust eating first his cinnamon toast, then the *foie gras* sandwich. Then, as no one came near him, his awkwardness abated, and he felt gradually free to indulge in small idle thoughts. He contrasted his friend-the-Bust in this corner with the live head of Hamnet diagonally opposite. He tried to envisage Hamnet in marble. That draped-up mouth would n't chisel very well; and the eyes, though so shining, were small, and would seem insignificant above the not quite firm fullness of the cheeks! Christopher thought again about Miss Peabody's check; then about the other contents of her bag, which he felt were somehow pathetic. So unlike the idea her manner gave you. People were a lot more incalculable than the stock market.... His friend Johnny Cotton said: "People only act like themselves nine tenths of the time. The other tenth they act like the self they might have been — " Christopher started thinking about Johnny, who was out on the Coast now, being a cheerful failure at something or other; and Ellen, his wife, out there with him, seemingly more proud of each one of Johnny's failures and losses. But he had n't seen Johnny for a long while; even when he 'd been East. Alice had n't liked the Cottons.

Now Alice was coming towards him. "Here, Christopher, I want you." Christopher started, and went to her at once — "Christopher, I want you to come and meet Mr. Peabody. Mr. Peabody, this is my husband — he came specially for the lecture, did n't you, dear?"

"How do you do? My wife brought me along," said Christopher.

"But I remember you quite well, Mr. Columin. That perfectly delightful party at your home that Mrs. Columin and I have just been speaking about."

"I remember it too," said Christopher. "It was most pleasant." But before he could make another uninteresting remark Alice took him away from the Lecturer again. And when they were out of the press of women she said: —

"I don't think you have to stop any longer, dear. . . . And now, dear, you'd best run around to Ellman's, as it's Saturday and he's coming to dine tomorrow, only a few people I've asked — just a small intimate dinner — and order some champagne. I happen to remember that we don't have any in the house . . ."

"But do we have to give Mr. Peabody champagne?" Christopher asked, gently. For they seldom had it since the "depression."

Alice gave him a forbearing glance. "Well, dear, it would be rather strange if we were the *only* people that didn't give it! Considering that he has been entertained by the Best People everywhere . . ."

When Alice said this one of Christopher's momentary mild fits of obstinacy seized him. "And did they *all* give him champagne?"

"Why, yes, I — "

"Then maybe he'll have had enough? — "

They were standing now in the outer lobby beneath the Zorn portrait of Mrs. Cary Kimmins (the founder of the Club).

"Christopher," said Alice quietly and gently, "I've had a slight headache all day — "

Out on Egremont Avenue the Packard was waiting by the curb. Christopher nodded to his chauffeur and took a taxi down to Ellman's, where he ordered a case of champagne.

The social column of the *Herald* on Monday published a photograph of Hamnet Peabody, and a paragraph stating that "an informal dinner was given for him last night by Mrs. Christopher Columin at her home on Maple Street"; and that "the other guests were Mr. and Mrs. Philip Van Zoon, Mr. and Mrs. Ellsworth Kimmins, and Mrs. Nantucket Lee." In the *Evening Telegram* there was a special interview accorded to "Diana Devonshire" by Mrs. Columin herself, relating how Mrs. Columin had had the privilege of speeding Mr. Peabody on his departure three years ago, and now of welcoming him once more on his return. "Diana Devonshire" reported that Mrs. Columin had received her "in a simple black gown with touches of white, and pearls," and that she was "in her beautiful library, a very dignified room containing various antiques collected by Mrs. Columin herself." Mrs. Columin had said that Mr. Peabody's talk on last Saturday at the Women's Club had filled her with "*Wanderlust*." When asked if she intended going abroad again this year she had said: "No, I'm afraid not." But she had shown the interviewer an oil painting that she had bought in Naples, years ago, from a poor artist.

"Diana Devonshire," otherwise Mrs. Henry Green (who had two children at home with flu, and a husband without a job), did n't report that Mrs. Columin had kept her waiting an hour and a quarter — so that she'd sat in the beautiful library wondering if she'd get the interview written in time (no twenty-five dollars if she did n't). And wondering too if the children's temperatures were up again by now? . . . Nor that, when the interview was over, Mrs. Green stood outside the house on the sidewalk of Maple Street wondering if she should afford a taxi down to the *Telegram* offices to get her stuff written there, in time; and how a man came after her, out of the house, and said he knew she must be late, and he had his automobile here, and she must let him drive her wherever she wanted to be: and that he had turned out to be Mrs. Columin's husband. And that by the time they got to the *Telegram* offices she had told him about the children having grippe — and about Henry having no job.

Next afternoon — the same afternoon that the interview appeared (1500 words — twenty-five dollars, thank heaven!) — they called Mrs. Green from the *Telegram* offices and said they had a Western Union messenger there wanting her, and should they send him to her private address?

He arrived with a parcel of picture books for the children, and a couple of cowboy outfits (labeled "For Convalescents"), and a bottle of champagne.

Chapter III

A WEEK later Alice told Christopher that Hamnet Peabody was coming to stay. She told him this in the hall as he was fastening his overshoes before leaving the house in the morning. He looked up with a flushed face and said he was delighted. But as he did n't seem at all surprised Alice said: "Well, it 's wonderful, is n't it? Actually, Mrs. Lee had asked him to come to her, and Lilian Van Zoon kept calling him up and trying to get him to go there . . ."

Christopher fastened his second overshoe and stood up. "Well, he evidently prefers to come here," he said simply; and his tone gave Alice the tribute she expected — implying that she would naturally attract the best minds to her house.

"He wants to *write*," said Alice, "and I 've told him he shall have all the peace and quiet he needs here. He can have your study — "

Christopher's study was a small room next door to the library. It had been chosen for him by Alice, when they bought "181" two years after their marriage. It was she who had had its paneling painted olive green, chosen the curtains of English chintz, its brown carpet, its couple of high-backed armchairs, its roomy desk and green-shaded reading lamp, and had plans submitted for the inset bookshelves on either side of the chimneypiece. These had held, ever since, an edition of Bret Harte's complete works which Alice had not wanted in the library.

But though his study was an expression of elegant but manly comfort, Christopher seldom sat there; for when he was home from the office Alice had always felt he should be with her in the library. In the first years she had had the idea of sometimes reading passages from her favorite authors aloud to him after dinner. And though this idea had failed, through Christopher's being "unresponsive," the habit of his being around had persisted. (For Alice had a tendency to believe that whatever she did by habit was unquestionably right. This tendency had made her always patronize the same shops, dress her hair the same way, and cross the ocean, when she went, always by the same shipping line.) In the matter of Christopher's study her habit of preventing his enjoying its solitude was supported by another habit — of using it as a coat-room for guests. On Tuesdays the ladies who came for the Discussions left mink and muskrat, squirrel and pony, heaped across the chairs and the settee. And for dinner guests there was a silver-framed looking-glass stood up on the desk, and in front of it a bowl of face powder, a brass tray of invisible hairpins, a red brocade pincushion, and two combs. These remained on the desk except on Mondays and Fridays when Mrs. Rigger, the sewing woman, was put in there to sew, when the housemaid had instructions to put the powder and pins away.

So when Alice said, in connection with Hamnet Peabody's coming, "He can have your study," Christopher's reply was: —

"But where will Mrs. Rigger go on Monday and Friday?"

"Oh — Mrs. Rigger — she can go upstairs." Alice leaned forward, presenting her cheek and holding her morning's sheaf of letters against her white satin blouse. Christopher kissed her, then fastened his greatcoat and turned to go.

As the door banged behind him the wind sprang at him as if it had been lying in wait. But as he stepped out along the sidewalk, he felt a kind of zest in its violence, and a relief in its clean and bitter cold.

Wherever Mrs. Rigger did her sewing the next week, or the one after, or the one after that, Christopher never knew. Anyway, he forgot about Mrs. Rigger. For the arrival of their house guest changed the atmosphere of 181 Maple Street from dullness to excitement, affecting even Ericson the butler, Coral the housemaid, and Helen the cook. Ericson, a great reader, got his copy of *Young and So Fair* out of his trunk in the hope of getting the guest to autograph it. Coral, after having put out all blue guest towels and blue soap and blue bath crystals in readiness for Mr. Peabody, had had a crisis of indecision and then, agitated, had changed her mind and put ready mauve towels, soap, and crystals. And Helen, who had read that Mr. Peabody was planning "to settle down," let herself get into a dreamy state, imagining how Mr. Peabody would say he had never tasted such perfectly delicious food, and when he left get the idea of asking her — if she ever wanted a different job — with a bachelor . . . Even William, the colored chore man, stoked the furnace up so, on that Monday morning when the celebrated guest did arrive, that the temperature of the living rooms was nearly eighty and caused a flush on Alice Columin's face.

So, when she greeted Hamnet, he observed this flush and was emboldened by it to greet her by her Christian name — "Alice, this is *too* kind!"

Alice had prepared a sentence of welcome ("Mr. Peabody, I want you to feel you 're not a guest, just an inmate!") but she was so much surprised and then, secretly, so much exalted by the intimacy of his coming right in and calling her "Alice" that for a moment she could n't answer him — and then just said, "How do you do," and asked him to sit down. She did n't even remember to refer to the book she 'd been reading when he came in, but sat down herself and then got up again, and rang. And it was n't until Ericson had brought in the cocktails that she quite regained her poise and could say when he raised his glass: "Mr. Peabody, I want you to feel you 're not a guest but an inmate!"

He looked down at the rim of his glass and then at his own signet ring. "Why not Hamnet?"

It was really wonderful, Alice recounted to her friends in the ensuing weeks, really perfectly wonderful, how Hamnet fitted in! (They had never gone back from the chore man's intimate footing. Also by the end of two days Hamnet was calling his host "Christopher." And at the end of ten, Christopher said "Hamnet" when necessary.)

Indeed a routine was established that pleased everybody.

Christopher breakfasted, as usual, at eight-fifteen. Alice then, in one of her new satin wrappers, did her usual telephoning and answering of letters, until ten o'clock. Then she went and inspected the tray that was to be taken up to the guest. Grapefruit, coffee, plenty of cream, hot rolls, bacon and eggs, one morning; kedgeree another; sausages another. She and Coral were equally anxious that the tray should look attractive; using a different one of the little breakfast sets each morning, and a different-colored tray cloth and serviette. Sometimes Alice stood a carnation or rose in the glass of ice water; sometimes, this as their friendship progressed, she would lean an envelope against the coffeepot containing a typed-out copy of a poem, or passage in a book, that they had read together.

Towards eleven o'clock a fragrance of lavender the first week, of rose geranium the next, hung in the landing outside the guest's bathroom. And about midday, sometimes sooner, Hamnet would appear. He always came to Alice's own little boudoir, where he would find her reading, and came over to the Empire sofa (on which she looked "like Madame Récamier," he'd said) and took her hand and said: "And how is my Egeria this morning?" Then she would ask him if he slept well — and if his breakfast had been all right? This gave him an opening to mention the rose, or the typed missive. After ten minutes or so of these interchanges Hamnet would say that now he really must go and write before lunch. Sometimes he went to the study, where a log fire was always lit ("these vestal flames," he called them). Sometimes Alice would suggest "just a small cocktail, or an old-fashioned," before he settled down?

They lunched off Helen's most provocative cooking, at one-thirty. They had found a common antipathy against the "provincial habit" of lunching at one. By this time Alice had changed, and wore one of her new spring suits or dresses sent up from New York. He always noticed her clothes, and said he wondered how she managed always to look as if she dressed in Paris.

During luncheon she consulted him on his afternoon plans. "I know you have to work most of the time;

and you know I would n't *dare* to disturb you. But if you do feel that maybe you 'd like a little drive? And Angela Dane is having a little cocktail around six o'clock that I suppose I should *have* to go to . . ."

Sometimes Hamnet felt he sort of needed a little drive. And now and then a cocktail party seemed to break the strain, and give him fresh ideas. And Ericson kept up the log fire in the study, so that if Mr. Peabody was in and wanted to write —

Hamnet talked quite a lot to Alice about this new book, which he was going to call *Kinship with the Stars*. He showed her the quotation in Meredith: —

> Not till the fire is dying in the grate,
> Look we for any kinship with the stars.

When, one dinnertime, Alice revealed this title to Christopher, Christopher said: "But won't everybody think it 's about Hollywood?"

It was this remark that caused Hamnet to say to Alice, when Christopher had gone up to bed, that he was "a dear fellow, a heart of gold — and yet, in some ways, kind of coarse-grained."

How regretfully Alice agreed.

Chapter IV

Christopher might have gone on indefinitely, disliking his guest, playing golf all Saturday afternoon and Sundays, and respecting Alice's superior judgment of literary men.

But about a month after Hamnet arrived Christopher received a note from Mrs. Jabish Peckett asking him to tea. "Please," she wrote in a small hand with pretty, fanciful capitals, "come to tea on Saturday." There was a P.S. "There is a forecast of more snow. So you will not be missing your golf!"

Christopher telephoned that he would be delighted to come. A maid took his message. Evidently Mrs. Peckett, who had proved herself on the afternoon of Hamnet's lecture so delightfully eccentric, had had a little fit of eccentricity again. For no woman in Green Plains of Mrs. Peckett's social position had ever asked Christopher to tea (except with Alice).

It was a tribute to Mrs. Peckett that she could live in the house she did, and yet maintain her distinguished position. For "nobody" except Mrs. Peckett lived over on Jefferson Street; except Miss Peabody, who happened to live right opposite the Pecketts and who was considered halfway between "somebody" and "nobody." (No formal invitations were ever sent out from Miss Peabody's little dark brown frame house, with the peeping pink frilled organdie curtains at each of the six windows, but invitation cards were delivered there, from time to time, by the same postman that delivered Mrs. Peckett's large mail opposite.)

Mrs. Peckett's was a much bigger frame house, surrounded by a wide porch and approached by wooden steps. The paint on the shutters was grass green, but had scabbed off, leaving grey marks underneath. The curtains in the windows indicated that she had had different ideas about the decoration of every room: royal-blue velvet showing at one of the lower windows (the drawing-room), thick primrose-yellow satin at another (the dining room), scarlet plush at another (Jabish's library; Mrs. Peckett had strong ideas about keeping men gay — since she considered them by nature either choleric or lethargic). . . . The upper windows hinted chintzes, checked cottons, and flower-sprigged muslins.

Christopher noticed the scarlet plush curtains as he approached the house. They seemed richly to redeem the ramshackle façade. He rang the bell and was admitted by a small boy and escorted by him and a little girl with pigtails into a room with yellow satin curtains. The little girl told him that Grandmamma would be right down; and then both the children went out and shut the door.

Christopher had only had time to notice two canaries in a cage, two Japanese goldfish in a jar, two white mice in a box lined with dark green fur, and a bowl of most beautiful blue hyacinths on a green glass table in the window, when his hostess came in.

Somehow he had expected to see her in brown beaver as she had been at the Club — but it only took him a moment to decide that what she had on, which was equally soft, brown, and snug, was just right.

She was perfectly *delighted* to see him; and she made him sit down in the most comfortable armchair he had ever sat in in his life. It was large, and shabby, like everything else in the room (except the animals, the flowers, and the yellow satin curtains) — but capacious and yet supporting, profound and yet resilient. Then Mrs. Peckett's stout maid, Biddy, brought in tea, followed by the little girl with pigtails carrying a dish of hot biscuits, and the little boy carrying an enormous black ginger cake; and Mrs. Peckett herself cut large slices of the bread and stuck them on a toasting fork, and, pushing a plate of butter toward Christopher across the little table that Biddy had set between them, instructed him to "get ready to do the buttering."

Biddy vanished, and so did the children (after they had visited the mice).

"They always come here and have tea with Jabish on Saturdays!"

"Really?"

"Yes — and then — there's a nice piece to butter

— put on a lump and let it melt and *then* spread! And try some of Biddy's strawberry jam."

Mrs. Peckett noticed what nice hands he had. As nice as his nose! she thought — and then started telling him about the animals and their lives and dispositions: how highly strung the female goldfish was, how irritable the gentleman; how fond the lady canary was of peppermint creams; and how devoted to one another the mice were. While she told him these things she was thinking just how she should broach the matter she had to discuss. She could never have made herself do so had it not been for the two happenings: seeing Hamnet in Westlock's obviously making a decision between one gold cigarette case and another, and finding poor Mary Peabody in tears after her nephew's half-hour visit to her yesterday evening —

But she waited until Christopher had finished his last piece of ginger cake and settled himself back with a cigarette, before she spoke: —

"Mr. Columin — "

He felt so relaxed that he could answer her quite as if he felt her equal. "Mrs. Peckett?"

"Mr. Columin, I am a lover of birds."

"Yes, Mrs. Peckett?" She had told him many entrancing facts about furred and feathered creatures in the last twenty minutes. But he was ready to hear more.

"I am a lover of all birds except the cuckoo," she went on, eyeing him warily, with her smooth small head a little on one side. "I very much dislike the habits of the cuckoo. Its moral habits. I consider it a more harmful bird than a vulture, for instance. Harmful and despicable."

Christopher nodded.

"Despicable," she repeated. And now her head cocked over on to the other side. She seemed to be waiting for a response. So he said: —

"Why, certainly — I imagine so."

"You don't even have to *imagine*," she said. And waited again. And then, quite irritably: "Or do you like parasites?"

"I imagine I would n't," said Christopher.

" — And vampires who make furtive meals off solitary old women?"

"My *dear* Mrs. Peckett!" Surely this was something more than delightfully inconsequent ornithology? Surely Mrs. Peckett — poor Mrs. Peckett . . . ?

But she cut short his own doubts by throwing up her little hands — "My *dear* Christopher Columin, I suppose that it's life with Alice makes you — so literal. In fact," and here she ceased looking amused, and Christopher saw that she was both distressed and angry. "In fact, my dear Mr. Columin, Hamnet Peabody is living on you!"

Christopher's response disconcerted her.

"Of course," said Christopher mildly. "Of course. I quite realize that. And," he continued, "the conclusion I came to, after the first few days of his visit, was that there's no reason why he should *not* do so! I have quite enough money for three. And we — have no children." He paused for a second. "You see, it gives Alice pleasure, to have him there."

"Yes," said Mrs. Peckett.

"Well?"

She met his mildly inquiring glance by a series of sounds that were like an angry chirrup. Then she sat forward on the edge of her big chair, clasped her hands around her knees, and, staring sidelong at the crumby carpet, said: "Christopher Columin, I am naturally curious. Indeed I know it, I am inclined to be inquisitive. But just for this reason I have always been specially careful not to become a busybody. But I'd like you, please, dear Mr. Columin, to believe that I would n't say what I have to now if I — if we — "

"If *we* — ?" demanded Christopher. For all she might say he felt angry; and had an unpleasant vision of the President and members of the Club in a kind of scrum, heads down, over a poor morsel of gossip that was himself.

"Jabish and I," she said.

"Oh," said Christopher.

"Naturally," she said. "I would not have discussed the matter with anyone else. And he agrees with me that when it comes to Hamnet Peabody not only exploiting you — and Alice — but still keeping poor darling Mary on a string — "

"You don't *mean* he *still* — "

"I do."

"From — Miss Peabody?"

"Exactly."

"Are you *certain?*"

"He visited Mary last evening, and when I went over to call on her, soon after, she was in tears — and I made her tell me."

"But, surely — Why, he *can't* need her money. Why, only yesterday he gave Alice — "

"A gold cigarette case!"

"Why, yes . . ."

"*Exactly,*" said Mrs. Peckett once again. And then followed a sustained angry chirruping until Christopher expressed his full realization of what, indeed, his guest had been at, by saying: —

"*Well!*"

"*Yes,*" said Mrs. Peckett, "that's just the way Jabish and I feel!"

Christopher got up. "This has to be stopped!" he said. "This must be stopped right away!"

Mrs. Peckett looked up at him. In his agitation he had taken off his pince-nez; anger made his eyes look tawny, and set his jaw, making his chin look obstinate instead of polite. (Mrs. Peckett reflected that Christopher Columin should be angry, or something like it, much more often.) She said: —

"Yes — but *how?*"

"Well," said Christopher. And then, more calmly: "I think it should be quite easy."

"How?"

"I shall give Peabody a definite allowance!" Christopher sat down, now. He was quite gentle again. He put on his pince-nez. "It will be perfectly simple. The allowance will be on one condition, that he no longer worries his poor aunt — "

"But — *why* should you do this, anyway?"

"Because Alice likes him."

"But what if she does?"

Christopher looked at Mrs. Peckett gravely. He was no longer shy, and behind the courtesy of his next speech there was severity: —

"Mrs. Peckett, I don't like to discuss Alice behind her back. But I 'd like to say that Alice has always asked very little of me — and when I can do something that 'll give her pleasure . . ."

"He 's going to buy Peabody for Alice," said Mrs. Peckett to Jabish when Christopher had gone.

Chapter V

It is possible that at the bottom of Christopher's heart, below that standardized blend of worship and obligation which he felt for Alice, he had, for her, a real tenderness: a sensitive melancholy-sweet residue of a greater emotion that he had felt, long ago, for the woman in Alice, who was n't there —

But whether Christopher was prompted by this tenderness for a ghost in his own heart, or only by his principle as a husband, he, anyway, decided on his walk home from Mrs. Peckett's that he had been *right* in what he had said to Mrs. Peckett about Hamnet. If Alice liked to have an author around, and he, Christopher, could afford it, why ever should n't she? The only complication was the quite separate compassion he felt for Miss Mary Peabody. And surely a settlement could be made by which he could protect her and gratify Alice at the same time? Neither of the ladies, of course, being bothered with the financial transaction, which would be simply between himself and Hamnet — from a business point of view Christopher reckoned that Hamnet was n't likely to risk the substance of perhaps around three hundred dollars a month from him, for the shadow of small sums from his poor aunt . . .

Christopher was so intent on these thoughts and decisions that he found himself in his own porch more quickly than he expected; and Ericson was opening the front door while Christopher was still deciding between weekly and monthly payments to his guest. ("Weekly" seemed somehow humiliating for the recipient; yet a man like Hamnet, paid by the month, would certainly have spent every cent by the end of a fortnight — !)

"Your *shoess*, sir!" said Ericson.

Christopher's abstracted gaze followed Ericson's concerned gaze down to his own feet, on which the shoes, a pair of black Oxfords, were encrusted with snow.

"Your *rubberss*, sir!" said Ericson.

"Why, yes — but I surely went out in them?"

"Yess — you went out in them, sir.".

Now and again Christopher forgot his rubbers. (He had done so ever since he could remember — now and again. His mother used to scold him.)

"Why — then I must have left them at — Mrs. Peckett's." And as he now saw the clots of snow beginning to melt on to the parquet — "I'd best take these off down here."

He sat down and did so. While Ericson, waiting to take them below stairs, was supposing that Mr. Columin had not been to Mrs. Peckett's at all (he never went out for tea!) but had certainly had a "date" that had been interesting enough to make him come away forgetting his rubbers. Ericson liked Mr. Columin and hoped that this was so. He and Coral often wondered that a good-looking man like Mr. Columin did n't have any sort of love life "on the side" — for who would blame him? (The Hungarian cook that left last year had said of Mrs. Columin: "Herr heart ees as cold as a dog's nose!") Ericson took the shoes. They dripped. . . .

"Thank you, Ericson. . . . Very foolish of me."

"Nossir," said Ericson, respectful but friendly, and went back to the kitchen. (Being a reader, he would have liked his employer to have brought a "faint but lingering perfume" into the hall.)

The door of the library, on the landing just above, was open, and Christopher could hear Alice's voice.

She might have guests. Christopher went even more on tiptoe, calculating that he must be careful to step over that board on the landing that was apt to creak . . .

He paused on the last carpeted top step, carefully surveying the landing, which amounted to a run of open country. And as he did so he heard Alice's voice speak the following sentence: —

"You see, Hamnet, my dear, I can't forget that I mean *everything* to Christopher! He needs me in so many ways."

And then Hamnet's voice, full of a syrupy sadness: —

"But I need you, Alice. I need you so very, very much!"

And then Alice: —

"Hamnet, *dear*."

It was an hour later that Christopher, still up in his bedroom, heard the Packard driven up to the front door. He looked out of his window, saw Alice getting into the car, in her evening cloak, and Hamnet following her, in a black cloak and an opera hat. He remembered that Alice had told him she was taking Hamnet, instead of himself, to Mrs. Jefferson's dinner; as she knew he would rather have a quiet evening.

The next morning, when Alice came down to breakfast, Christopher had n't appeared.

He was occasionally late on Sundays, although she specially had a nine o'clock breakfast hour for him. But it was one of her rules to avoid making difficulties; and to-day she was especially determined that she would n't let Christopher feel the least flaw in her behavior. As she had said to Hamnet last night, as they drove back from Mrs. Jefferson's, at least she had always done all she could for Christopher. And that, if things ever *had* to come to a crisis, Christopher would have nothing to reproach her with.

When she 'd referred to the possibility of a crisis,

Alice knew that, if there was to be a crisis, she would have to make it. And secretly this prospect alarmed her. She was not, of course, afraid of Christopher. But she was afraid of large decisions and big changes. (She did not know this; for she was so accustomed to be tyrannical in petty matters that she imagined herself to be strong in great ones. And mistook her real fear of decisions for sensibility.)

This morning she repeated in her own mind the thought that Christopher should have nothing to reproach her with. And sat sentinel behind her coffee-pot and waited for Christopher to come down.

At ten minutes past nine she rang for Ericson.

"Tell Mr. Columin his breakfast will be getting cold."

Ericson glanced at the electric hot plate, then back at Mrs. Columin. Then he said: —

"Mr. Columin has had his breakfast, ma'am."

Alice took in what he said, and then stared. "*Had* his breakfast?" She looked across the table and saw that his place was not laid.

"Yess, ma'am," said Ericson. "He had his breakfast in — the study."

Considering that Alice was by nature unfitted for the unexpected, she took in Ericson's words with dignity. She said: "Oh. In the study," with some dim idea of making Ericson think that she felt that Mr. Columin's having his breakfast up in the study was quite all right.

"And — "

"What is it, Ericson?"

"And Mr. Columin said, ma'am — " The boy flushed. (He and Coral had been asking each other "What next?" and laughing, back in the pantry.)

"Said what?"

"That he — wanted to spend the day in the study, ma'am, and did not want to be disturbed."

Ericson went.

She sat trying to accustom her mind to the idea that *Christopher was in the study not wishing to be disturbed.* And trying to think of an explanation of such a fact.

But soon her efforts at thinking gave way to increasingly frequent fits of feeling; and soon to a general condition of angry agitation.

Finally she decided to consult Hamnet. He was, of course, still in bed. But she felt that in a crisis one rose above conventions; and gathering her wrapper around her she went upstairs. She passed the study door with her head held up, deciding that it was more dignified just to take no notice of Christopher. Though, when she had passed the door, she turned to stare back at the door itself — and to listen. There was no sound. She would have been reassured by the shuffling of a foot, the scraping of a chair. There was something unpleasantly indifferent about his silence.

She proceeded upward to the top landing and knocked at Hamnet's door.

"Hello? Yes?"

"Hamnet — it's me — Alice."

A second's pause. Then: "Yes? What is it?"

"Hamnet, could I come in and speak to you?"

Another pause, of several seconds during which there were slippy, soft sounds of pillows being shifted. . . . "Just a moment — all — right — come in."

She went in as his left hand was replacing a pocket mirror face downward, on the table beside the bed.

"Alice *dear?*" he cried, surprised into a high tone of voice. For her agitation was making her wide pale pink lips, usually set complacently, quiver like the edges of a rug when a draught comes under the door. "Alice dear, *what* is the matter?"

Hamnet was wearing a new pair of pale green pyjamas with dark green collar and monogram on the pocket. (He was glad of this; for he had lately been taking advantage of his secluded life at the Columins' to wear up an old blue pair.)

But at this moment (his Shelleyan upturning lock of hair was newly combed, he held a pencil in his right hand) Alice was in no state to register. "*Hamnet! Christopher's in the study!*"

Hamnet looked shocked and pained, because she did.

"In the *study?*"

"*Yes!*"

"What . . . !"

" — And," continued Alice, "*and* he's sent a message by Ericson that he does not wish to be disturbed!"

For a second Hamnet hesitated. Then, leaning a little forward, and with a very gentle smile, raising his upper lip softly from the lower, and with his eyes fixed on Alice, he just said: "Alice — dear." But conveying, with the most sympathetic, the most understanding delicacy, that, since she had turned to him, he was there. He added: "You must n't worry too much, dear."

He might as well have said this to a puppy madly preying upon a felt slipper.

"But what does it *mean* — what does he *mean* by it?"

"Perhaps," said Hamnet, "he just wants to be alone. There are times when every man has to be alone. Why, I know myself — "

"But not *Christopher!*" she broke in. " — Why, he 's never in all his life — "

"Even Christopher — " Hamnet interrupted. "Even Christopher," conceded Hamnet, who was rising on the wings of his own thoughts and would, if necessary, take off from Christopher. "Those times, Alice, when perhaps one feels one is up against a problem that no other human soul can help with — " There was a knock at the door. His mouth shut down like a hatch.

"Come in," said Alice.

It was Coral, her pretty face flushed.

"Please, Mrs. Columin — "

"What is it, Coral?"

The girl held out a slip of white paper. "Mr. Columin pushed this — under the door."

Alice took it. On it was written: "Ericson is to bring my lunch in here, please."

Alice handed the paper to Hamnet.

"*Well*," said Hamnet uncertainly. This message made him feel that a situation had arisen. He bent over the slip of paper and seemed to ponder over it; then said with mild common sense: —

"Alice, dear" (she turned and told Coral to go), "Alice — this is just one of those things — Christopher just wants a little solitude. Now what you must do is go and dress yourself and perhaps call up Rachel or Mrs. Van Zoon or one of the girls, and go around there and have luncheon with them."

"But *you*, Hamnet — ?"

"Why — did n't I tell you? I promised to spend to-day with the Lees. I wish I had n't — "

"Can you put her off? You *must* put her off — "

Hamnet looked quite troubled.

"Alice dear, you would n't have me hurt Mrs. Lee's feelings — "

"But in *this case*, Hamnet, you can call up and tell her that — that — I'm not at all well."

"No dear, I could n't. It would n't be true."

Alice decided not to humor Christopher by taking any notice of his behavior. So, when she had said good-bye to Hamnet just outside the study door, saying very clearly, "I suppose you won't want the study then, to-day?" she retired to the library. After this she came out at intervals on to the landing, but never crossed it to the door which enclosed the man who had been her husband, without any trouble, for twenty-one years.

Her nervous state was not good by lunch time. Down in the dining room Ericson's presence irritated her. But when he was absent she imagined him carrying trays to the study upstairs. She ate only half her grapefruit, left her chicken untasted, and refused any ice cream. When Ericson brought her coffee she forced herself to ask him whether Mr. Columin had had his lunch. Ericson replied matter-of-factly that he had.

"And — how does — Mr. Columin look, Ericson?"

"He looks all right, ma'am."

"He ate his lunch all right?"

"He ate up every bit, ma'am."

Ericson turned composedly to go.

"Oh, and, Ericson? Mr. Columin did n't say if he would be — coming out, this afternoon?"

"Mr. Columin ordered hiss tea for fife o'clock, ma'am."

"Thank you, Ericson."

Alice drank two cups of coffee, but it gave her no stimulus. She went upstairs again feeling sick with temper, self-pity, and irresolution.

What should she do next? How was she to go on

"taking" this behavior of Christopher's? She tried to steady herself by reflecting that to-morrow morning he would have to go to the office and everything would be normal again. But she could not feel steady. And when she thought of Hamnet lunching with Julia and Nantucket Lee she could have screamed.

In fact, as she had been several hours alone, she was worked up to such a need of a scene with *somebody* that when she reached the first landing she stopped outside the study door, and forgetting her ideal of dignity and her determination not to humor Christopher, she called out his name.

"*Christopher!*"

"Yes, dear?"

"Christopher! *What are you doing?*"

"Drinking my coffee, dear."

She paused, thinking that to walk in unasked would be humiliating, but to stay out here perfectly absurd.

"Christopher, I want to *talk* to you."

There was a momentary pause. Then, very gently: "I'm sorry, dear. I've locked the door again."

"Then unlock it."

An equally gentle: "No, dear."

"What d' you *mean?*"

"I think I'd rather not."

Alice tossed up her head with a little throaty gasp of: "Really!"

But she could not continue to stand outside the study door.

By three that afternoon Alice retired to bed. (Spoiled women, capricious monarchs, and the Wolf in "Red Riding Hood" have always known that unjust power is increased, and seems less unjust, when wielded from a bed.)

Alice went to bed in a big way. Keeping up a kind of hysterical calm, she made (the now openly hysterical) Coral help her put on her nightdress and a blue satin bedjacket edged with blue marabout, and had all her small lace-covered pillows assembled behind her back. She had one hot-water bottle at her feet, another upon her stomach, made Coral draw the curtains, excluding the last daylight, and took bromide, and sniffed smelling salts, and put pale powder on her cheeks, and lay back, and sat up again and took more bromide — and sent for Christopher.

Coral went down and came back, and said she had knocked at the study door and Mr. Columin did n't answer.

"Go down and knock louder."

Coral went down and in a moment returned again.

"He does n't *answer*, ma'am!" Coral was sobbing openly now, and she felt that everything was getting more and more like a tragedy in the newspapers.

"Did you knock?"

"Yes."

"*Loud?* He might be asleep." (Anything seemed possible now, and she could well imagine this new and perfectly Mephistophelian Christopher sleeping while she —) She said to Coral: "You must *go in,* then!"

"But the door's locked, ma'am."

"Then Ericson must *break it down!*"

"But — "

"But what?"

"Ericson hasn't come back yet, ma'am. He's been gone *two* hours." Loud sobs choked her.

"What d' you mean? Where to? What did he go for? Stop crying like that!"

"He — Mr. Columin, ma'am, sent him some kind of an — errand. He slipped a paper to him — under the door — and ca — Ericson w-went out, right away."

While Coral was still choking out her words Alice was getting out of bed. Very calm now in her manner, she slipped a wrapper over her jacket, put each foot into a mauve mule, crossed the room, and went downstairs to the landing below.

Coral leaned over the banisters and watched her.

She stopped outside the study door, and on a last superb note of forbearance said: —

"Christopher dear — unlock the door, please."

But there was no reply. Alice put her hand on the handle and gave it a nervous jerk (acting on the specially feminine belief that locked doors will respond to a dictatorial manner).

In this case the door opened. For it was not locked.

But Christopher was not inside.

THE ADVENTURE

PROBABLY no later happenings astonished Christopher quite so much as the simplicity of his own departure.

It was like the sensation of a man who bends, with every muscle in taut and agonized anticipation, to lift a weighty box; and lifts it up — empty. His mental reaction had the same lurch-back, and reel and stagger. After that mere walking downstairs and across the hall and out of the front door and into the first taxi — which took him quite impersonally to the station, where an equally impersonal train took him to New York; after the "mereness" and the matter-of-factness of every single incident (the entering the Guaranty Trust Company, the ten minutes in Cook's on Fifth Avenue, the attainment of a visa at the Battery — after the dispassionate manner in which the legendary *Queen Mary* received him into a cyclamen-tinted cabin on A deck) Christopher was more utterly breathlessly astounded than if he had been sleuthed to the bank by a private detective, chased from Cook's to the Battery by cops in an armored car, been fired at twice as his taxi left his hotel, and finally come on board to find six members of the Supreme Court crouching like tigers-about-to-spring in his stateroom!

He sat on the edge of the bed, on a cyclamen satin cover, and felt that to be as astounded as he was could not possibly go on much longer; and must end either in waking up or in some abrupt and frightful retribution.

But the *Queen Mary* sailed at her appointed time: carrying Mr. Christopher Columin upon her deck; bearing him down the widening blue spaces of the Hudson with a superb and colossal ease which, gradually, as the battlements of Wall Street dwindled, affected Christopher himself, and became a part of his own sensations. (Indeed, as he passed Liberty, the elation of his spirit and the slightly intoxicated facility of his thought made him fancy that she pointed an encouraging finger toward the Eastern horizon — and that there was even a slightly confederate expression in her eyes.)

Next morning Christopher woke early. The strangeness of his surroundings made him sit upright in bed, his heart going faster than his reason; as it used to early on Christmas mornings when he was a child . . . when the beginning of joy was like fear.

But Christmas mornings had been dark and this was light. A light, clear, yet pale, in the cabin.

He stared at three round things in turn. The clock

above his bookshelves, which marked ten minutes past six, and the two portholes across which a line moved slowly up and down, making them alternately the color of honey and the color of hyacinths.

Christopher gazed, but his thoughts — troubled, tremulous, pleased, and doubtful — were without order. And became soon so like emotion that he began to feel it his business to subdue them and bring them to order. At the same time he considered that he must try and get to sleep again. For seven-thirty was the time he usually got up.

But when it occurred to him that there was no reason why he should not go on sitting up, he did so. And as the light in the cabin became more golden and as the portholes continued to display to him alternately sample discs of two most lovely elements, it occurred to him that there was also no reason why he should not get out of bed.

He did so. And went straight (tipping forward faster than he expected) towards the left-hand porthole. He stood upon his suitcase and leaned his head out; salt air sprang against his face, incredible cleanness filled his nostrils, a great brightness rushed into his eyes, and for a second his heart and lungs seemed both to stop and a word danced in his brain — which was "Morning."

He remained at his porthole but still, intent, taut, like a dog pointing. . . . And then, moving deliberately, swiftly, he dressed, and within ten minutes — shaved, in his white starched collar, his tie perfectly tied, his shoelaces in double knots — he was out of his stateroom, down a narrow alley, along the corridor and up a rubber stairway, across a prairie of Axminster, up one staircase and yet another, intent, eager, unwavering, until, across a black marble space, through two more alleys afforested with doors, he was out — the deck under his feet, white rails, dark sea, and the whole Atlantic morning shining and tearing and singing and throbbing about his ears . . . !

"*Golly!*" said Christopher — "*Golly, golly,* GOLLY!" And the wind, in the ecstasy of its own mood, whisked the new-laid "gollys" off his lips and scrambled them in the air.

Christopher turned right, plunged his hands in his pockets, and walked a hundred yards up to the bows of the ship and leaned upon the mahogany rail. There were several decks below him; as if he were standing high up on a wedding cake. He whispered one more small "golly" to himself and just stood there, noticing detail after detail of the decks below, of cables and rigging, funnels and masts above.

He had been there some five minutes when he suddenly heard a deep voice say: —

"Glorious!"

Christopher turned. Next to him stood a woman, in corduroy trousers, a seaman's jersey, with her grey hair splayed in the wind. She had small, rugged, brownish features, and very light grey eyes whose gaze, fixed at this moment upon Christopher, was gracious but impersonal. Her look passed over the sea and sky.

" — Could n't be more glorious — I 've been up since five!"

"Really?"

"Yes." She leaned her elbows on the rail beside him. "Just been talking to one of the sailors. Boy from Greenock. Tells me his mother drinks, father 's in jail. Fine type, though. I asked him if he 'd like a job as third gardener. Said he did n't fancy it — liked the sea. I told him Adam was happy enough on dry land — *American?*"

She turned her head and again her grey gaze, amiable and intent, yet so indifferent, was on Christopher.

"I — "

"I saw you were. Collar, chin, jaw. But eyes might be — French — Gaul — "

"I had a French grandmother." He noticed that her corduroy trousers were tied round her spare waist with a rope, one of whose ends was fastened down by a large diamond brooch in the shape of a crescent moon.

"Pleasure or profit?"

He stared.

"Your trip?"

He caught it. "Oh — well. As a matter of fact — ugh — *Pleasure*," he brought out.

"Good. Right. Pleasure at the Prow! Swimming?"

"Well . . . Sometimes."

"It's the men's hour now — went down and was turned back. Angel with a fiery sex prejudice. What's your job?"

"Wool," said Christopher. "At least it was. I retired — recently."

"Sheep or pants?"

"I — we — marketed the yarn. Supplied our factories very largely."

"Retired young — eh?"

"Well . . . !"

"Forty-two?"

"Forty-seven!"

"Don't look it. Bones. Good bones. *Wife?*"

"N-no."

"Not sure!" She smiled. White beautiful teeth.

"No," said Christopher, firmly now and with a queer jolt of his heart. "No wife."

"Play deck quoits?"

"I never have."

"We'll have a game, later. Massage now. Nothing like it. Limbers you." She lifted back her left arm and caught her flying hair, and producing a large black beret from her pocket pushed the hair into it and pulled it down over her head. Then she nodded — a brisk gracious bend of her head — and strode off; and Christopher watched her straight back and her shambling corduroys retreat down the deck and vanish into a doorway.

Twinges of guilt and phases of bewilderment afflicted Christopher during this long, diversified, idle Thursday. Now and again he would think: "At this time I should be getting off the trolley car . . . !" Or now Miss Bax (his secretary) would be coming in and taking his replies to the morning's mail. . . . Sitting down to lunch in the gigantic restaurant of the ship, he thought of his usual table at Kelly's — and (perhaps as an admission of guilt, perhaps as a commemoration) he ordered the lunch he usually ate there from the *Queen Mary's* steward: "Steak — rare — French fried potatoes — salad with Roquefort dressing — a glass of buttermilk — " (Alice's "rule" for him.)

Out on the deck afterwards, lying on his chair, his legs tucked in a blue-and-scarlet cover, he had glimpses between the swerving gulls, of — the office in the afternoon, the sunlight falling on the carpet in front of his desk, the concrete roof of the building opposite in shadow from the higher Western Electric building beyond that —

As he lay out here the people pacing past him down the deck against the blue had the vivid fast-flowing quality of a dream; and the breeze and the warm afternoon sun were contained inside the huge shining precarious bubble, and within this bubble the steward brought him a tray of tea and said: "Do you care for buttered toast, sir?" with alert, yet self-respecting deference.

His acquaintance of the early morning did not fulfill her notion of teaching him deck quoits. And he did not see her again until she came into the restaurant at dinnertime, dressed in pale blue satin with a low *décolletage* and a train, the headwaiter gamboling before and about her. Christopher noticed that her hair had evidently been in skillful hands, for it was waved, curled, and built up on her head and surmounted by the diamond crescent and a red carnation.

She sat down several tables away, near a pillar. While she was ordering, a small, deft, brown-moustached man with tortoise-shell spectacles came round the pillar, seized the chair on her right, and sat upon it with an air of a self-satisfied kitten.

When Christopher was starting to eat his ice cream his friend caught sight of him and sent a steward over. "Her ladyship," said the steward, "would be very pleased if you would join her after dinner in the Chinese lounge."

He did. He discovered her name to be Lady Charlotte Jenkyn; and that the little kitten-faced man was a Professor of Archæology from Cambridge, England, called Tombwell.

Lady Charlotte said: "Brandy for everybody? or

port? or curaçoa or what? Muggy night! We're in the Gulf Stream. Coffee? Slept all day. My maid sick as usual, poor Button. Sick at the sight of a funnel."

She made Christopher sit beside her. She had on magnificent pearls, and brooches here and there on her dress, and Christopher saw that she had put rouge on, with a fine indifference to its situation. While she was talking Professor Tombwell also began a dreamily spoken discourse full of detail which seemed to be a comparison between Carthage and New York. "A Phœnician woman," he said, "translated to the Ritz Tower . . . the same rhythm," he crooned over his green chartreuse. "Each of the Mediterranean civilizations," he said to Christopher — "superb luxury . . . c-corruption . . . d-dust in Helen's eyes — "

Christopher's imagination picked up the phrase "Mediterranean civilizations." It flashed and sparkled like one of Lady Charlotte's brooches.

When they went out on deck the air was warm and heavy, and the sea hissing down in the dark. Lady Charlotte walked beside him and said: "Where are you going?"

He said he was going to London, and he had an idea of looking up some relations of his in England but didn't know how to find them. "You should try the Personal Column of the *Times*," she said. (Professor Tombwell was talking now about buried cities.

Christopher caught "Helen's eyes silted up with sand. B-buried b-eauty . . .") "Everybody finds everything they want in it," she said — "dogs, love — money — salvation at the top of the column, cigarettes at the bottom. . . . Burglars communicate. . . . Bishops bless." She explained to him that he must put in a message telling the Cornish relations to write to him.

She said that Button, her maid, would put it in: "Give her something to think about — stop her vomiting. . . . Organizer Button. Vomit her one fault. Inherited. Father drank. Butler."

Professor Tombwell put his arm through Christopher's. "At this very moment we may be p-passing over the courtyards of Atlantis. Agreeable fancy? Don't you think? D-don't you?"

To Christopher the fancy was most agreeable.

"Another agreeable fancy," murmured the small man — "the hull of this vessel a shadow passing across the sky of their f-future. That we — you and I, Mr. Columbus — "

"Column."

"Mr. — forgive me — that we, you and I, existing as we do in the unimaginable f-future of the Past . . ."

They all three leaned on the rail.

"Tropical," said Lady Charlotte. "Fine moon."

Christopher felt something soft against his hand and glanced down and saw Lady Charlotte's head and the carnation and sparkling crescent. Then he saw that it was her wig, which she was holding in her hand.

"Failing the *Times*," she said, "the *Landed Gentry* might help."

Queen Anne's Mansions had been suggested by Button to Lady Charlotte for Mr. Columin to stay at in London. The porter there was benign, broad-chested, and white-moustached. At the back of his mind Christopher detected a secret assurance that it was an excellent thing to be English. But there was also a respectful certainty in his manner that it must be an excellent thing to be American! And most especially to be ("If you would just write in there, sir") Mr. Christopher Columin of 181 Maple Street, Green Plains, Mass. ("Thank you, sir. Your luggage will be sent straight up, sir.")

A shy young man escorted Christopher up in an elevator. They went down long carpeted corridors. The white doors with brass knockers looked exactly alike. Christopher asked if there were no numbers and was told, shyly, that people did not like to have numbers. Christopher said that must make service difficult. The young man admitted: "Well no, sir."

But one of the white doors mysteriously intimated to the young man that it was assigned to Christopher. They went in. Christopher was pleased at once, for the windows of the sitting room looked over the trees in St. James's Park. The young man ventured to say that he could see Whitehall on his right hand, if he leaned out, far on the left the roof of Buckingham Palace, with the Union Jack flying over it.

The sky especially pleased Christopher and he said, "What fine clouds," for they were festooned about in every pearly shade against the palest sky. The young man said, "Well, not all visitors like our clouds," and seemed pleased. And when Christopher and he had smiled at each other, over the hedge of their mutual shyness, he went away.

When Christopher had done gazing at his view, he drew in his head and examined his apartment. It was white-walled, clean, and most solidly comfortable. It seemed very manly after the exotic beauties of the *Queen Mary*. Soon his luggage was brought by a man in a baize apron, who said, while he was upending the wardrobe trunk: "Better weather we've had to-day, sir," and "Thank you very much indeed, sir," when Christopher gave him half a crown.

When he had gone Christopher sat down in the leather armchair and looked at his *Evening Standard*. He decided he would go and see a play. As he was doing this a housemaid let herself into the apartment and went into the bedroom to turn down his bed. When she came into the sitting room and patted the cushions on the sofa and chairs, Christopher said: "Good evening."

"Good evening, sir." She added: "It's been nice weather to-day, has n't it?"

When Christopher had selected a play he telephoned down to the porter to reserve him a seat. Later, he ordered dinner up in his apartment. A noble-looking elderly waiter served him with a perfect mixed grill and a bottle of excellent claret, followed, at the man's own suggestion, by a glass of richly good port. When he brought the port Christopher said what a beautiful day it had been. The man looked most gravely interested and agreed.

The theatre was all crimson and gold and tarnished. Christopher was glad he had put on his tuxedo. Everybody around him was in evening dress. He thought how Alice would have felt at home in all this elegance. The play itself slightly bewildered him. He could n't get the hang of the characters at first. They were not at all like the people in the movies he went to sometimes, or in the plays Alice had made him take her to when once a year he went with her to New York. These people seemed like real people that wandered on to the stage and were living their lives there, though in old-fashioned clothes. But towards the end he was fascinated but vaguely saddened — as if the house and the orchard had been his own. Going out he noticed on the posters round the theatre that it was a Russian who had written the play and wondered if he had written anything else.

The following morning Christopher received a cable from his lawyer in Boston informing him that Mrs.

Columin was coöperating in the divorce. While he was reading this, at breakfast in his sitting room, the telephone bell rang. It was Button to inform him that his advertisement was in the *Times*.

He thanked her and took up his copy. And there it was! Halfway down the first Personal Column. Above it was a message: "*Solomon. Return or desolation lies ahead of us. Sheba.*" Below it: "*To let — Georgian House, 7 bed, 3 recep., Bombproof stabling.*" Christopher's own advertisement made him feel vaguely exuberant, but he could not imagine that anything would come of it.

In the next two days he visited several museums and picture galleries. But these visits made him think how much more Alice, who understood Art, would have enjoyed them. So much inchoate and unrelated beauty disturbed his feelings without satisfying them. He enjoyed more walking about the streets and looking at the people. He had not imagined that an English crowd could look so startlingly un-American. A broad demarcation that he could make out was that one section of Londoners was rosy, the other anæmic. After eleven o'clock St. James's Street and Piccadilly and Bond Street were so full of roseate men, young and old, carrying furled umbrellas that Christopher felt conscious of his own biscuit-tinted complexion.

He had bought half a dozen soft shirts at Austin Reed's; an umbrella, furled, at Brigg's. And ordered himself two pairs of shoes in a shop in the Burlington Arcade.

The third morning he came in to find an envelope, typed address, on his breakfast table.

"Better weather this morning, sir."

"Y-yes." Christopher picked up the envelope.

"Looks as if the rain was going to keep off."

"Why — yes."

"Nothing more I can bring you, sir?"

"Nothing, thank you."

"Very good, sir — thank you, sir."

The envelope contained another thin envelope addressed: "Christopher Columin, Esq." The letter inside was headed "St. Tad's Rectory, Cornwall."

Dear Sir, —

I have been sent your advertisement in the *Times* and hasten to write to you. My wife and I would be only too delighted if you will pay us a visit any time when you are in this part of the world. Columin, as you will see below, is my name. My family has been settled in these parts for the last four hundred years. We have a family tree, to prove it, and I know that one John Columin did leave this country and go to Massachusetts, in the first half of the eighteenth century, though I cannot trace the date. He was the brother of my great-great-great-grandfather, Simon Columin, therefore a collateral ancestor of mine. But all traces of him were lost.

My parish is the village of St. Tad's. But should you think of coming to this part of the world the station is Tremayne, seven miles away. I hope this letter may sound

as truly welcoming. A relation from the other side of the globe is no common occurrence. And be assured that whatever I can do for you in any way I am most ready to do so.
Yours very sincerely,
BENJAMIN COLUMN

P.S. — Should you seriously be thinking of coming, send us a wire confirming hour of your arrival and I will meet you in the trap.

Christopher had scarcely done wondering about the "trap," and begun upon his grilled kidneys, when the telephone rang again. Professor Tombwell was announced and then appeared, mewed a small gracious "Good morning," and detected, in the proportions of the room, a negation of all the principles of the eighteenth century. He then observed that Whitehall, from these windows, looked like Moscow; then he said softly: "Sh — Charlotte has sent me. She is in love with you."

He sat down, pulling up an armchair.

Christopher put down his coffee cup.

"It be-began on the b-boat," said Tombwell, looking round the room, and then getting up again and going gingerly to the fireplace. "She s-suddenly w-wants things. The English aristocracy have always been like that. F-full of charming predatory whims — d-don't you think? Don't you?"

"Why — I suppose so," said Christopher. "But what exactly does she want?"

Tombwell went on, stroking the plaster-relief design of the chimneypiece. "That's what makes her a Big Game Hunter. S-suddenly lions, or elephants appeal to her, and she goes out and shoots them. Magnificent, don't you think — d-don't you?"

"What does she want — now?" repeated Christopher.

Tombwell leaned closer to the design of the plaster and murmured: "N-no feel for c-curve . . . curves inhibited . . . Design must feel — *des seins, des fesses* — "

He broke off. "Want? Marriage, of course. She always marries. I told her I thought you would look very well in the j-jungle. Only you must give up those g-glasses — she thinks so too. They d-don't look well on f-features — "

"I am very farsighted," said Christopher, seizing on a minor issue.

"She's sending you her masseur. She told me to t-tell you that all eye things can be cured with m-massage — Kidneys! — May I take one? My fingers will do — Excellent. I came across a Sicilian r-recipe for cooking kidneys — or was it liver! S-swan's liver perhaps? (Now — is n't that the K-Kremlin? — With the sun on it?) But — anyway, Charlotte told me to tell you that she 'll be abroad for the next f-four months — and — won't settle anything practical until she gets back . . ."

"That gives us a little time," said Christopher. "As it happens, I 've an engagement to go to Cornwall."

"Excellent," said Tombwell. "One more kidney if you can spare one — and — dear me, it's eleven now and I must go to Christie's. There are some exquisite snuffboxes." He seized Christopher's hand. "I'll tell Charlotte what you say . . ." and went (leaving Christopher wondering what he had said).

Christopher felt that the distance to Tremayne, Cornwall, had been much exaggerated. The hall porter at Queen Anne's Mansions had hoped he would not arrive too tired. And Christopher thought he detected in the nice housemaid also a stagecoach attitude. The journey was hardly longer than from Boston to New York.

When he arrived and got out of the train there were several people waiting on the platform. But none of them looked clerical. So he moved towards the barrier with the crowd and passed through a waiting room whose doors were all open and where a pleasant fire burned, and out into a yard where two automobiles waited, and several elderly taxis, and a kind of low tub-shaped cart harnessed to a plump white pony. In the cart, almost filling it, was a very rubicund man in clerical clothes and a straw boater with an emerald-green and purple riband round it. He stared hard at Christopher and then waved his whip and shouted in rich, jolly tones, "Forgive me, I can't get out," but urged the pony to come up to where Christopher was.

"Mr. Christopher Columin? I thought so! I could tell in a trice. Welcome, sir ... You're very welcome." The Reverend Benjamin Columin passed his whip and reins into his left hand and thrust out the right one. Christopher shook it. It was like shaking hands with a man in his bath. "Now *then*," said the Reverend Benjamin. "Now then, now *then* — ?" His eyes, choleric in their blue brightness, yet gentle in actual expression, turned from Christopher to his luggage — which his porter was now assembling beside him. Christopher said quickly that he would have his luggage sent straight to the hotel. (He gathered that his relative's idea of "meeting" him would involve also driving him.)

"*Hotel!* Hotel! Fiddlesticks, my friend. You're coming to *us!* We're expecting you! We're *delighted!* As for your luggage . . ." His hearty tones dropped into a vague doubtfulness. Then he brightened. "Why, it can come out with Polzeath to-morrow night. To-morrow's market day, you know . . . Come in, then. Come in. Bring your little case if you can — *that's* it — under my feet, porter — that's right, my boy. Shilling you've given him! Great heavens! You'll prejudice his immortal soul." (Twinkle here in those glass-blue eyes.) "Squeezed in all right? You see why I couldn't get out. Regularly sandbagged, ain't I? What's inside 'em, did you say? — Just hold tight while we go round this corner. Kitty detests this corner, always has, gets a whiff of the slaughterhouse, y' know — "

Christopher gripped the edge of the pony cart on his side as the pony's grey rump took on a wild vitality, the Reverend Benjamin gripped his reins, and the little tub-cart swung rattling over cobbles round the corner of a high wall.

" — In the sacks?" continued the other — and the pony was going sedately up a steep small hill. "Well, oatmeal in one, corn in another, rabbits in the other." He added: "My dear life, *rabbits!*" with one of his changes of voice, this time there being a tang of rich melancholy. "*Rabbits,*" he repeated to himself.

"Is that the Cathedral?" said Christopher.

"Yes. But the Bishop's away, I'm afraid."

"I'm — sorry — " began Christopher.

"He always is at this time of year. There's the old gate — and that's our biggest grocer in these parts — famous for his cheese, and rightly so. I have to stop here — " He drew rein. Immediately a bald man in a white coat and long white apron ran out with a parcel in his arms, and coming round to the back of the vehicle respectfully bent down and set the package among the sacks.

"Thankye — thankye."

"Good day, sir — " The man hovered respectfully until they had driven off.

"Now the pork butcher. I do hope you'll forgive me — er — you see, we seldom come into town and wife had a lot of things she wanted got — "

They drew up again. A young man in a white coat with a long white apron dashed out, nipped round to the back of the cart, and zealously placed a brown-paper package next to the other.

"Sausages!" said the Reverend Benjamin. He pointed his whip toward the shop, fronted with green glazed tiles. "Famed for their sausages! And rightly so! *Eh?*" he added to the youth, who grinned and blinked.

They drove off again. Stopped at two more shops, each time eliciting an eager figure in white. Then they started up a long steep hill between houses as grey as the Cathedral, but not ancient or picturesque.

"If only these rabbits would n't *fidget* so! Well — well!" The Reverend Benjamin glanced down, shook his head, gave a deep sigh followed by a blue flash of laughter in his eyes, and demanded what sort of journey Christopher had had.

"Excellent," said Christopher.

"Not too crowded? Some of these express trains get appallingly crowded."

Christopher said no, he had been very comfortable.

"And London? How 's London these days?"

"Well, you see, I scarcely know London."

"Of course not, of course not. Pretty crowded, I should say?"

"Why — yes."

Soon they got up above the town and into green country, on either side of the road grass, deep ditches full of flowers and beyond each ditch high leafy hedges. Christopher commented on the flowers.

"It was a wonderful year for primroses, but of course they're over now."

Christopher said: "I was very much delighted with your letter."

His relative's answer was in cogitative vein: "They say the Americans have been getting along all right without us all this time! What is your opinion? Old Polzeath's son went out there — Pittsburgh, they say it was — and has n't been heard of since."

Christopher found it difficult to think of a concise answer for this question. But now a shower began, and the parson got out a big umbrella from a cane umbrella stand fixed on the front of the cart, and put it up and asked Christopher to hold it over both of them. And after this he talked to Christopher of the villages they passed through, the dissolute or curious characters in them, and of his two children, — one called Sabrina, aged sixteen, and one called Waterloo, — of their ponies and their prowess at school; and at the end of an hour and a quarter they arrived in the village of St. Tad's, and Kitty suddenly bolted up a drive, between laurel bushes and rhododendrons, and they came helter-skelter in sight of the Rectory, tore past its front door, the little cart rocking and swaying, and crashed round a corner of the white low house into the stable yard.

"*Dulce 'Domum*' — " said the parson. And a girl bathing an Aberdeen terrier in a zinc tub on the farther side of the yard looked up and smiled, and a small boy rushed out of the stable shouting: "*Did you bring them?*"

"Your manners, Loo!" said the Reverend Benjamin. "This is our cousin — Mr. Christopher Columin."

The boy flushed and came up to Christopher and held out his hand. "I — I'm so sorry. I'm awfully sorry. How d'you do?" He had a charming freckled face, with a sensitive mouth, an impudent cleft chin, and eager dark green eyes. His fair brown eyebrows seemed to move up or down, peaked or level, according to his feelings (during the moment that he was shy they stayed level), above his uncertain gaze fixed on Christopher; then, when he turned again to his father, their outer corners peaked and, drawing a quick breath, he demanded: "But *did* you bring them?"

At this moment the girl called out: "How do you do? *Please* forgive me not coming."

"My daughter Sabrina," the parson said. He and Christopher were both out of the cart now and Christopher smiled uncertainly in her direction. "If you'd be so good — " said his relative, and Christopher found his arms piled up with parcels. Then a woman in a flowered smock and riding breeches ran out of the back door and was introduced as "my wife." She said "How do you do?" in an eager, flustered way and began taking the parcels off Christopher's arms and asking him if he'd had a nice journey and hoping he was n't too tired, and calling out to her husband in between her kind, flurried inquiries: "Did you bring the candied cherries, Benjamin? — Did you have time to go about the sewing machine? — Was the town *terri*bly crowded, Benjamin? — Did they say if Sabrina's shoes would be ready — ?"

While she was speaking a bent man with a red moustache came out of an alley of wild currant bushes and started unfastening the pony's harness; and the Scotch terrier was lifted out of the zinc bath by Sabrina and rushed across the yard shaking his small black barrel form madly, and yapping; and Loo gave a scream: "*Oh* — he'll *get* them," and Christopher, turning sharp, got his arms again full, suddenly, of something, and this time it was a sack — full of warm, struggling round things, and the little boy threw himself between Christopher and the advancing Scottie screaming: "He'll *get* them, he'll *get* them!"

But Christopher, summing up the entire situation in a flash, made a rush indoors, banged the back door after him, and then, very gently, set the sack upon the large table of a clean large kitchen smelling of marmalade. . . .

When the others came in (except the Scottie) the little boy thanked Christopher for his rescue of the rabbits.

Then he escorted him up to his room. They went up a steep staircase, along a whitewashed corridor, down steps, across a low-ceilinged room, up other steps. Everywhere there was whitewash, and oak beams, and sloping dark oak floors, and cool shadows. There was a clean chill smell everywhere like a dairy, but now and then a whiff of lavender, or of bluebells that were set in bowls here and there on the sills of the latticed windows.

Christopher's room was also low-ceilinged, its white walls dyed green-gold by the light reflected upward from the garden. There were bowls and vases of wild flowers set on every table — beside the bed, by the fireplace, on the writing table, on the dressing table; also on little wooden brackets that were stuck on to the heavy oak post that came up through the worn linoleum on the floor and disappeared into the ceiling.

Loo informed Christopher that supper was at half-past six and left him. The red-moustached man brought up his luggage and Mrs. Columin came in for a moment and said she expected he'd like to rest a bit, and went away.

When he was alone Christopher noticed that there was a kettle on the big marble-topped washstand, and proceeded to wash his hands.

Then he unpacked. There was a walnut tallboy

against one wall, and he put most of his clothes in its drawers. But when he opened the door of what he supposed must be either a hanging cupboard or a bathroom, there was a set of shelves littered with the bones of birds and small animals.

Christopher was trying to find his way down to supper when Sabrina came out one of the many doors along the corridor he was in, and piloted him downstairs.

They went into a long room with many tall windows, and filled with chairs and armchairs and sofas, some of them of horsehair, others upholstered in worn green or yellow velvet. At one end of the room was a fireplace surrounded by a club fender — brass with an upholstered leather rail. At the other end of the room a big circular table covered with a white cloth and set for supper. Around it were mahogany chairs with horsehair seats. Beyond the table was an immense sideboard covered with china dishes, biscuit boxes, a decanter, a Sheffield plated urn, and several silver bowls, teapots, and coffeepots of Georgian design. On the wall above hung a gilt-framed battle scene as wide as the sideboard itself.

"If you mind ferrets, say so," said Sabrina. But as she spoke a ferret that had been poised on the sill of an open window darted out on to the drive into the dusk; and the parson came in carrying a lamp, newly lit, so that the domed glass shade was pale yellow like a cornelian. After him came the boy, Loo, his hair damped and brushed neatly sideways across his candid forehead.

"My dear life!" said the parson, his expression a mixture of jollity and distress. "*My dear life!* . . ." He stood the lamp on the table. Christopher, standing wedged between two armchairs, asked what was the matter. Sabrina went out of the room.

"If we have any eatable strawberries this summer we shall be *lucky!* — *Drought!* — And those new plants we had last year, all the way from my brother at Penzance — hardly a flower on 'em. How do strawberries do over with you, Cousin Column? Dry soil, I should say? Very dry? — Dust storms too, ain't there?"

Before Christopher could reply Mrs. Column and Sabrina came in carrying laden trays and they all sat down at the round table.

Christopher perceived many appetizing things upon the table, as well as four silver shells filled with pink and yellow primroses. There were glass dishes containing jam and jelly, thick golden Cornish cream, a plum cake, cold dark red ham, and a brown dish heaped with slipper-shaped hot crusty things which Mrs. Column explained were "Cornish pasties" (pronouncing them "pah-stis") — and made specially for Christopher's arrival. They contained potatoes and chopped meat that tasted spicy and very good. Christopher ate two. Then Sabrina said: "Will you have a scone?"

"Skon?" asked Christopher, puzzled, and they were all delighted to discover that Christopher called scones "hot biscuits," and biscuits "crackers"! And Loo giggled and choked over his tea. And after this Christopher felt less awkward; and increasingly amused. He began to observe his relations with real pleasure, to observe how the soft light of the lamp which stood in the centre of the table beamed upon their fresh complexions; to listen to the music they had in their voices: the parson's bass rolling out, Mrs. Columin's little practical remarks having a lyric freshness — and the children both speaking with most sweet voices, and, in Sabrina's case, unusual turns of speech.

As the meal progressed he watched. He had a fancy that Sabrina seemed at one moment like a flower, the next like a puppy. Looking at her face it was impossible to say whether prettiness or mirth possessed it more often. Her expression was ethereal sometimes, and sometimes rollicking; evidently, as Christopher was to know later, corresponding to the extremes of her mood, which varied between poetical detachment and an intense pleasure in jokes. A great deal of her was drawn in long lines. She had long legs, long arms, long eyelids, — rather slitted over the bright blue long eyes, — and a long mouth that curved up at each end. Christopher supposed that the amount she ate must make her long instead of wide. For at supper she consumed three "pasties," and an unbelievable quantity of scones and jam and cheese and cake, and cup after cup of tea. But all the time she ate she seemed to be watching out of her long eyes; and whenever anything funny or gay or odd fluttered into the talk she gave a start, as if her attention were a butterfly net.

But she seldom spoke directly to Christopher. Nor did her mother, who kept offering everybody different dishes and filling up plates and cups, and offering again before they were finished, and getting up now and again to give a morsel or a saucer of milk to the various animals, both in the room (as were the Aberdeen terrier and the two cats) and presumably out in the back yard. So the conversation consisted of Benjamin Columin and his son, Loo, asking Christopher questions about America — Benjamin's questions founded on the general assumption that America must be in a poor way (showing as it evidently did no talent for self-government). But Loo was ready to believe it a land of wonders, including Niagara, Red Indians, the Grand Canyon, steak for breakfast, and gangsters as thick as primroses. He had just been reading *Uncle Tom's Cabin,* but when he tackled Christopher about slavery he stopped suddenly at his sister's look, and she said: "English people were working little children in factories at the same time." So

Christopher said quickly that that was all a long time ago. And that "everybody" (and here he recollected a phrase of Alice's) "was more humane now."

After supper Mrs. Columin and Sabrina cleared the table, carrying the dishes away on black tin trays, and the parson took the cloth off the table, and, carrying it to one of the windows, pushed up the sash and shook the crumbs out into the night. When he had folded the cloth and put it in a drawer in the sideboard, he set the lamp upon the table, which Loo had meanwhile polished over vigorously with a yellow cloth. He bent down to examine the surface and muttered, "Shows every scratch!"; and shook his head with that same air of jovial discouragement that he had had during supper for the Cheddar cheese, the time of the year, and the distance to New York.

Then he came over to the fire, put one or two more logs upon it, sat down in the horsehair armchair opposite Christopher, and took his pipe off a brass rack beside him on the wall. The firelight burnishing his face orange on the one side, and the more distant lamp-light gilding it upon the other, he looked across at his guest and said: "*Well!* — Well, well, well!" — each "well" sounding more richly, thoroughly cordial than the last. And then: "Cousin Christopher, to be sure!"

This is the nicest man I ever met, thought Christopher. But he only said: "It certainly is strange!"

The parson filled his pipe out of a jar held by Loo,

who was now seated beside his father on a three-legged stool.

"Strange! You're right — " The parson pulled at his pipe. "It is strange," using the word so that it implied satisfaction more than surprise. He then asked Christopher if he remembered Tremayne Cathedral, and regretted that the Bishop was not in residence, and (by a series of sentences which dealt with the Bishop's wife, her good sense as a woman and a housekeeper — and her attitude towards the tradesfolk) arrived at the information that the lamp oil you could procure in Tremayne was cheaper and better, mind you! than the village store used to get specially for him from Exeter.

Now the logs in the grate began to flare up. And when Mrs. Columin and Sabrina came back they all sat in a semicircle about the fire, and the animals — the Scottie, three cats, and eventually the ferret — lay upon the hearth. Mrs. Columin, in a high-backed horsehair chair, took stockings out of a box covered with rosy cretonne and began to darn; and Sabrina to embroider in petit point, a white unicorn upon a crimson ground. Loo took a knife out of his pocket and became intent on hollowing a small piece of wood, and Christopher lit a cigarette, and the talk settled to a contented ebb and flow, and the furry stomachs of the drowsy animals went up and down in the firelight. Later the parson fetched a jug of ale and two glasses. And Mrs. Columin asked Christopher if he minded having his bath in the morning, and Christopher told her that that was the time when he always took his bath.

Loo was in bed when Sabrina came in, in her pyjamas, and said: —
"Well, what d' you think of him?"
"*Very* nice. But he seems a bit timid."
"He can't help that."
Loo understood quiet or shy or sad people better than Sabrina did; though he was n't yet old enough to understand why they were so. He said sleepily: "Perhaps it 's because he 's American."
Sabrina shook her hair so that it sheened in the light of the candle she was carrying. "Americans are n't *reputed* to be timid! Just the opposite! Pioneer Blood boiling and bubbling in their veins — "
"Still — there must *be* quiet Americans!"
Loo was getting drowsier every second.
"Perhaps he just needs 'bringing out,'" said Sabrina, recollecting her headmistress's advice on treating new girls at school.
But Loo was asleep.

Christopher lay and considered a magnolia looking in at his window, and listened to the close-by singing of a thrush, the peaceful far-off rattling of a lawn mower, the gay small scuttling of mice in the wall behind his head. Then there was a knock at his door and Loo came in very gingerly, carrying a small tray. On it was a fragile cup of Sèvres china, rose, white, and gold, containing tea as dark as molasses, and a bright, silver jug of milk.

Loo came slow, on tiptoe, and set the tray on the bedside table. Then, after letting out his breath, he returned Christopher's good-morning — "And I put three lumps in the saucer."

"Thank you."

"I hope you slept well?" — real interest and solicitude in his tone.

"I had a beautiful sleep, thank you."

"It's a fairly fine morning, but I *hope* it is n't going to cloud over for you!"

Christopher's sense, at that moment, was that all the clouds in the firmament would not dim the contentment that lay like a vague radiance over his inner thoughts and outward perceiving.

"I did n't bring your tea before, because Mummie said you would be tired, but I wish I *could* have because one of Dovey's new Alderneys got over the ditch into the garden, and you could have seen her from your window! — Shall I put the sugar in *for* you?"

"All three!" said Christopher. (And for a second a wraith, in hair net and wrapper, flickered across the sloping floor. For Alice, herself in danger of obesity, always made him take saccharine.)

Christopher leaned up and lifted the exquisite cup,

and saw, on the other side of the saucer, a very small pale blue egg flecked with pink; and realized that Loo was watching him.

"A robin's egg," Loo explained. "I — have n't blown it yet. But I will. I'd awfully like to give it you — if you'd like it, of course . . ."

"It's just perfectly beautiful — "

A rapping. Sabrina's voice: "The water's up." She put her head round the door, her eyes festal slits, her smile festooned from one cheek to the other. "You'd better drink that down and come while it's hot." Her head vanished.

Christopher drank his tea and Loo got him his dressing gown, and collected his sponges and loofahs from the washstand. "Oh, and Mummie is bringing your shaving water in a few minutes."

Christopher followed Loo, and after labyrinthine ups and downs he was in a wide room with a steep sloping ceiling. In the middle of the floor was a hip bath with brown ears and a high back, set upon a pink blanket. Steam emerged from the bath, and beside it stood tall cans swathed in towels. A trapdoor in the boards opened and up came the red-moustached man in a bowler hat, and then the rest of him in shirt sleeves. He set a brass kettle upon the floor at his elbow. Then shoulder and head vanished down again.

"If you want any more cold water," said Loo, "will you please just bang on the floor?" He added: "Be-

THE ADVENTURE OF CHRISTOPHER COLUMIN

cause underneath is the kitchen, you see." Then he, too, opened the trapdoor and vanished — shorts, blazer, smile, and brown round head.

Christopher could smell that the kitchen was below while he fitted himself like a Buddha into the bath. Appetizing aromas came up between the boards and he could hear the bubbling and sputtering of frying, and heavy footsteps going to and fro on a stone floor.

Down at breakfast, Mrs. Columin, in riding breeches, with a blue checked duster round her head, was reading *David Copperfield* aloud; the children were eating fried potatoes; and the parson, in a fisherman's sweater, was drinking out of a cup the size of a small *pot de chambre* patterned with cherries. They all got up when Christopher came in, and busied themselves supplying him with tea, scones, butter, fried potatoes, and hot grilled ham. "Own pigs and home-cured," recommended Benjamin. "Fanny cures ham as well as anyone in the West Country." Christopher, tasting the ham, said she certainly did, and that the potatoes were delicious.

"Glad you like 'em," said the parson, "they're one of my specialties. . . ." He explained that he always cooked the breakfast except on Sundays and Feast Days.

Mrs. Columin went on reading the chapter in which David pawns his waistcoat; and Sabrina passed Christopher three glass dishes of plum, apricot, and raspberry jams, and Loo pushed a pot of marmalade, heading off the fleet of jams, and whispered "Ha-ha" to Sabrina when Christopher took marmalade. But Sabrina only sank into a trance of amusement and helped herself to raspberry.

After breakfast Sabrina prepared bread and milk for the ferret — whose name was Milly. Loo went out to feed his rabbits, and Mrs. Columin told Christopher that she had lit a fire in the drawing-room and hoped he would make himself comfortable there.

"I daresay you'll find all sorts of books in there that you haven't seen over in America!" said Benjamin, as he crossed the tapes of his cotton apron over his back and tied them in a bow on his broad stomach. "Fond of books?"

"I'm not much of a reader, I'm afraid," said Christopher. "Somehow I never seem to get around to it." He thought of Alice and of how he had never finished *Young and So Fair* — and suddenly his diffidence returned.

"Well — well — I don't suppose you get much reading matter out there — except newspapers, of course — I understand you get a lot of them! — of a sort. Gracious! — past nine already — and Saturday again — well, well — *Fanny?*" he shouted to his wife, who was out in the hall — "FANNY?"

Mrs. Columin scuttled in.

"Yes, Benjamin?" She had put on her flowered smock again over her breeches. Her wispy gold hair had begun to escape from under the duster turban.

"Has Chilton brought the joint yet?"

"Yes, Benjamin."

"Well, well — that's *one* good thing. But — here, bring me a *tray*, dear! — what about my *sermon*? Not a word written yet! I shall never get it done — and *then* where shall I be? What would the Bishop say? My-dear-life!" His jovial jeremiad continued in this strain while he stacked plates, and knives, and forks upon his tray. . . . To his wife his exclamations were evidently as familiar an accompaniment to Saturday morning as the arrival of the joint of beef. Taking up one of the cats in her arms, she led Christopher to the drawing-room, which was on the "Charles I" side of the house. It was an oak-paneled, low room, smelling faintly of dry rot and full of formal mahogany and satinwood furniture of an endearing Victorian ugliness, and, inevitably, set about on the many little tables, on the ebony and mother-of-pearl escritoire, on the cherry-wood work table, were more bowls, vases, and little jars full of flowers; even more than in the other rooms — including peonies and pink camellias which Mrs. Columin said she had picked early this morning. And Christopher saw that the peonies still had dew like bright tears among their flushed petals.

When he was alone he examined the bookshelves, and some magazines upon a yellow brocade ottoman, which all proved to be copies of the *Poultry Breeders' Review*. He had settled down to read an article on

"Roup in White Wyandottes" when Loo came in and brought him a paper called the *Scout,* and while he was telling Christopher the story of the serial in it to date, Sabrina rushed in with a cablegram.

While Christopher read it the children watched him. He looked up and saw their anxious looks.

"I *hope,*" said Loo, "that it is n't bad news?"

"I hope it 's all right?" said Sabrina.

Christopher glanced at the message again (it had been forwarded from Queen Anne's Mansions). "Am marrying Hamnet Peabody as soon as divorce is completed most wonderfully happy Alice."

After a moment's pause Christopher said: "No, not bad news at all," and crumpled the cablegram and threw it into the bright flames of the fire.

Christopher stayed a week at the Rectory. And then, somehow, he stayed on.

He stayed because they did n't want him to go. And he did n't want to leave.

By the middle of May, when the children were back at their day schools in Tremayne, he was so much a part of the family that Mrs. Columin said she did n't miss Sabrina in the house at all! For Christopher proved to be very deft at washing up, dried glasses so that they shone, learned to polish boots as well as the parson himself, and eventually fulfilled his ambition (though discouraged by Mrs. Columin) of "turning out his own room" — wielding broom, dustpan and brush, and dusters, with a fierce and intent dexterity that made the parson, watching, tell him that he'd recommend him to Saint Peter for looking after the "glassy floor."

Not that the stages were n't gradual between Christopher's first drying of a vegetable dish and that great eventual triumph known as "Cousin Christopher's Corn Muffins" (when Selfridge's, in London-Church-Town, were written to and sent a recipe; and Christopher, having promised a surprise for Sunday breakfast, baked late on Saturday night — with the tactful help of Mrs. Columin — and produced, at 9 A.M. on Sunday, — for Loo, ravenous from an early gallop on Kitty, and the parson and Sabrina eager empty after early service, — a dish of hot golden crisp corn muffins worthy of Fannie Farmer herself).

It was n't long after his "settling in" that Christopher had begun to help "Cousin Fanny" with Sunday breakfast. She began by teaching him to fry sausages — an art which he realized he had lost since boyhood. The wielding of the heavy iron pan and the savory sputtering recalled, queerly, summers up in Maine . . . the aroma of pines . . . his mother in a linen riding habit sitting on the grass cutting bread, and such a zest and glory and wonder in the sun and air. . . . And in due course the parson said he did n't know "how they'd ever got through Sundays without him." For it was Christopher who gave that last look at the joint before they all went across to church to *look* better too! — "A bit of color in his face — " (Benjamin's own prawn-pink glow set a vivacious standard of male complexion.)

"Mrs. Dovey says," remarked Sabrina, "that he's a very handsome gentleman."

"He has a very *nice* face," said Loo.

"He's much less shy — *that's* certain," said Fanny Columin, who had been shy herself as a girl, but had been so busy ever since as to lose the habit.

"He's begun singing in his bath," said Sabrina.

"He sings out in church a bit — which is helpful," said the parson.

Mrs. Columin, having finished her own tea, rushed out to the rosy box for one of Loo's grey stockings. "And I must confess, Benjamin, with all due deference to *you*, that the boots have *never* been better cleaned!"

The Reverend Benjamin nodded a friendly "That's all right, dear — of course Christopher can give as much time as he likes . . ."

Loo said: "He's written for some new sort of polish he's read about. If you get enough coupons from tins of it you can get a tea set or a portable wireless or — I think it's a free steamer trip to Boulogne for the week-end — "

His mother asked him: "And which will you choose, Loo?"

"Steamer trip, of course."

Sabrina said: "Christopher knows *all* the wild flowers

now. And about half the garden ones. ... He knows *some* of the wild ones from when he was a little boy in America. But lots of their flowers are different, as well as the names of ones that are the same — insects too. He calls a cricket a katydid."

"What cricket did at school," said Loo.

"Lovely joke, Loo," said his sister appreciatively.

" — Or a Katy-did match," said Loo, "or a Katy-did eleven — or — "

"Nuff, Loo," said Sabrina. He had a way of going on with one of his good jokes until the last one was so threadbare that he depressed himself with it.

At this moment Christopher came in from a solitary stroll which had been made sociable every two minutes by his various friends in the village. He sat down and cut himself a slice of bread.

"Some of *my* strawberry jelly," said Sabrina. "Try it." She pushed the jar across the table.

"It looks gorgeous. By the way," he turned to Fanny, "Mrs. Dovey's sending up a tin of cream."

"She wheedled you again, Christopher!"

"Well, yes. She started telling me about her trip to London-Church-Town once again and I had to get away — gracefully."

Sabrina asked: "Did she tell you that hat she wears on Sundays all piled up with flowers and fruit is the same one she got in London that time? It's beginning to look like the week after Harvest Festival."

"Now then, Sabrina!" cautioned her father, looking

upon her as usual with a mixture of sternness and adoration.

"I hear you're going to experiment with a new boot polish?" said Fanny, with one of her little quick half-teasing glances.

"I am, Cousin Fanny! . . . It seems from an advertisement in that excellent newspaper, the *Scout* — "

"I gather," said Benjamin, "that if you go on cleaning our boots with it long enough, Cousin Christopher, you'll also be giving Loo a taste for foreign travel."

Christopher looked puzzled and Sabrina explained about the free trip to Boulogne.

"I see," said Christopher — "every muddy walk 'll bring Loo nearer France?" He smiled at Loo and cut himself another slice of bread.

"More tea, Christopher?" asked Fanny.

He put the bread on his plate.

"More tea . . . Christopher?" she repeated.

Christopher took up the butter dish and balanced it on the palm of one hand. Then he realized that Fanny was looking at him and saying — what? He saw Sabrina laughing at him.

"More tea, Christopher?" asked Fanny once again.

"Thank you — yes." Christopher let her take his cup, and became absent again.

"Penny, Cousin Christopher?" said Benjamin, who had himself been abstracted for the last three minutes, deciding whether he should, or should not, bring in any obvious reference on Sunday to those continuous thefts of old Dovey's eggs that had been going on. . . . Would n't do any harm to make them remember that there was one Eye on them (Text: "Thou God seest me").

"Well — " began Christopher.

"A penny-farthing!" said Sabrina.

"*Well*," said Christopher, "I 'm getting a kind of an idea."

He began to tell them . . .

So it was revealed, discussed, and amazedly, jubilantly, decided that Christopher should take Sabrina and Loo on a trip abroad for their summer holidays. The mere proposition so convinced his cousins that he must be, almost if not quite, a millionaire that they did n't even think of objecting to the cost of such a plan. Fanny's only fear was that he might find the children a "handful." And Benjamin's that the climate of "some of these places in Europe was very treacherous," and that they would all of them catch bad colds — "and of course you won't get the wholesome food you get here — all kinds of *messes*, y' know!"

However, the table in the nursery was spread with maps. Christopher wrote to Cook's for guidebooks — and he and Sabrina and Loo juggled with the countries of Europe: France; Italy; Switzerland; as if they were so many colored balls; repeated the names of places from Calais to Constantinople like incantations. . . .

Three days before they left Sabrina asked Christopher: "Do you *know* anybody in Europe?"

He said he believed he had some French relatives somewhere called Lacaze. He knew that an uncle of his had returned from New York to found the Lacaze Line and live at Le Havre; and he had heard, vaguely, that that uncle had had children. Urged by Loo, he decided he would write, anyway, care of the Lacaze Line, to Le Havre, "because," said Loo, "you might find more cousins like us." So Sabrina, who was good at French at school, dictated the letter to Christopher. In it Christopher asked his relations, if there were any, to write to him care of Cook's in Paris, where he would be making his first stop. After some indecision they addressed the letter to a *"Monsieur Lacaze, care of The Lacaze Line, Le Havre, France."*

"But supposing there *isn't* a Monsieur Lacaze?" said Loo.

"Then he won't get it," said Sabrina. She added: "What d' you suppose he looks like?"

"A black beard, certainly," said Christopher. He had just signed his name and was putting the cap on his fountain pen.

"Yes," said Loo. "A black beard."

"And peaky eyebrows," said Sabrina, "with a few of the hairs stretching forward — like beetles' antennæ — and brown eyes — brown deep-set eyes — rather nice eyes and *little* and vastly agreeable."

"Of course — if he's a cousin or anything he *might* look like Christopher," said Loo.

Sabrina said: "Well, *we* don't look like Christopher, do we, Christopher?"

Christopher said: "No, but maybe if I was to grow a beard *I* might look like Monsieur Lacaze."

"But your beard would be *brown*," said Sabrina.

"Your eyes are hazel."

"Your eyebrows don't have antennæ."

"You're tall and he's little," said Loo.

"And you say funny things in a grave way — and he says ordinary things in an excited way that makes you want to laugh at him."

"Evidently," said Christopher, "I am a more attractive man than my cousin Mr. Lacaze."

Christopher's phrases on the importance of travel, on its power to broaden minds, enlarge viewpoints, and increase experience, were derived from Alice. But such an eloquence and eagerness lit these platitudes that soon there was an answering glow in Cousin Fanny's imagination; the romantic in her (the young woman who had named her daughter from Milton and made her son commemorate her girlhood's passion for the Iron Duke) triumphed over the mother. And she spent the weeks before the children's departure equipping them to face the wide, and surely wonderful, world. Her sewing machine whirred late into those summer evenings to achieve one striped pink and one spotted blue cotton dress for Sabrina, and three new shirts for Loo out of the silk that her brother, the Judge, sent her from China. And she made an entire Saturday's expedition into Tremayne with the children — where she bought them each a pair of sandals, a pair of rubbers, brown fabric gloves, and grey felt fold-up hats. On the same expedition Loo bought himself a new compass, a ball of red string, and, at Smith's Library, six new films for his No. 1 Brownie (thus leaving himself still with fifteen shillings in the post office). Sabrina bought a thermos flask in a scarlet imitation-leather case, a plait of colored silks, a case of mixed needles (Egg-Eyed Sharps), and three colored chiffon handkerchiefs from Woolworth, one rose, one pale blue, and one violet. When they were leaving and Kitty, her solid buttocks quivering and straining, was pulling them up the hill, Fanny remembered about getting the new wick for the methylated stove in the tea basket: so they went back, and while she was in Kemp the ironmonger's, the Bishop, who had been in the post office opposite, came up and congratulated the children on the Great Good Luck of their "impending journey." He looked at them in his sweet-old-lady yet quizzical way. They told him they were going first to Paris, and then were going to follow their noses or "prick the map with pins" (citing Christopher). The Bishop then said that as a young man he had dined on the Eiffel Tower, then the fashionable rendezvous, and seen a lady shot from a cannon at Luna Park. Then he gave each of them a new, crisp ten-shilling note, said something about the art of travel being to "take as much wonder as you seek," and turned away; and proceeded down the street, his black-gaitered legs a little bowed, his shovel hat shadowing his gaze, which was fixed, as that of a spiritual lord may be, upon some aspect of his Invisible Estate. Perhaps, with the Columin children's souls still fresh in his sight, he contrived to reflect, passing the tub-cart, upon the real nature of travel. And how men (save those that shift blind and mouthing from Ritz to Ritz) travel in two dimensions. He may have pondered on the odd fact that body and spirit do not always arrive in a place at the same time, or wondered, regretfully, that travel in space should be so easy while we must stay at home in Time —

Fanny Columin bought not only the wick, but an extra straw basket that might be useful. It was of green straw, and the ironmonger, an old friend, had let her have it for one-and-eleven.

"It will be nice and light to take in the aeroplane," said Fanny as she got in the trap, and handed it to Sabrina and took up Kitty's reins again, for Christopher had arranged that they should fly as far as France.

But if Fanny was able to delight in the prospect of the children's journey (since it accorded with her fundamental assumption that magic and good are identical, and both a part of everyday life), her husband's view was less simple, and alternated between a most hearty and wondering gratitude to Christopher for his generosity, and forebodings as to the inconveniences, pains, disasters, that overtook those who went abroad. It was he who insisted upon packing Sabrina's winter vests, supplied Loo with a sheaf of telegraph forms, and presented Christopher with a first-aid outfit in a metal box marked with a Red Cross, "in case of railway accidents." He shook his head, apostrophizing "his dear life" over the sly dishonesty of the French, and warned Christopher against the Italian habit of serving, with macaroni, a dark sauce made of chopped horseflesh. Towards Germany he expressed a steady unchristian hostility, tempered by flashes of jovial contempt for "wurst," and a tolerance for Munich beer. And when Christopher tried to reassure him by describing the number of people he knew who traveled in Europe in the summer, Benjamin merely reiterated his special fear that they would "find the Continent most dreadfully crowded."

They were to leave on a Monday, and on the Sunday before, the parson chose as his text: ". . . And immediately the Spirit driveth him into the wilderness."

It had been decided that Fanny should come to Tremayne Station with them, but that Benjamin should escort them as far as Croydon; and "the car" was ordered from the livery stables in Tremayne to fetch them, a Daimler of mid-Edwardian design with a weather-beaten Mickey Mouse tied to the radiator cap.

They all sat inside the car, Sabrina and Loo in brown mackintoshes and their new grey felt hats; Loo holding his Brownie camera and Sabrina carrying the green and red basket containing fresh pasties, raspberries, peaches, ginger biscuits, milk chocolate, and a bottle of milk. The parson wore an oilskin, but unbuttoned, over his clerical clothes, and Christopher — in the same pale grey suit in which he had left 181 Maple Street three months ago — wore a red rose, presented to him by Mrs. Dovey, in the lapel of his coat. On the top of the car were piled their suitcases — the children's brand-new — and the immense brown round hatbox that Fanny had used — and not since — on her honeymoon.

On the drive to Tremayne Sabrina wriggled and beamed, and Loo looked a little startled.

At that station Sabrina got some extra toffee out of a slot machine, and Fanny bought Loo the *Scout*. When the train was signaled Sabrina embraced her mother with smiling impatience — her kisses being more a celebration than a farewell. But Loo clung to her suddenly, and clutched his arms tight round her neck.

Then his father hustled him into the train. And as the train moved out Benjamin and Christopher and Sabrina all waved to Fanny, and she stood on the platform waving to them. But Loo sat very still in a corner of the carriage staring down at his own tight-locked hands.

While they waited at the aerodrome Loo was so pale from excitement that all his freckles showed; and Sabrina was flushed and silent with joy, the cupid's-bow ends of her mouth turned up; but Christopher, having been carefree and amused in the train, began to feel the load of Benjamin's paternal anxiety shift to himself — and observed that Benjamin, morose at Paddington, doubtful and nervy at Victoria, had become calm in the motor coach, and was now quite detached from his children, his attention enthralled by the planes on the field. He kept drawing Christopher's attention to departing or arriving machines. "Look at that one now . . . ! Blue! My goodness! And that great huge thing there coming down. . . . Well, well, it's a miracle to me how they manage not to run into each other. Good gracious — in the war it used to be a different matter — running into each other was part of the risk, poor souls. But — now look at *that* one! Where's that going to, my man?" He addressed an Imperial Airways pilot who was standing near. "India, padre." "Well, well — " said Benjamin. "My dear life, what next?" He turned and gave the young pilot one of his great chuckles: "We'll be going higher still in aeroplanes soon! Eh?"

"That's it, padre — *if* we're upward bound, of course!"

Their chuckling exasperated Christopher, who was now having pang after pang of self-reproach, self-doubts. Suppose anything *were* to happen to either of the children? Supposing that Loo was to be sick? Or Sabrina to feel badly? Or —

Sabrina turned a shining gaze into his.

"Oh, Christopher! I feel as if I was going to *burst* with excitement."

A man in uniform was saying: "All aboard, please." And Benjamin was slapping all their backs. Christopher felt a hand slipped in his. A glance at Loo's face, and he said quickly: "Come on, son — it's going to be grand fun . . ." and felt steadier himself. There was a responsive clutching of his hand — a swift upglance, a sort of silent, quivering thank you — and there was the girl, taking it all, kissing her father goodbye, climbing in: "Here, Loo. . . . Step in — we'll see what kind of places we've got."

They were inside. "Twenty, twenty-one, and twenty-two," said a steward. Christopher got Loo beside him, Sabrina opposite.

"There's Daddy so fat and large," said Sabrina, "and soon he'll be a mere speck — a fly crawling upon the surface of the earth — a mite — a maggot." She took her new spotted handkerchief out of her pocket to wave.

"Look there, Loo — up there — you can watch

the altimeter — you'll see when we're climbing —" Christopher kept his arm through Loo's. "Now — we're off —"

The machine started across the field — faster — noisily. "Good-bye — good-bye!" — Sabrina was screaming and waving. "Oh, look at Daddy . . ."

Christopher put his handkerchief in Loo's hand so he had something ready to wave. Now the green and salmon-pink houses beyond were tearing past — now they were off the field — up — the white-tired wheels still whizzing in the air.

"Now, look, we're getting higher," said Christopher. Loo's profile nodded.

"Look — *look* at Daddy now," murmured Sabrina — "his face is a little pink blob — it looks like a wild strawberry —"

Christopher saw Loo swallow. (It occurred to him for the first time in his life that women might be the insensitive sex.)

"Seven hundred feet already," said Christopher, pointing. "Soon we'll be above the clouds."

There was the smallest interval, then the child's mind caught "above the clouds." "Above the clouds?" Christopher felt the arm clutched in his relax. "Oh," he said — "*oh!*" And thank heaven he was looking at that darned altimeter! . . .

"Eight hundred, over eight hundred now," said Christopher to Loo, as though he were repeating a charm.

But it was Sabrina who felt air-sick. Not, as she explained faintly through white and still vaguely smiling lips, that she "really minded vomiting" — but what she did mind (she explained that afterwards) was "*him* seeing her . . . !"

"Him" was the Beautiful-Young-Man-with-red-brown-suède-shoes. He was sitting across the gangway from them, reading something called *La Nouvelle Revue Française*, and as soon as Sabrina saw him (and until she was "overcome") she began to look at him with long smiling admiring eyes; and when he, faintly, smiled, she smiled back a long curling enchanted smile; and when the Beautiful Young Man leaned across and asked Christopher, in English, with a slight French accent, if he might offer "Mademoiselle, his daughter," one of his papers (he had *Vogue, Harper's Bazaar, The Bystander*, stacked in front of him), Christopher could n't refuse — and would have allowed Sabrina to be his "daughter" as an extra precaution if Loo had n't explained at once, shouting very loud because of the noise, that he was "their distant cousin from America." The young man — he had brown eyes, brown moustache — seemed amused. And Christopher was rather liking him but trying to get in a warning look at Sabrina (for he certainly had not reckoned on her using her gay and airy witchery on just anyone) when Sabrina began to be "overcome."

In fact the situation she provoked was one of the most practical knight-errantry. For the young man produced chewing gum and after a time persuaded her to chew it, and this eventually brought her round again. But Sabrina would rather have been saved from something more romantic. And though in the last part of the flight the Beautiful Young Man actually sat with them, and ordered them all tea, and ended by winning Loo's liking, and Sabrina herself sat up and ate buttered toast, jam, cake, and "squashed-fly biscuits" ordered by him, she could n't help being aware of what had nearly happened to her. However, his manner was so gallant, his clothes so lovely, his eyelashes so thick, his eyes so romantic, that she had forgotten almost everything else when the steward said, "We're getting in now."

When the plane did come down at Le Bourget, the Young Man helped them out — he took Sabrina's hand (like a courtier, she thought). But the moment they were on the field and going toward vast white cement buildings, a lot of men carrying cameras rushed at the Young Man and surrounded him. . . . And when they saw him again at the *douane* he was being followed by these men and several others.

"Press," said Christopher.

They asked him what he meant. He explained that the Young Man's arrival was getting Publicity and that he must be well known.

"*Rien à declarer, monsieur?*"

"No," said Christopher. And now they moved out through a barrier and there, out in the yard, was the

Young Man, and stepping out of a large motor was a lady, so exciting, ravishing, and peculiar that they did n't even see if she was pretty. She was even narrower and taller than Sabrina, in a black dress and black gloves and a little bright pale and pink colored face, a tiny hat right on the top of her golden screwed-up hair, and out of the hat waving immense black plumes (like horses at a costly funeral, Loo said afterwards). She held out her black-gloved hands to the Young Man and he kissed her on both cheeks — and camera men rushed up. And then he got into the car with her and they drove off.

"*Golly!*" said Loo.

"Come," said Christopher, "we have to get in the autocar."

Sabrina followed him — dreamily because her dream of Romance with her Beautiful Young Man was changing in her imagination to a dreamed-of tiny hat that she could wear on the very top of her head, and the immense plumes growing out of it would be — not black — but all different colors —

"What's byrrh?" Loo was saying. "I wonder who that fellow was?" Christopher was saying. "It does feel queer driving to the right," Loo was saying. ("Blue — and pink — and mauve — and white — and pale, pale green plumes — " Sabrina thought, still dreamy . . .)

Faithful to the principle of not being "planny," they left their suitcases at the Imperial Airways Terminus and walked up the Rue Auber and stood enthralled, but vague, in the Boulevard des Italiens.

Christopher had been to Paris once, on his honeymoon. He remembered Alice's taking him to Notre-Dame and to the Louvre, and that they had stayed in a hotel in the Avenue Montaigne. He was determined to avoid all three of those places. And he remembered that he had wanted to sit in a café under an awning and that Alice had been upset at the idea. (He remembered her telling him that Oscar Wilde had been ruined by sitting in cafés in Paris.)

The evening was hot. And he was just weighing this piece of remembered information against the charm of the awning and all the little tables outside the Café de la Paix when Sabrina said she was thirsty, and Loo said the airplane had made him hungry, and they all three went to the café, found a table, and sat down. Loo said it was like the Annual Church Outing from Tremayne last year when Mummie had put little tables out into the drive.

The waiter spoke English to them. Sabrina ordered a strawberry ice and a lemonade, Loo a tongue sandwich (he had difficulty in getting this understood), and Christopher a whiskey-and-soda. They all felt madly excited again, Loo talking incessantly about the shape of the buses, the colors of the taxis, the people on the pavement. Sabrina's ice cream looked so good to Christopher when it came that he ordered one for himself and then Loo wanted one also.

When they had all finished their ice cream Christopher said they must find a hotel. Sabrina suggested they should explore until they saw one which seemed right. This idea pleased them all. For the streets were cooler now, and there was a feel of excitement in the warm pale violet air.

So they began to walk. The shop windows were full of flowers, or satin and gold lace boxes of chocolates, and what Sabrina said must be "filmy garments." ...

They reached the Church of the Madeleine. There Christopher looked at his *Blue Guide* and decided to take the direction of Montmartre, where he thought they might find a hotel at a healthier altitude. For he felt very responsible for the children. And was quite unaware that they felt responsible for him.

As they went as the *Guide* seemed to direct, they passed a big shop that surprised them all by being called the French for "spring," and a railway station outside which huge posters urged them: "*Visitez l'Angleterre.*"

"Ha! As if we *would!*" said Loo scornfully.

Now the shop windows had either quantities of boots and shoes or heaps and tiers of foreign-looking food in them.

"We must keep moving gradually on an upward gradient," said Christopher.

A lot of small and narrow streets seemed to be going upward and they chose one.

"You forgot to go to Cook's for your letter," said Loo.

Christopher said he could go in the morning. The dusk was gathering and he began to wonder if he should n't have booked rooms ahead in an unoriginal way. He had an idea it would be wrong to take children walking about a city like Paris at night. So he stopped and started to look in his *Blue Guide*.

"What's the matter?" said Loo.

"Maybe it will tell me of a good hotel."

"Of course it will — hundreds," said Sabrina. "But — "

"I don't think you should be out late," he said, looking from one to the other and thinking that their faces looked most strangely lucid and fair in this narrow street where everybody seemed to be wearing black.

"Well, then," said Loo. "What about that?" He pointed across the street. Christopher read in gold letters on a black marble plaque the word "Hotel." There were windows with nice fresh-looking lace curtains, and little balconies outside all the upper windows, and the whole façade, on examination, though modest, looked agreeable. And the shutters had been freshly painted a light blue-grey which made it look cleaner than the neighboring houses.

"It looks rather nice," Sabrina said.

Christopher glanced at the plaque again to read slowly in smaller gold lettering that there was "all comfort," and "hot water at all hours." This decided him. His little pangs of responsibility were quieted by the idea of the children having hot baths. He said to them:

"You wait here while I go in and ask." So he crossed the road and went in.

When he came out again he said: "Yes, she can give us two rooms between us. I wish my French were a bit better . . ." Loo noticed that he was flustered trying to make French explanations. Sabrina wanted to laugh when they went in with him and saw the lady he had been explaining to, she had so much bosom, and hair the color of marigolds, and she looked at each of them in turn with such boot-button eyes. But the hotel was more luxurious inside than out. It was, Sabrina thought, what the Lamb's Head at Tremayne tried to be; red plush and gilt and mirrors, but much more really elegant.

The lady led them upstairs. She was very scented, just as Mummie had said Frenchwomen would be. Sabrina noticed that she had sand shoes on. She and her fragrance preceded them down a corridor. She opened first one door, then one next to it. Then she went into the first room and they followed. "*Voilà*," she said to Christopher, and some more. Sabrina understood that it was her best room. It had a wallpaper striped purple and gold, and the huge bed was covered with purple velvet and round bolsters covered with the same velvet, and there was a large pink silk lampshade with gold bobbles round the bottom of it.

Loo exclaimed he had never seen such a beautiful room, and stared at everything in turn.

"*Et à côté*," said the lady — and led them out of this

to inspect the next room. It was smaller, with a deep red wallpaper covered with pink-and-gold roses, but an equally enormous bed covered with brown velvet — and bolsters to match — and red silk tassels at both ends of each bolster.

"I like this best of all," said Loo, deeply impressed.

"*Mais, madame* — " Christopher stuck. He turned to Sabrina. Would she please say that there were only two beds? Sabrina said it. The woman became exasperated at once and said that already downstairs she had explained all that to Monsieur. . . . "But that, *enfin* . . .*"* She became voluble, and her hands flung up in gestures of renunciation — dismissal — and farewell. But Sabrina felt that she was really determined not to let them go, as she certainly meant to overcharge Christopher in the morning. If Loo had understood this he would have flared up in anger, but Sabrina always knew by instinct when to shrug. So she said: "*Bien, bien, madame,*" and smiled, turning up the corners of her mouth while Madame quieted down. Then Sabrina said to Christopher: —

"Loo and I can *easily* sleep in one bed. We often have." She turned to the woman. "*Je couche avec mon frère,*" she said as reassuringly as possible.

The woman's boot-button stare met hers, then shifted to Christopher, then to Loo. Then she changed her cross expression to an ingratiating one, and smiled tightly and was about to go when Christopher said: "Tell her I'm going to fetch our valises." Sabrina told her this and it seemed to surprise her. But she only said: "*Tiens, tiens, tiens,*" and went out.

Christopher made them have the purple room and left them in it, and said he would get a taxi and be right back. They went out on to their balcony and looked down three floors into the street and saw him come out. They shouted down to him but he did n't hear because a bus came past filling the whole width of the street. It slowed down at the next corner down the hill and to their surprise they saw Christopher run after it and leap on. "He has quite an adventurous streak," said Sabrina. "He did n't mean to go by bus and suddenly he felt its wild call."

Then Loo poked her. A lady had come out on to the balcony next to theirs. She was young, with dark, curly hair and very, very pretty, and was looking at them with an amused smile. She wore a Japanese mauve dressing gown with pink irises growing up it, and she had on red slippers.

Sabrina smiled back at once. And the lady said: —
"I spik Eenglish."
"Oh, do you?"
She came to the side of her balcony nearest them.
"You Eenglish? You Americain?"
"We 're English. He — *le monsieur* — " Sabrina pointed down to where the bus had halted — "*il est américain.*"
"Oh, ho! *Vous parlez française, mademoiselle!*"
"A little. I learn at school."

The lady leaned her elbows on the iron rail and her sleeves fell back, showing that they were lined with crimson. "And you, ma honee?" She spoke to the now admiring Loo.

Loo shook his head. "I don't speak French."

She gave a high little laugh — a pretty noise (like the glass Japanese things that you could hang in windows to tinkle in the wind, Sabrina thought).

Loo felt rather embarrassed but went on liking her.

"*Et — le — monsieur* — 'e 'as gone awigh?"

Sabrina said: "Only to fetch our luggage. You see we 've only just arrived. We 've never been to France before — or to Paris, of course."

This time a perfect gale tinkled the glass music of the lady's laughter. "You come — you come *to-digh?*"

This time Loo was annoyed. He did n't laugh like this when strangers came to the Rectory. He was just going to lose his temper when the lady turned her head and shouted: "*Oui, oui — mon chou —* " And then a man's voice inside her room said something to her, and she smiled at them, blew a kiss to Loo, and disappeared.

"I expect her husband thinks she 's catching cold," said Loo — feeling a vague masculine approval for the acts of discipline that recalled ladies given to irrational mirth. "Still," he said — "she *is* pretty."

But Sabrina had gone dreamy. "There 's a lovely poem — a French poem about a balcony — I don't really understand it, but I learned it."

"You're always learning poetry you don't understand," said Loo. He knew she was going to begin saying some, which was one of her habits that always made him feel prickly and yet fascinated him. So he seized her hand and pulled her back into the purple room so that at least she would n't be seen looking so dreamy. She sat down on the purple velvet and began saying the poem: —

"*Les soirs illuminés par l'ardeur du charbon,*
Et les soirs au balcon, voilés de vapeurs roses.
Que ton sein m'était doux! que ton cœur m'était bon!
Nous avons dit souvent d'impérissables choses,
Les soirs illuminés par l'ardeur du charbon.

"*Que les soleils sont beaux dans les chaudes soirées!*
Que l'espace est profond! que le cœur est puissant!
En me penchant vers toi, reine des adorées,
Je croyais respirer le parfum de ton sang.
Que les soleils sont beaux dans les chaudes soirées!"

"I hate French," said Loo. Then: "I wonder where the lavatory is."

Sabrina did n't notice him so he walked to the door and looked out, and then went to explore.

Sabrina, feeling quite choked with inexplicable feeling, got up and went out again on to the balcony. The houses opposite were in shadow now, and the pansy-dark sky above their chimneys was beginning to have a lovely pink glow all over it. She stood for a long time and then she heard Loo's voice behind her in the room:

"I got lost — but the pretty lady directed me. Her husband's quite nice — he was going out. As they were so kind I asked if they would both come to breakfast with us to-morrow morning. I explained we were leaving before lunch. She said her husband would n't be able to, but she would like to very much . . ."

At this moment Christopher came in followed by a man in a green apron. The man put on the light. Sabrina said to Loo: "You 'd better tell Christopher."

Loo began to gasp a little. "Oh, Christopher," he began.

By now Christopher knew the signs of Loo's being troubled in his mind. So he put his hand on his shoulder and said: "What is it, son?"

Loo explained that he had asked the lady. "You see — she was very kind — "

"And it seemed neighborly — eh?" said Christopher. Sabrina could n't tell if he was laughing inside, or not. But he said: "Well, that could n't be nicer, anyway. We 'll order a swell breakfast for her."

"Oh, thank you," said Loo.

And now Christopher produced the parcel containing the lunch they had n't eaten in the aeroplane. He said they must eat it for their supper as it seemed there was no restaurant downstairs, and he did n't want to take them out at night.

So they ate the pasties and drank milk, all sitting on the immense purple velvet bed, and feeling intensely gay.

In the morning Sabrina made the bed so that the room should be tidy for the visitor. Christopher came in and said he hoped they had both slept well; he had been disturbed at intervals by people coming in late and banging doors and talking in the corridors. Also he had woken early to reflect on the responsibility of the children, and feel worried again. But he was reassured by the sight of Sabrina in her pink and white striped cotton patting the velvet tasseled bolsters, and Loo, whistling, and setting chairs around a wicker table on which he had spread two of his clean pocket handkerchiefs, edge to edge, and put the last peach, saved from the evening, upon a pink ash tray in the centre.

So Christopher set about ordering breakfast, he and Sabrina shouting together into a telephone in the wall; and Loo prepared to fetch the French lady: "Oh — and her name is Nicolette, she told me."

"Nicolette what?" asked Sabrina.

"She did n't say."

"But her husband must have a name!"

"Yes," said Loo. "I asked her. But she did n't seem to understand."

"Then I guess we 'll just have to call her Mrs. Nicolette," said Christopher. He sat down and wiped his brow after the ordering. A lady lacking a surname was simple compared to making that dame downstairs understand that bacon had to be crisp. And Sabrina was still shouting into the box on the wall about orange juice.

"If we don't find any letter from Lacaze at Cook's to-day," said Christopher, "I think we'll make for one of the coasts. It's too hot to stop in Paris, anyway."

Loo came back with "Mrs. Nicolette," no longer in her Japanese wrapper, but very smart in a black dress, short and tight-fitting in a pretty way, and white shoes and a bunch of white gardenias pinned at the neck. Loo said: "This is our cousin Christopher." And Christopher rose and shook hands courteously, and she said: —

"I spik Eengleesh," and smiled brilliantly at him; and sat down in the armchair, and crossed her hands on her lap, and bent her head back to laugh at Loo, who had got one of the cushions of the bed to put at her back.

"Eh! *Mon petit cavalier?*" She turned to Christopher: "'E is nize, your young cousin, is n' 'e?"

"*Oui — oui, madame,*" said Christopher. She seemed a delightful little creature, so friendly and different from the types of Englishwomen he'd seen around in Queen Anne's Mansions.

There was a knock at the door and a rattle outside, and then the man in the green baize apron came in, his chin covered with dark bristles, carrying an immense tray, on which were an array of little white jugs, a quantity of rolls, a little melting butter, and a bottle whose label was translated by Sabrina into "Orange Flower Water."

"*No bacon?*" shouted Christopher at the man.

The man looked at him with bitter indifference, set the tray down, and went out.

"*Pas de bacon!*" said Christopher, turning, full of anxious apology, to his lady guest. "Why, it's a terrible breakfast to offer — and —"

But Mrs. Nicolette was shaken by one of her own gales of tinkling laughter — caused, it seemed, by the orange flower water. "For you — it is — for you?" she demanded of him.

Christopher took off his pince-nez and blinked with bright owl eyes at Sabrina — but she smiled and sat down and said, "It can't be helped," and began to pour the coffee out of the little jugs.

"The peach is for you," said Loo to the lady.

"Aha, *une pêche* — but that is *nize!*" And she began ripping the skin off.

"All the same," said Loo, "I wish they'd understood about the bacon." He and Christopher both looked so shaken by a sense of their lack of gallantry that Sabrina said, "I'll try once more," and went to the box on the wall and took up the receiver and said: "*Madame, j'ai dit cochon! — COCHON!*" But the receiver only clicked downstairs, and just when Sabrina was sitting down again the door banged open and in came *Madame la Propriétaire,* her marigold hair on end, and her face pallid this morning and squdged up with what seemed to be rage, speaking for several minutes very fast, the word *cochon* recurring. Sabrina turned to their guest, who was biting off mouthfuls of her peach with an air of good-tempered enjoyment. "What is she saying?"

Mrs. Nicolette smiled. "She say you insult 'er."

The proprietress was raging and breathing over by Christopher, her bosom close to his left ear. Christopher, more and more distressed for their beautiful guest, tried to sign that he would deal with whatever the situation was after — or out in the corridor, finally indicating Mrs. Nicolette, who was now drinking her coffee, with a protective and shocked gesture. But this gesture only produced a second's pause, during which Madame drew a snarling breath, set her hands upon her hips, and then with angry-pig eyes on her pretty countrywoman began another tirade, and among the shrill words and exclamations Loo and Christopher could detect the old word *cochon* — and: "Ha! Nicolette!" several times, and Sabrina made out the word *fille*. . . . But during the tirade Mrs. Nicolette remained dignified, smiling faintly, and dipping her roll in her coffee. And when at last there was a panting pause in the tirade she turned, drew herself up with tranquil charm, and said to Christopher: "Do not 'ear 'er — she is an old dog-woman."

But when the proprietress began again, Nicolette got up and said something which made her flush and then grow pallid again and at last, muttering and declaiming and pointing her finger back at all of them, she went out of the room.

Nicolette then sat down again, grinned prettily at

Loo, and dipped the last piece of her roll. "Aha — *mon petit cavalier*, that woman!"

"I hope your husband will come back and be very angry with her," said Loo, scarlet with chivalrous indignation.

"Aha! You bet 'e will, *mon petit chou* — you bet." She turned to Christopher: "I tell 'im what she say. There are many many gentlemen *camarades* to me that they will come and smack 'er bottom!"

"Well — " said Christopher after a moment's pause, "I certainly hope they will!" He put down his cup and added that he would n't at all mind being one of them!

So they packed up rapidly after breakfast. And Nicolette stood by while Christopher paid his bill. For which he was sincerely grateful to her, although Madame seemed quite to have forgotten the unpleasing scene at breakfast, and was carrying on a loud but ingratiating conversation with a lady and a smart-looking colored man in a pale grey bowler hat who had just arrived. (Nicolette seemed to know the colored man and smiled at him and added: "*B'jour*, Thomas!")

Then Nicolette was very kind, and said she would escort them to Cook's; for she was both startled and amused that they should not know where they were going until they had been to Cook's and found a letter there. She said "You fonny-boy" several times to Christopher about this. And when she was helping him shut his valise she gave her little peals of laughter and once chucked him under the chin and said he was a "*grand bébé.*"

She went to her room and returned looking astonishingly French in a small white hat tilted forward over her eyes and a black spotted veil, and white gloves with black flowers embroidered on them, and a white bag decorated with the silhouettes of two black cats and a black crescent moon.

She went out in the street with them and called a taxi from the rank on the corner. The driver evidently knew her and they seemed to say some jolly good-mornings together in a thick friendly raucous sort of French of which Sabrina did n't understand one word.

When they got to Cook's there was a letter at the *Poste Restante* for Christopher; but it was not from Monsieur Lacaze. It was from Alice. Christopher read the letter while Mrs. Nicolette went over with the children to the Foreign Exchange Department, as Loo wished to exchange the Bishop's ten-shilling note for francs.

It was curious to Christopher to see the dark-grey embossed heading of the notepaper, "181 Maple Street, Green Plains, Massachusetts," and to read Alice's firm yet spidery handwriting.

DEAR CHRISTOPHER:

I am sure that you had my cable of almost two months ago in which I told you a piece of news that my heart is still too full to be able to speak about. We rather hoped for a reply from you just to make me feel anyway, Christopher dear, that you were not harboring any resentment. I will not go into the matter fully, for words can say so little. But maybe you realized for some time that our marriage was not ideal and that we were so differently keyed, as Hamnet puts it. However, dear, I won't go into all this now but let bygones be bygones. I hope that you have not suffered too much in facing up at long last to what you probably knew in your heart quite a while ago, that is to say that you were not the man for me although I did my best, and always tried to put a brave face on it. On the other hand we live in a modern world and I hope we will always be able to be good friends. As Hamnet is anxious to have a little talk with you about certain practical matters that have to be fixed up before our marriage (in the autumn, I hope!) we are taking a little trip to Europe — a sort of "preliminary platonic honeymoon," as Hamnet put it! And Hamnet thought maybe we could meet somewhere in France, as I hear *from Mrs. Peckett* — who told me she had a card from you — that you are leaving England and planning a trip for August. Hamnet and I are to be in Provence from August 5th until August 23rd or 24th. And Hamnet suggests that we might "foregather" at Nîmes, where we are stopping three days for the bullfighting (which Hamnet intends to use in a chapter of *Kinship with the Stars* — which he intends to start writing next spring). We will be going to the Hotel des Arènes — so the best will be if you will telegraph us there, and let us know the day of your arrival. Of course if you cannot possibly fix up this plan telephone us there and we'll see what Hamnet can arrange.

Your affectionate friend,

ALICE

P.S. We sail on the *Normandie* on July 30th.

"I got fifty-six francs and twenty centimes," said Loo.

"Fine," said Christopher vaguely.

"And now where are we going?" said Sabrina.

"What is the date?" said Christopher to the young lady with "Visit Paris at Night" written up behind her counter.

"The second of August, *monsieur*."

"Yes," said Nicolette, who had been smiling at the *commissionnaire*. "It is the second of August. I know it was yesterday the first."

"Then we are going to Nîmes," said Christopher, and went over to the *commissionnaire,* who told him that one bought tickets upstairs.

They all went up in the *ascenseur,* and Sabrina said: "I wish Nicolette could come too," holding Mrs. Nicolette's hand.

But Mrs. Nicolette smiled and shook her head. "*À Nîmes?* Mademoiselle is very kind, but I have to stop 'ere — *à Paris.*"

"Of *course* she has!" said Loo as they got out of the *ascenseur.* "She has to stay with her husband."

Mrs. Nicolette glanced at him for a second and smiled faintly. Then she went and stood beside Christopher and helped him to buy "*3 billets, 2me classe — à Nîmes*" and look up a train. There proved to be one before *midi.* So she drove with them to the Gare de Lyon, and joked again with the taximan, and found them two porters and seemed to joke with them also, for they immediately became very gay and obliging. And when Mrs. Nicolette advised Christopher to buy some luncheon to take with them on the train, "or they would have to go in the *wagon-restaurant*, which would cost a 'ell of a lot," the porters helped with the purchasing — escorting them to the buffet, where Christopher bought some *croissants*, hard-boiled eggs, bunches of little greenish grapes — and Mrs. Nicolette bought, and insisted on presenting them with, a bottle of wine.

When they were in the train and leaning down from the windows of the corridor to say good-bye, Loo thought how *very* pretty Mrs. Nicolette looked standing below them between the two nice laughing porters: and he suddenly felt sharply though not deeply sad — and there went through his head a vague confused idea about leaving people hurting just because loving or liking them was so exciting. . . .

Christopher too felt an emotion — of surprise and gratitude that linked up with a general feeling that somehow there seemed to be unexpected gay or kindly or delightfully odd people waiting around every corner of existence. Sabrina waved and blew a kiss and kept shouting: "We shall come and see you on the way back — " And just as the train was moving remembered that they had n't any address — and shouted, "*Adresse*" frantically, leaning out and stretching her long arms so that the two porters shouted: "*Prenez garde, mademoiselle!*" But Mrs. Nicolette dashed up, her bag open, holding out something white.

" — Here!" screamed Sabrina — and clutched down and got the visiting card just in time.

And then they all waved and Mrs. Nicolette waved and waved, standing between the porters in their blue blouses, who waved also.

At last, when they sat down in the smoke-smelling sun-hot carriage to read the card it had

MADEMOISELLE NICOLETTE
34a Rue d'Amsterdam

printed on it, and in one corner "English spoken."

"What a sensible idea," said Loo with admiration, "to put about speaking English, is n't it?"

But Christopher looked preoccupied.

After they had lunched and Christopher had drunk most of the bottle of wine, and the children had tasted the wine and disliked it, Christopher fell asleep in a corner of the carriage, and Sabrina and Loo went out into the corridor, and stood with their arms on the rail of the wide windows and watched green poplars and silver rivers and grey-turreted châteaux flying past, and Loo said: —

"That letter, Sabrina, that Christopher had. . . . I don't think he liked it or something."

"It's like traveling through a tapestry," said Sabrina. "I like France. Perhaps it was from his wife! It had a mauve American stamp, I saw, with a little picture of the capitol, I think it must be."

"His — *wife*, Sab!"

"Yes. I asked Daddy and he told me Christopher *did* have a wife but they 're divorced — " Loo looked so distressed that she said quickly: "You know divorce has nothing to do with sin in America. It 's just a way of showing displeasure."

"I see," said Loo. "But then — who was — displeased?"

"What d' you mean?"

"I mean Christopher or his wife?"

Sabrina said: "Both. Mutual consent, Daddy said. She 's marrying again."

"I wonder what she was like? . . . Christopher's wife, I mean."

Sabrina pulled the two front pieces of her hair and tied them vaguely under her chin, and let them curl loose again.

"He told Daddy that she 's a very brilliant and intellectual woman. 'A pard-like spirit, beautiful and swift,' I expect. Not like him at all. . . . Look at that man fishing for French fishes."

"But Christopher 's not stupid," Loo flared.

"No, Loo — I did n't mean that."

"What did you mean, then?"

"Well. He 's just what Mummie calls 'a dear,' and probably she 's a sort of Cleopatra. Perhaps it was like in Browning and he was 'the spray the Bird clung to.' "

"Well, it must be lonely for him, though."

"He might marry again, too."

"What? *He?*" Loo exclaimed.

"Well — look at Mrs. Dovey's father. He was seventy-nine when he remarried. And Abraham —"

"You can't judge by Abraham," said Loo.

When they went back into the carriage Christopher was awake and reading the *Blue Guide*. He said: —

"Why don't we stop off at Avignon for a day or two? It seems it's full of remarkable sights."

"Two popes quarreled to be Pope," said Sabrina, "or something like that, and one went to Avignon. And then there's the song of course." She began to sing it in spite of Loo, who didn't see how the ladies in the two other corners could fail to wake to the shaming spectacle of Sabrina doing "*Les beaux Messieurs font comme ça*" — and bowing with Christopher's straw hat upon her disheveled head.

She stopped abruptly.

"Yes — Avignon." Then: "Christopher!"

"What, dear?"

"Where are your glasses? You're reading without your glasses."

"I — lost them," said Christopher. "I — dropped them — in the hotel, perhaps — I don't know exactly. Anyway, I happen to be farsighted so it doesn't really make much difference —"

"It makes a great deal of difference," said Sabrina. "It makes you look quite handsome — and it makes you look *much* less — less —"

Loo's shout interrupted her: —

"*Great Scott!*"

"Why, Loo?"

"Daddy's right about French people," said Loo. "I *saw* him as we went out —"

"Loo darling, what?"

"Just imagine him *daring* to —! I thought he looked different."

"Whoever, Loo?"

"The man with the bristly chin — who brought our breakfast! Did n't *you* notice, Sab? — When he brought our luggage down?"

"A pair of familiar glasses gleamed upon his noisome nose?"

Loo nodded.

"*Well!*" said Sabrina.

Loo stood in the middle of the compartment on tiptoe with anger.

"We ought to go back — or wire or telephone or — something."

"On the other hand, Loo," Christopher interrupted, "just supposing it was the Hand of Destiny — that chose this way of making me into a really handsome man!"

"Of *course!*" said Sabrina. "That's just what it *is!* . . . 'Earth has not anything to show more fair' than Cousin Christopher without his glasses!"

A few moments later Christopher's train of thought brought him to a question, thrown out quizzically at Sabrina: "Less what? . . . You said — not wearing them made me look less —"

"Oh — *darling* Christopher," said Sabrina, "I was only teasing!"

"Less what — exactly, Sabrina?"

"*Well,*" said Sabrina, "I think less awfully — *gentle-manly!*"

"*Gentle-manly?* Then what," he demanded, "what would you rather I was?"

"*Well* . . . Perhaps it's your white starched collars —"

"Well?"

"You see I love you anyway, Christopher darling — we — all do. But I *should* like you to look a Supremely Romantic Figure . . ."

"I — see —" said Christopher. "Like — Clark Gable, for instance?"

"More like Lord Byron."

"As far as I remember, Sabrina, Lord Byron was — a bad man?"

Sabrina nodded, and her long eyes gleamed like shavings of aquamarine. "I should love you to be *bad*, Christopher!"

Loo bounced across the carriage, sat close up against Christopher, and looked at his elder but incalculable sister with a stare of reproving common sense.

"I would n't . . ."

Leaving Hamnet to bathe his mosquito bites, Alice Columin fetched her gloves and her *Blue Guide* from her room, and went out to get her first impression of Avignon.

She followed the directions of the clerk at the desk, and proceeded through several narrow streets that smelled at one moment of onions and stale wine, the next, as she passed the bead-curtained door of a *coiffeur*, of chypre; and the next of something she did not like to think about. As she went this latter smell persisted and became part of the character of the town.

Alice stopped twice to consult the *Blue Guide* and hold her handkerchief to her nose.

When she emerged on to the steep sunlit square, surrounded by the striped awnings of its cafés, she saw the Palace of the Popes. It rose, vast, and of a remarkable golden-colored stone, above the far end of the square. Its cinnamon-colored tower made the sky seem dark blue, like gentians. Alice felt the thrill she had expected to feel; and advanced slowly up the square, thinking that she would sit down at one of the cafés, and order herself an orange juice with ice in it, and sip that until it was time for her to meet Hamnet at the Restaurant des Papes.

She began to glance from one café to another, wondering which would be cleanest, and was finally attracted by one that had a red and white awning, four bay trees in front of it, and a group of Americans already sitting there. Alice selected a table in the corner. It seemed even hotter here under the awning than out on the square. But she was glad to sit down. She ordered her *"orange pressée"* and *"de la glace."* She was glad she had chosen this one. The café next to this looked cheaper, and was crowded with the type of tourist she and Hamnet always tried to avoid — noisy, mostly young — many of them wearing shorts and carrying rucksacks. . . . Of course, as she'd said to Hamnet that day at Versailles, it was nice to think of people traveling even if they were poor, but . . . ! A good many of them were lunching there, and what they ate gave off odors of hot olive oil and garlic. Once more Alice got out her handkerchief and sniffed *"Extase."* . . . Hamnet had chosen the scent for her that first day in Paris, and this started her thinking about Hamnet . . . about his difficult nature. Maybe he'd be less easily worried, feel more himself, when he did get his secretary back. It was all nerves, she was sure. . . .

The waiter brought the orange juice. He was young, with a picturesque face and fine black eyes. Alice gave him a good tip and he said, *"Merci, madame,"* and gave her a smile that she might have found bold if it hadn't vaguely pleased her. She spooned two lumps of ice into her glass; they tinkled coolly; and her thoughts now fell into a pleasant sequence: she thought of the delicious luncheon that she and Hamnet would eat in another half hour; of the experience it would be to visit the Palace of the Popes during the afternoon; of the description she would give of it in later conversations. ... For one of her satisfactions on this journey was anticipating her return, when she would say: "Hamnet and I saw — did — thought — " and "Hamnet has a way of revealing new beauties in the things we've all seen many times." (Here she would refer to the "Mona Lisa," St. Mark's, to Mont Blanc perhaps.) ... And she would add some such phrase as "That's what being an artist means — isn't it?" And Alice smiled, in advance, the sweet intimate smile that would light her face as she spoke.

At this moment — perhaps it was a specially loud rattle of plates, or scraping of chairs in the café next door, perhaps it was the rich, fishy, olive-oily steaming of a bowl of bouillabaisse that a waiter was carrying to some noisy party there that caught Alice's attention and made her glance over her shoulder and see, at a small table ten yards off, a man in sun glasses sitting with a girl in a straw hat, and a small boy. All three, the man, the girl, and the boy, wore crimson cotton shirts, open at the neck, and the man wore purple rope-soled shoes, and all three were laughing.

It took Alice an entire minute to realize that the man was Christopher. ...

And when she did fully realize this, her amazement changed at once to intense, silent anger. And the more she looked at him the angrier she became. She looked from his shirt to his trousers, which were pale greyish and dirty, then at his feet, then at his bare arms, then at his hair — which she had never seen except pomaded modestly down into a smooth grey-brown cap, curvetting up here and there from his forehead and above his ears, thicker, wavier, a good deal browner than she had supposed it, and behaving as if it had never known thirty years of daily and reputable extinction beneath a derby hat —

Then Alice looked at his companions. The girl was extremely pretty and could not be a day more than seventeen. Alice's breathing quickened. The boy was less easy to explain. Alice stared at him so intently that he caught her look, and a smile that had just begun to spread over his face stopped, his cheeks flushed, and, averting his look from hers, he leaned close to Christopher and made some inaudible remark. Alice saw the girl smile; and then Christopher's gaze, hidden behind the dark glasses, turned in her direction. Then he stood up. She went towards them.

"Why — Alice?"

"I — did n't expect to find you here, Christopher!"

"Well — ugh — well, you see, Alice, I — we 're on our *way* to Nîmes . . . where I was to meet you, you know, Alice . . . I had your letter . . . I found it at Cook's in Paris, and so I decided — or rather — we decided that —"

"You have n't introduced your — friends to me, Christopher!"

Christopher, still gripping his spoon, said: "Sorry —

oh no — no — of course — Alice. . . . This, these are my cousins! My cousin, Miss Sabrina Columin. . . . And Waterloo Columin — "

Alice continued to hold her handbag and guidebook against her stomach, and said: "I suppose, Christopher, that you imagine you 're being — amusing — ?" She bent a pale steely glance upon Sabrina: "Cousin! — I should *say* so! — And — and — Waterloo!"

Sabrina leaned across the table and smiled upward at Alice. "You see, Mummie hero-worshiped the Duke of Wellington."

Alice stared icily: "I am afraid I don't see."

Sabrina tipped her head on one side and looked upward at Alice through her gold-brown eyelashes. (It was a charm-trick she had used instinctively ever since she was a year old and it had never failed.) "Perhaps you 're like *me?*" she suggested — "Perhaps you adore Napoleon madly?"

"No," said Alice curtly, "I do not."

Her tone would have discouraged anyone else. But Sabrina only shook her hair, curled up the lovely corners of her mouth, and asked: —

"I wonder who is your favorite hero in history?"

Alice said to Christopher: —

"We are at the Grand Hotel here. As Hamnet is very anxious to see you — you might as well have your — little talk here? You could come in some time this evening . . ."

Christopher said that he would come. And continued to stand awkward and troubled, holding his spoon, while Alice, with a sharp, "We'll expect you then —" turned away, passed between the crowded tables, put up her parasol and proceeded up the square, and disappeared round a corner.

When she had gone the children looked at Christopher. Loo was startled, Sabrina confused between her delight in a new specimen and her troubled feeling for Christopher.

Loo said: "Well — what a *beastly* lady!"

Sabrina said: "Christopher, your bouillabaisse."

"What did she mean when she said '*Cuzzn, I should say so*'?"

"Shut up, Loo."

Christopher withdrew his stare from the corner where Alice had disappeared. He gazed down into the glistening yellow-green bread in his bouillabaisse and the tiny crabs and the *écrevisse* claws.

"Please don't tell us anything," said Sabrina, "if you'd rather not."

But Christopher said: "She used to be my wife —"

They looked at each other. For a moment they felt shy of him because he was, suddenly, a person to whom something bad had happened.

Christopher looked up and saw their shyness, and behind this shyness their troubled fear of something vaguely ugly. (He was to perceive more precisely, later on, Sabrina's idea of human ugliness; which was

— though she did n't herself know the definition — "people with no love in them.")

"But she 's — " Loo broke out.

Sabrina snapped: "Shut — "

"What, Loo?" said Christopher very gently. Loo's surprise had changed to emotion now; so after being red he 'd become pale. "I — only — "

"Go on, Loo — "

Loo breathed: " — but — did you — " His dark green eyes were bright, the pupils expanding. Then he suddenly breathed out: "But were you in *love* with her?"

Christopher warded off the dreadful simplicity of the question.

"Why — Alice is no longer young now. After all, I myself . . ."

"Mother is not young now," said Sabrina, "but Daddy is still in love with her."

"And Queen Elizabeth was n't young . . ."

"And Ninon de Lenclos . . ."

"And Cleopatra."

Loo said: "Anyway, you divorced with her because you did n't love her *any more*, did n't you?" He went on sympathetically: "I expect she *has* changed a lot from the days of your courtship."

"But Shakespeare says — " Sabrina hesitated.

"What, Sabrina?" said Christopher sharply.

". . . Love is not love
   Which alters when it alteration finds."

Christopher looked from one to the other; met Loo's devoted troubled gaze; Sabrina's lovely questioning lucidity. Then he thought of Alice. Alice now. Alice twenty years back.

"It never was love," he said.

When he had said this the children bent over their bouillabaisse and began to eat it fast and talk to each other. They felt as if Christopher had gone into deep mourning before their eyes.

The fact that Hamnet had grown fatter was not concealed even by his Lanvin dressing gown, and his blond face was punctuated and flushed with mosquito bites. He was looking very cross when Christopher arrived, Alice was evidently distressed, and the room smelled of oil of lavender.

Since midday Christopher had been thinking of Alice with bitterness; for as she stood over him and the children in the café he had perceived her suddenly as a pretentious dull woman, who had consumed the best years of his life as if they were a bag of peanuts! And during the afternoon (while the children insisted upon paddling in the Rhone) he had sat on the hot stones on the shore and hated her (since it is natural to hate those whom our own lack of judgment has made harmful to us).

But now Christopher noticed her manner, now that she was with Hamnet — a new nervousness, an unfamiliar unsureness of herself. . . . And he saw — in that first ten minutes since Hamnet had held out a damp limp hand and begun talking — that Alice, in her immaculate pink shantung suit, her white hat, her double row of pearls, and her condescending glances, was mentally in a condition of disarray. . . . She began several sentences and left them unfinished. She sat down first on one chair, then on another. She pulled her gloves off and then started drawing them on again. . . . And then, quite suddenly, between one of Hamnet's sentences and another, when Alice had begun to speak, and been disconcerted by a glance from him, Christopher saw that she was n't, after all, the domineering, hard, malicious, slave-driving, conceited vampire of a female he had hated as he sat beside the Rhone on the hot pebbles, but just a rather stupid woman, suffering pathetically in middle age from the excesses of her early self-esteem. And as he made perfunctory replies to Hamnet, refusing a cigar, he found himself contrasting her with Fanny Columin, who must be around the same age.

" — Spiritually confining," Hamnet was saying now, "for a man of Creative Ability to be harassed — not to say exasperated, by financial worries — "

"You see, Christopher," said Alice — "what Hamnet would *like* to have arranged is — "

"Alice dear." Hamnet's upper lip lifted. "Alice dear, let me explain to Christopher."

" — No really fine Work," said Hamnet, "can be done under such conditions. . . . This — er — trip

— is in the nature of a 'calmant' — a rest cure, as a preparation for Future Work — "

Christopher crossed his knees and lit a cigarette. Alice was staring at him. She said in parenthesis: "Christopher, where are your glasses?"

"They were stolen in Paris. Now see here, Hamnet — "

Hamnet moved restively at something unfamiliar, even casual, in the tone of his future wife's ex-husband.

" — what you 've been getting around to telling me, Hamnet, is, I should say, that you 'd like me to settle some more money on Alice. Is that so?"

" — Dear me — " breathed Alice. She stared down at Christopher's purple rope-soled *espadrilles.*

Hamnet took his cigar out of his mouth and gave a faint, distressed, but comprehending smile. The delicate approach, the fine interpretations, were not, that smile indicated, of course to be expected . . . from Christopher. But he only said, very gently: —

"Alice has been accustomed to every luxury."

Christopher mentioned the sum he had already settled on Alice, through his solicitors, and stated that he had only left himself with an income of four thousand dollars. At which statement Alice gave a soft low cry of: "Well — you did n't have to quit working!"

"No," said Christopher, "no — "

A vague gleam in his eyes turned to a smile, the smile slowly to a grin, and the grin to a chuckle. Then he said, tempering his tone to her anxious angry stare: "On the other hand, dear, I'd made quite a bit! And there is such a thing as overproduction . . ." He added, turning to Hamnet: "Why — just think what things might have got like if *Creation* had gone on another seven days!"

There was a pause.

"Evidently, Christopher," said Alice, "you have been in queer company."

"And all Alice asks of you . . ." Hamnet went on.

"You see, Christopher — there are all sorts of extra expenses."

As Alice spoke the door opened and a slender little man came in on tiptoe, talking very fast in a soprano voice, and carrying a dispatch case, an overcoat, and yellow-backed books. He was Hamnet's French secretary, who had just arrived from Paris, where Hamnet had engaged him.

Christopher shook hands with him. Alice ordered him a cocktail. Now that his secretary had arrived Hamnet became much better tempered, and Alice consequently more gracious. And in an atmosphere of slightly hysterical amiability Christopher agreed to make over to Alice an extra sum of capital; thus leaving himself with three thousand dollars a year.

(He reflected that the entire Column family at the Rectory managed to be happy and high-spirited on a yearly stipend equivalent to fifteen hundred dollars.)

On saying good-bye to Alice he referred to her going on to Nîmes. But she told him that their plans were now changed and that Hamnet had decided to go a short trip to the Adriatic, and then return to Paris, where they would stay a little time before returning to America to get married.

Hamnet escorted Christopher downstairs to the lounge, where the children were waiting beside a dusty palm.

Their brief introduction to Hamnet caused Sabrina to refer to him ever afterwards, for no reason Christopher could make out, as "Mr. Peregrine Pickle." But Loo urged Christopher to leave Avignon soon, lest they should meet him again.

So the next morning when Loo had taken a photograph of the Palace of the Popes with his Brownie they departed for Nîmes.

At the *Poste Restante* at Nîmes there were three letters.

One was from Fanny, to the children, containing the news that another five rabbits had been born, that Mrs. Dovey had been to Tremayne and bought herself a fashionable grey satin blouse, and a diamond ring from Woolworth's; and that Milly the ferret, after stealing a treacle tart out of the larder, had had a bilious attack, and been on a diet of junket for three days.

One was for Christopher, which had been forwarded from Queen Anne's Mansions to the Rectory. It was from Professor Tombwell, written from Italy; a most amiable letter saying that he had been so very sorry not to see Christopher again in London. But that he was now in his Italian home, where he very much hoped that Christopher would, if he could fit it in with his plans, come to visit him. He added that Lady Charlotte also, who was on her way back from the East, would be staying at the villa, and would also certainly wish to see Christopher again.

The third letter was the long hoped for, yet no longer expected one from Monsieur Lacaze.

Villa Candide,
L'Ile d'Argent, Var

Dear Mr. Columin,

I received, with immense pleasure, your letter, which has been forwarded to me by quite a series of our mutual relations, finally reaching my summer residence here. I shall remain here until the end of September, when I return to Paris. If you, and your young cousins, whom you mention you are traveling with, should come in this direction by any chance, I shall be enchanted to receive you. Also so very much interested and delighted to meet a member of that branch of our family that went to America two generations ago. I remember from my childhood, in Le Havre, hearing charming anecdotes about your grandfather Lacaze, whom you mention — also letters from them all at Christmas time!

Yours sincerely,
S. Lacaze

This island is about an hour's journey from Hyères. There is a service of autobuses to the coast, and a launch twice a day from the coast to the island.

The smells in the streets of Nîmes (and the obvious reasons at every corner, for them) astonished Christopher, made Loo feel a little sick, and though they amused Sabrina caused her to buy a bottle of strong scent, labeled "Chypre" — with which she soaked her blue chiffon handkerchief and held it at her nose whenever they went out of doors. (She changed the Bishop's ten shillings to buy the scent.)   Nor did Christopher like the hotel, where he found fat, pale, slug-like things crawling up between the tiles of his bedroom floor. When he complained the manager said: "*Tiens* — what would Monsieur?   These beasts were natural."

So they decided only to stay over for the bullfight the next afternoon and to telegraph Monsieur Lacaze that they were coming the day after to Hyères.

The bullfight, which took place in the Roman Arena, was a drowsy and good-natured affair. A dusty bull walked into the Arena looking preoccupied, and though the crowd shouted and a local toreador flapped a cloak, and prodded his rump with a stick, it seemed difficult to attract his attention. After a time the toreador seemed to get irritated, partly by the lethargy of the bull, partly by personal insults shouted by some members of the crowd, and once he turned and, very red in the face, charged in the direction of the insults, but was ordered back to the bull by a man in a tail coat and a soft shirt who stood at the side of the Arena mopping his face.

Loo had his Brownie with him and took photographs of the bull (which came out well, as the bull had not moved).

Just towards the end Christopher felt his arm gripped suddenly by Sabrina.

"Look — *look!*" And she pointed out, opposite to them, alone in one of the boxes, and wearing a striped black and white singlet and a white cap with a large peak, the Lovely Young Man who had given them tea in the aeroplane!

Sabrina was quite flustered. "He has n't seen us! D' you think he will? Which entrance d' you think he 'll go out by? I wonder why he 's here? Oh, I *wish* we knew his name!"

She unrolled her blue chiffon handkerchief and put it around her neck. It just tied round in a scrubby knot.

Christopher said he was sure that in a little place like Nîmes they 'd be bound to run across him during the evening, even if they missed him with the crowd going out.

But when the bull had drifted out and everyone rose to go, and the toreador was bowing to the applause, the Lovely Young Man rose and went from the box opposite, departing with movements of exquisite grace. Sabrina saw him go. And by the time they got out themselves he had vanished.

"I 'm sure we 'll see him later on," said Christopher, kindly and anxiously, for he had been watching the clouding up of Sabrina's face.

"I 'm *sure* we will, Sab!" Loo took her hand. Sorrow in Sabrina was rare and correspondingly alarming to him. He could vividly remember her very few griefs (whereas his own, that had been many, half of them known only to himself, had been absorbed into his character and been themselves forgotten). "Prob'ly he saw us, and is looking for *us*, Sab!"

He might as well not have spoken. For Sabrina's hand lay limp in his, and her eyes, usually the blue gates of a most certain heaven, were darkened, screwed almost shut. A sob shook her angel-like torso, rose upward, choking her, and became a sound ... a gulp, a sharp moan. And suddenly her face was quivering and streaked and running with tears; as if the rain of an entire thunderstorm had descended upon a single jonquil. ...

Christopher's embarrassed and frightened expostulation, Loo's desperate whispering and patting, had no effect. Once in tears, Sabrina became the very element of tears. About her, *provençals*, in black, and stout with much wine and olive oil, stared at her and made little clucks of genial interest; English tourists moved away from such exhibitionism of grief; and American ones remained, hovering but not obtrusive (sure that this grief, like all grief, must be curable), while the Roman Arena towered behind her, perennial testimony to the Civic Smugness that was Rome, and stonily indifferent to the vanishing of Beautiful Young Men, or the first contractions of a brand-new romantic heart beneath an exterior of blue-spotted white cotton, or to the choking down of sobs behind

THE ADVENTURE OF CHRISTOPHER COLUMIN

the knot of a blue chiffon handkerchief from Woolworth —

Loo turned a despairing look on Christopher; and Christopher, trained to "nerves," if to little else, in women, said: —

"What she needs is a nice cold drink!" And taking Sabrina by the arm he led her across the *Place* to the nearest café, sat her down, sat down next to her, keeping hold of her arm, and summoned the waiter.

"Only — of course — *not* WATER!" said Loo, for they had all been following Benjamin's warnings never to DRINK WATER ABROAD. (The bottled kind being only a heinous form of CROOKED DEALING.)

The phrase seemed to penetrate through Sabrina's quivering and blinded consciousness, for she suddenly opened her already swollen eyelids and said hysterically: "*Not* WATER!"

Christopher kept his hand upon her arm. "Why then, dear — let's have something else." He looked rapidly round to get an idea from what other people were drinking. Coffee did n't seem the right thing. Beer obviously was n't. But at the next table two men in blue blouses were drinking some refreshing-looking pale green cloudy stuff with ice in. He asked Loo's opinion "why did n't they try some of that."

"It looks nice and cool," said Loo.

They made a dumb show to the waiter.

In the bottle it was a transparent yellow-green, like a chrysoprase.

"Well," said Christopher, keeping a special optimistic note in his voice for Sabrina, "why don't we try that? And if we don't like it we can sample something else!"

"It looks nice," said Loo, as his was poured out, and turned cloudy with the water. "It smells like liquorice. . . . Oh, it *is* nice. Do try, Sab!"

Once more Sabrina's poor eyes opened. She tried to say something but could n't yet. She stared blindly at her glassful of jade: and then, feebly and with a shaky grab of a gesture, reached out her hand, touched it, hesitated while she gave a long quivering sniff — and lifted the glass.

Loo watched as tenderly as a nurse a convalescent child.

Christopher, quite ready for her to throw the glass down and break into another fit of sobbing, was reassured to see her sip; and sip again. (Sabrina had always had a passion for liquorice.)

"You try, Christopher," said Loo.

"Evidently," said Christopher, smiling into the gathering southern dusk around the café, and at Sabrina's radiant flower face, and at the waiter (and feeling no scruple, no scruple whatever, in confiding in the waiter, for you could see from his face that he was one of the best fellows in the world — one of the very best — a really worthy man). "Evidently," Christopher repeated. He beamed, and when the waiter, serviette in hand, leaned over, Christopher went on, "Evidently — there's nothing beats — liquorish — for setting you up!" For, evidently, here was just the kind of fellow you could trust, the kind of man you could tell just anything to — "Th-there's nothing beats — liquorish. . . . Carry on, old boy — another all round — that's quite O.K. with me! If it is with you? . . ."

"Poor — poor Mrs. Nicolette — " Loo was muttering with gentle melancholy — "if only she had n't had to stay in hot Paris. Oh, Sab, *do* you think that red-haired Old Woman will be unkind to her . . . ?"

" — When I think," confided Christopher to the waiter, "that people imagine that cocktails will do the trick — alcohol, you know — why, it's all *nonsense!* — Alcohol's poison t' most people — let's be frank an' admit it! Why ifyoucanget — *liquorish* to do the trick — but, of course — trouble is they don't have it . . . back home . . ."

Sabrina's elbows were on the table, her hands cupping her face. Her sweet vague voice went on, murmuring and bubbling: —

> ". . . What is the use of the lip's red charm,
> The heaven of hair, the pride of the brow
> And the blood that blues inside the arm —
> Unless we turn, as the soul knows how,
> The earthly gift to an end divine?"

"Of course Alice," said Christopher, "never did agree. I can tell you that," announced Christopher to the waiter's retreating back. "Alice is a woman who has t' have sh — champagne! — or nothing! But what *I* say is — " he leaned across and tapped Loo's hand, "and you may as well know it, son — what I say is that champagne is an A1 drink for — poor folk that need to — well, to feel things are better than facts warrant! See? D' you see, son? That poor girl, f'r instance — noospaper woman hell of a life . . . Kids sick . . ."

"Poor Mrs. Nicolette," sighed Loo.

"That's wha' I say — give her champagne. But you an' me, son . . . why, are n' we feeling jus' grand right now? . . . Perfectly grand?"

"The passionate pale lady's face . . . passionate . . . pale lady's face . . ." murmured Sabrina.

The dusk was night now. A half moon was pale yellow above the Arena.

Genial and trustful, Christopher overpaid his bill, shook hands several times with the waiter, then he and the children set out across the *Place*, past the Arena, to get back to the hotel, Christopher still talking, Loo now in a state of forlorn melancholy, holding on to Christopher's arm and blinking like a little owl . . . Sabrina wandering by herself, and chanting: —

"With how sad steps, oh moon, thou climbs' the sky."

When at last they got into the hotel Christopher took up Loo's idea, repeated in a drowsy voice, of having a little sleep before they had supper, and they started to go upstairs to their rooms.

THE ADVENTURE OF CHRISTOPHER COLUMIN

Christopher opened his eyes and realized that he was looking at a man in pyjamas bending over and throttling a lady in a yellow dressing gown. The lady's hair was the same yellow, and hung back disheveled from her bent-back head. On her face was an expression of slightly malicious satisfaction.

The man was breathing hard. Christopher made out the hissed words — "*will* kill you this time."

"That 'll be heaven," the lady said coolly.

" — To pretend you had — to sleep alone — in a beauty mask — and all the time you 'd planned *this!*"

Christopher now realized that he had such a headache he wondered if he had some mental delirium with it. And this was n't his room. The bed he was in was in a sort of darkened alcove.

Now he saw the man's hands slip from her throat to her shoulders. Now he was shaking her, so that her hair shook like laburnum in a storm. Then he stopped, but stayed bent over her, ferocious.

She said in a fragile sarcastic tone: —

"I can't think *why* you came in?"

"I woke up. I was dreaming about you. I thought of you — I supposed I had the right to come and see *my own wife* if I wanted to — and then — "

He broke off and with a mad snarl his hands were at her throat again, and in that same moment two realizations started through Christopher's aching, bewildered mind. First, that the least dangerous course was for him to go on pretending to be asleep; second, that the man was Sabrina's hero — and that the lady was the one who 'd met him at Le Bourget. He shut his eyes (still with an idea that he would open them again in his own room). But as he did so the Lovely Young Man's voice (that had that East-Side accent of a Frenchman's "americin") said: —

"To come in and *find you* — !"

Her fragile voice articulated: "Darling, you know quite well you found me very stiff and uncomfortable in this chair."

Christopher looked through his lashes. The Young Man had let her go now, but was close to her — a threatening and dramatic figure in lilac pyjamas.

She said: "I wish you *would n't* talk so loud. You 'll wake him!"

"*I 'll wake him and throttle him!*"

"I 've told you, darling. If you do that, I shall call the manager, and you 'd *never* get rid of the Press! There are three young reporters anyway staying in the hotel hoping to get a new story about you . . ."

Christopher did n't see what happened next, for he had got his eyes tight shut again and had furtively been shifting the bedclothes up so that they were over his nose. (He reflected that the dimness of the alcove around him was also a safeguard.)

But now there was an exclamation of some sort from the Young Man — a vague quizzical remark ending in "darling" from her. Then the swift slap of bare feet across the tiles of the floor; and the door banged.

A moment later, when he dared to look, the lady was coming towards him in her yellow dressing gown saying: "How are you feeling?"

As she spoke he took his arm out from under the sheet and saw his own coat sleeve.

"I'll give you some Alka-Seltzer," she said, and went away to her washstand, and came back with a fizzing glass.

Now that he was sure he wasn't dreaming he began to feel violently embarrassed. He sat up straightening his tie. She handed him the glass. She said, in her slightly foreign, unsurprised voice: —

"I found you when I came in. You were asleep. So I didn't disturb you."

"I — I don't know how to — apologize — I — "

"Please don't! People must never apologize. Everything that happens is just a happening!"

"I — must go."

She took the glass and walked back to the wash basin, the yellow folds trailing after her. Christopher got up. He saw that he had his purple *espadrilles* on.

She said: "Please me by *not* being embarrassed." She came up to him and gave him her hand.

Somehow he got away.

On his way back to his room he looked in to see how Loo had slept. (Evidently, he decided, that stuff they'd all drunk at the café last night must have been extremely alcoholic.) Loo was asleep, also in his clothes, on the top of his bed.

Christopher knocked at Sabrina's door. After a moment her voice answered.

He went in. She was lying in bed, pale to the lips, but serene. When she saw Christopher she smiled.

"Golly, I feel awful." She giggled faintly. "I think that stuff we drank at the café was —" She broke off. "Oh, Christopher, you do look distraught."

"I feel it, Sabrina."

"I think we were all 'flushed with wine' when we came in. I don't remember it all. But after you wandered off singing 'My country, 't is of thee' I —"

"Did I?"

"You certainly did. Well, poor Loo was awfully sleepy, was n't he? He fell asleep once at the top of the stairs . . ."

"You look terrible, Sabrina; dearie me, I feel so sorry. It was so *wrong* of me!"

Her pale smile was seraphic.

"Darling Christopher, you did n't know that liquorice would bring us to such a pass!"

"No," said Christopher. "I certainly did not." (He thought of throttling heroes and yellow dressing gowns.)

"Oh, *golly!*" muttered Sabrina. "*All* the same — we enjoyed it, *did n't* we? Except perhaps Loo. And he was enjoying his sorrow really —" She broke off. "I forget — we went after the bullfight, did n't we?"

Christopher wondered if by some queer incidence of alcoholic oblivion she *had* forgotten!

"You were upset," he said, suddenly firm. Better, if there *were* to be some inquiries, it should be now — and not, by any awful chance, caused by meeting the Young Man in a corridor . . . (He saw himself involved through Sabrina, and discovered to be the rival — the idea was n't amusing. What Christopher hoped for now was a clandestine departure of himself and the children as soon as possible.) "You were — upset over — the Young Man — "

"Oh — !" Sabrina sat up.

"Curiously enough," said Christopher, "I 've — discovered that he happens to be married, to a lady of my acquaintance!"

"Married?" She began to wilt back again.

"Why, yes," Christopher went on smoothly. "They 've been married quite a while — I believe they have a couple of delightful kids — "

Sabrina sank right back. And lay still. If she had had any impulse to what Christopher thought of as "acting up again," Christopher's information calmed it completely. (Early in his married life Christopher had avoided a situation in which Alice seemed certain to make a fool of herself by telling her that a certain young man at Miami was not a violinist but a bandmaster. He was in fact a violinist and Christopher knew it.)

No, to Sabrina, the idea of her idol being "married" and a "father" was, after a sharp moment of disillusion, completely sedative. All the Lovely Young Man's other attributes — his melting eyes, his long legs, his undoubted celebrity — were deglamored by the notion that far from being "Sir Galahad" and "Lord Byron" and the "Three Musketeers" incarnate in one superb six foot of manhood, he was, like Daddy! — like the Bishop! — like Albert the Good or even Dr. Watson — merely domestic — !

"Would you like your coffee sent up?" Christopher asked.

"I think," said Sabrina, with rather dreamy calm, "I think this morning I'd rather have tea!"

"Of course," said Loo, as the little launch sprang and rolled on the waves toward the island, "if we *don't* like Mr. Lacaze, we need n't stay more than half an hour, need we?" (He had heard his mother say that half an hour was the time you had to stay for a first call.)

"Whatever he's like we must be courteous," said Christopher.

Sabrina was shading her eyes and gazing towards an island, still distant enough to look deep blue, but with one or two pale specks on its edge that might indicate houses round a harbor. She said: —

"Anyone who goes to live on an island must be nice. I've always thought it must be heavenly to live on an island — with your own everything like a kingdom, and magic casements opening on the foam. Unless, of course," she added, after a moment, bitterly thinking of her hero Napoleon, "unless you're imprisoned on one!" She turned to Christopher. "It must have been on such a sea as this that he looked towards Europe — and chafed, like an imprisoned eagle!"

Loo said: "Birds don't 'chafe'!"

"Well, then, 'stare with melancholy golden eyes,'" said Sabrina good-temperedly. She turned to Christopher. "What d' you think he thought about at the very end? — At St. Helena?"

Christopher answered, after thinking more than a minute: "Maybe he wondered if the whole racket had been worth while — " He added — because the problem coincided with his thought of these last weeks: "Maybe that 's what some of the go-getters do think — when they have to sit back and reckon up just how they spent their energy — "

"*Look* — there 's a little boat — the one with orange sails, coming from the island. That must be the harbor!"

"Don't lean over so, Loo!" he cautioned.

The little launch veered and started plunging toward what was now clearly a little port, consisting of a wooden pier, a dozen pinkish and white houses, and behind them pine woods that sloped upward toward olive-terraced heights. The choppy waves slapped the sides of the boat, Sabrina's hair blew back, the two men in dirty blue cotton tunics (who appeared to be the "conductors" of the launch) said something to Christopher, which included the name of the island, and then pointed to a farther-off island westward and said "Port Cros!"

"There's a man in a white jacket on the landing stage!" cried Sabrina.

Loo screwed up his eyes, staring.

"D' you think that's *him*?"

"It might be."

It was n't. But it was Monsieur Lacaze's servant, for he came up to them at once and said he was from the Villa Candide, and escorted them to a battered little Ford car, and drove them from the port, up a shady, sandy road between pines. . . . Above the pines, high up among the olive terraces, he pointed to a plaster house with a deep-eaved dark red roof, and a loggia built around it, and shouted "Villa Candide" twice, and Christopher shouted "*Oui.*"

As they approached, they saw that there was a terraced garden below the house, and that the whole place had a serene and habitable appearance. . . . The garden was full of flowers; and they perceived now cushioned chairs and tables set out upon the terrace. Christopher wondered if his "cousin" were married — a condition they had none of them somehow imagined for him, his chief characteristics having been fixed in their imagination as a black beard, boot-button eyes, and a slight agile person. Sabrina had also referred to him as being "extremely foppish — but wearing a *béret basque* in the country."

The servant escorted them indoors and they were just looking about them at the long room, which was open on one side on to the terrace, when a woman in a blue dress came out of a door, and came up to Christopher and held out her hand, and spoke in English, giving him a charming smile. Then she turned and said how do you do to each of the children. Her glance was full of a lovely dark gayety. Then she said: "I am Mademoiselle Lacaze."

"I expect you know then who *we* are," said Christopher, feeling that was a foolish remark. (These were the kind of occasions when he missed Alice.) But she acknowledged this with a smile that made him feel that his words had been both considerate, witty, and altogether agreeable. He went on, as he sat down in a chair she motioned him to: "Your father wrote to me a most delightful letter!"

She sat down also. She returned Christopher's vivid yet slightly shy gaze with assurance and warmth. There was a very slight hesitation in her manner before she replied.

"I hope you received my letter?" She went on, seeing yet deftly not looking at them: "I wrote to Cook's in Paris — as you asked me to, with the idea that it would be forwarded to you — if you had already left . . ."

It was Loo who said: "Yes, thank-you-very-much — we *did* get your letter at Nîmes . . ."

"So we telegraphed from there," muttered Sabrina. She could n't look at Loo. (No beard! No button eyes! No *béret basque*) . . . She glanced at Christopher, who did n't look amused. Who was at last beginning a sentence: —

"I — you must forgive me — "

Mademoiselle Lacaze, with the same deft unseeing sweet glance, broke in: "But — what is there to forgive? You could n't have chosen a more perfect time to visit me — and except for my nephew Jean, I am alone. The villa, if you will permit it, is at your disposition — " She rose and went to a bell and rang it. "But first of all Marius shall bring us some tea — "

"Please," said Loo, who had got up politely when she did, and was now looking up at her with half-doubting delight, "please — do you mean that you would like us to *stay* with you?"

For a moment she did n't seem to take in the meaning of his question because her attention was caught by the child himself, and in that second something instinctively swift and loving in her responded to Loo's own lovable qualities, which were now, as always, so visible in his face. . . . Then she answered: —

"But naturally — " She turned to Sabrina: "It is understood that you will stay?"

"Oh *yes!* How *lovely!*"

"Then" — Mademoiselle Lacaze turned to Christopher, "you, *mon cousin*, must stay also? Indeed, if I keep the children . . . you will have to remain!"

The man in the white coat was there.

"Marius, tea for all. Also — wait! After tea you

will arrange how the luggage is to be fetched. Monsieur" — she indicated Christopher — "will give you all instructions. . . . And tell Eugénie to prepare the rooms . . ."

While she gave these orders, Christopher watched her, thinking that that little air of authority suited her, and accorded with the general effect she gave of being dignified without being hard.

As she sat down again and began to talk, a tall boy of about eighteen came in.

"This is my nephew, Jean Bernard."

He shook hands and bowed slightly to Sabrina, giving her a glance of gay interested admiration, then to Christopher, "Monsieur," and to Loo, "How do you do?" He spoke with an excellent English accent. He was slender, and had a brown, blunt, high-cheekboned face, witty peaked eyebrows, very white teeth, and a cleft in his chin. His nervous tapering fingers seemed at variance with the gayety, the health, the stubbornness, of his face — until his features were in repose, and their vivacity dimmed down to an expression of intent nervous thinking.

When tea came in (weak tea, and curiously brittle dry toast) Jean looked after Sabrina and Loo. He was entranced to discover the origin of Loo's name; and told him, teasing, that he was bold to travel in France with it. He told Sabrina that he was spending his summer holiday here; and that he was studying history and philosophy at the Sorbonne in Paris. He informed

Loo that there was a bay, on the south side of the island, where there was supposed to be a Treasure-Trove — though the only thing that had ever been found was the ivory frame of a fan on some submerged rocks. "Of Empire design," he added, "but of no value.... Tante Sophie has it."

While Jean was speaking to Sabrina his manner was quite different from his manner to Loo. Sabrina noticed this and found the difference exhilarating. She smiled so often at Jean in gratitude that he said (when he had watched her consume one relay after another of the crunchy toast) that he thought everything she ate turned to laughter....

After dinner the children went out with Jean down to the sea, and Christopher and Mademoiselle Lacaze remained on the terrace to drink their coffee and talk and watch the last colors of sunset fade out of the bay.

And when the night had come, and there was a sheen over the sea, and they heard the children's voices, returning, Christopher wondered that more than an hour had passed. For he had talked to his hostess and listened to her, as if they were dancing together, easily, and with grace and pleasure. And when once or twice she'd laughed softly at some observation he made he had felt a little glow, as if he had executed a successful pirouette.

The children came panting from the climb. And she rose and led them all into the house. When she was saying good-night, she remarked that to-morrow they must meet Herr von Strelsau. She added that he was an Austrian, and was her tenant down in the little house on the promontory, and also her most dear friend.

Before he got into bed Christopher stood for a long time at his window looking at the stars. Below was the dark swishing of the sea, and the soft night wind was fragrant with salt and pines.

Looking in the direction of the promontory, he saw a light and supposed that Herr von Strelsau must be awake.

Mademoiselle Lacaze, when her guests had gone up to their rooms, wrote: —

Dear Fritzl, —
There have arrived at my house a man of the most distinguished simplicity, a little boy with the heart of an angel, and a very young girl of delicious beauty. Will you lunch here to-morrow and make their acquaintance?
Sophie

The small square grey box in which Herr von Strelsau lived was cemented on to a rocky promontory of the island, and situated so directly on the sea that on rough days the spray came in at the window of the living room. If there was a storm the window had to be shuttered, and Herr von Strelsau inhabited his bedroom (the only other room), which faced toward a group of pines, and the olive-terraced interior of the island rising above them.

The official name of the "house" was the Villa Cunégonde, but it was known, down at the port, and by Madame Lacaze's servants, as "chez Monsieur de Strelsau." At a distance it was difficult to distinguish it from the grey rock on which it was built, and its charm was its romantic position and its inhabitant.

For when Herr von Strelsau came out of it, to greet them, Loo thought of Father Christmas, and Sabrina of Father Neptune. . . . His beard and hair shone like the edges of white clouds, and he had deep-set brown eyes, wonderfully clear like light in mountain streams. And the same quality of clear dancing light was in his smile when he came up to them holding out both his hands and saying: "Welcome! . . . Good morning . . . How do you do?" He kissed Mademoiselle Lacaze on both cheeks, shook hands with Christopher — "So delighted!" — and when he had shaken hands with the children said to Mademoiselle Lacaze: —

"*All* — your cousins? I felicitate you, Sophie," with a caressing, singsong Austrian intonation.

But while they all laughed Loo explained that he and Sabrina were only Christopher's distant cousins.

Then Herr von Strelsau led them back into his house to show it to them. It was as untidy inside as it was stark out. One whole side of the living room was the window facing the sea; the other three walls were hung with innumerable small and large pictures, oils and water colors, photographs of people and watering places and castles, strips of Chinese embroidery, antlers, a bear's head, a fox's mask, a cuckoo clock, a Dutch

THE ADVENTURE OF CHRISTOPHER COLUMN 171

seventeenth-century black-and-gold lacquer clock, an African skin shield, several small skins, and several modern railway posters grown battered from being pinned up unframed. Along two of the walls were low bookshelves filled with books and surmounted by endless photographs in silver or red velvet frames of men in uniforms or court dress, and ladies in tiaras or carrying fans and either looking like the Merry Widow or Queen Alexandra, or Female Snake Charmers. But most of the books were in heaps in the corners and stacked below the grand piano, which was open. As well as books on the floor there were rugs, several shoes, and little heaps of pine cones. And in the middle of the room an immense white-and-gold porcelain "stove," whose chimney vanished through the ceiling. About this ornate heritage from the German eighteenth century were wicker armchairs, wooden stools, and an oak settle.

Sophie said: "I know, Fritz, that you always refuse, but if you would only let me send down Eugénie before breakfast here. You would never see her."

A look of beatific obstinacy came into the Neptune face.

"Beloved Sophie, once a week is *enough*. To clean overmuch is a nonsense . . ."

Loo had found a ladder that led up the wall behind the stove, to a trapdoor. "On the roof," said Herr von Strelsau, "you will find an excellent telescope. Through it you can see what you will. . . . Sophie sees, for instance, what is beautiful; Jean sees what is there, and I," he beamed, "poor Fritzl, see what cannot be there!"

Loo said: "Are you joking?" . . . puzzled.

Sabrina said in the same breath: "*Are* you joking?" . . . delighted.

". . . I see, for instance, swart ladies from Carthage making a Cruise, and excellent Greek boats that go past rowed by many slaves, and also very many splendid pirates . . . that look for treasure ships."

"— Treasure ships?" repeated Loo, coming down off his ladder now and approaching Herr von Strelsau as a squirrel might have drawn near to Orpheus.

"Pirates?" cooed Sabrina.

"— Treasure ships?" said Christopher — and the forgotten but so eager little boy in Christopher drew near to their host — also.

Sophie Lacaze looked at them, all four. And said: —

"Come, *mes enfants* . . . if we are to go up in time for lunch . . . You can return afterwards to the enchanted telescope!"

After luncheon Jean offered to show the children round the island. Mademoiselle Sophie went up to take her siesta, and Herr Fritzl asked Christopher if he would like to come and spend the afternoon down at his house with him.

When they got down there Fritz got out a box of superb cigars, and they settled down on a shabby padded seat that ran along the open window on the sea. (The evidences of what seemed to be poverty verging on squalor struck Christopher as awfully at odds with the conversation at luncheon, during which it became clear that Herr Fritzl was paying for the keep and education of an entire family of his — distant — relatives, the problem being one of money remittance.)

Herr Fritzl brought out some benedictine and they puffed voluptuously at their cigars; and he asked Christopher various questions about his journey, his "so sweet-charming young cousins" — his home in America.

When Christopher said he came from Green Plains, Herr Fritzl took his cigar out of his mouth, and after a second repeated: "*Green Plains?*"

Christopher said yes, it was a town in Massachusetts. And Herr Fritzl nodded, looking out to sea and putting his cigar slowly back between his moustache and beard. But as he made no further comment, Christopher started to ask him about himself. For he was interested in how this man, picturesque and essentially elegant, — for all his frayed cuffs and dirty white canvas shoes, — had come to live here.

"That fellow Jean was telling me you had a magnificent *Schloss* a little way up the mountains?"

Fritzl shook his Jove-like head. "My father, beloved man, had a *Schloss* — altogether my blessed grandfather and my most saint-like great-grandfather (old devil that he was) also had their castle. But for me! What is titles, castles, and such things? — They are a nonsense!" His clear brown eyes beamed. "A full nonsense!" His smile shone like the sun between the white clouds of his moustache and beard. "*So* is it. *So* is it." He continued: "My elder brother, poor fool, drives a taxicab in Brussels; my older sister . . . vile woman, she has a beauty establishment, or some such a nonsense, in Budapest. . . . My younger sister, beloved girl, is for a long time established in heaven. And I — sweet-dear-Fritzl that I am — am here!"

"And you 're contented?"

Again the heavenly smile, and a quizzical half nod, half shake of the head. "Why should I not be so? I have a view — with a room attached to it. A piano — with my fingers frequently attached to it . . . I read . . . I eat . . . I wash my beard — and I have the friendship of my dear Sophie — beloved girl!" he added with feeling; paused; and then once more his faun-like gay air returned, and he got up and went to the piano, moving stiffly but smiling to himself with a flash of white teeth. "I will sing an English song to you — my favorite English song. Do you know it by chance?"

He sat down and played "Molly Malone," and sang the verses in a mellow voice with his eyes almost shut and his eyebrows peaked high.

> "She was a fishmonger, but sure 't was no wonder,
> For so were her father and mother before;
> And they each wheeled a barrow
> Through streets broad and narrow,

Crying 'Cockles and mussels, alive alive-oh.'
Alive, alive oh . . ."

"What a strange song," said Christopher, when he had done.

Herr von Strelsau's eyes opened, bright and challenging.

"You are meant to laugh? Or — " He turned now and added with the most droll and charming air, "or — do you not wish to, Herr Columin?"

"I — I should like to very much," said Christopher, "but maybe it's a little late now?" He added: "Curiously enough I was reflecting this morning, as I was dressing — "

" — Such a beautiful purple shirt, Herr Columin."

"Thanks. I like it myself. It comes from Hyères . . . I was thinking that maybe I'd had too little practice in laughing. You see, in business . . ."

"*Ach! Business? Ach,* my poor friend . . ." He looked at Christopher now with the most heart-felt solicitude. "It is not to wonder then . . . that you should not easily laugh." He shook his head. "I have known — of course — many businessmen in my life — very many. And *except* that they were in 'big' business, bankers and sowhat that could swindle *immensely*" (he made a large joyous gesture with his arms), "they had a *sad* time! . . . *Ach,* no! To spend one's most excellent years . . . and all the most excellent, and beautiful hours of *each day,* in confinement

— and with a telephone in *each ear* . . . That is a *nonsense!*"

Christopher felt what Herr von Strelsau said acutely; and he got up and walked about.

"First," said his host, "men have had the idea, which is partly true, that money will buy happiness! *Then* they have had another idea — less clever — to *make* money!"

"But somebody has to make it," said Christopher, anxious to be contradicted.

Herr von Strelsau shook his head, slowly, turning it so far round in each direction that Christopher saw first his sad left profile and then his amused right one.

"No, no, beloved Mr. Columin. People has to sleep, and has to eat . . . and has to make jokes — and has to love! . . . But to make *money!*" He hesitated, his full rumbling tones became dreamy. "At least, let us admit," he said, — and now he turned to the piano and his fingers began to move over the keys, — "that it is more agreeable not to . . . ?"

"I admit that," said Christopher.

Now he was playing — "D'Une Prison." And now he asked: "Do you know this, Herr Columin — do you know your Verlaine?"

He sang the poem to Raynaldo Hahn's setting.

He got up and shut the piano. "It is one of Sophie's favorites," he said. "Often she comes here to play and we sing together." He added: "She has an excellent voice — not big, but charming."

Christopher said that he would like to hear her. He had once been alone to a *Lieder* concert in Boston and enjoyed it, unknown to Alice. He remembered now the moving beauty of the singer's voice (though he could n't remember her name). He asked if Mademoiselle Lacaze sang any Schubert songs. And Herr von Strelsau said yes, she sang them "most excellently."

Christopher looked round the cosy untidy little hutch of a room and out at the blue splendor of the sea, and said: "Well, I think you have made a nice life here"; these flat words emerging from feelings he could n't express, or even define in his own mind.

The impression left on Christopher by that first evening's talk with his hostess grew still more agreeable in the subsequent days. In character she seemed a mixture of mystery and common sense; sympathy alternated with skepticism in her point of view, gravity with wit in her expression of it. Her manners were so excellent that she had no "manner"; and her conversation, which was plentiful, did not draw attention to herself, but to her subject. Physically she was plump, but graceful; her movements easy but dignified, her hands and feet white, small, and extremely pretty. What was constantly lovely in her was the oval shape of her face, and the way her head was set graciously upon her firm neck. And what was occasionally beautiful was the expression of her dark eyes.

In theory Christopher might have found her alarming. Her wide reading, her clear fine thinking, her hesitant, veiled humor, her little cool, pitiless opinions on mediocrity both spiritual and mental, might have made him diffident. But in fact he had never found a woman (or indeed a man either) such excellent company. He had had one glimpse, through Mrs. Peckett at home, that a woman might be amusing; but he had never imagined that a still young woman could be so unaware of her "self"; or so far removed from the state described by Loo and Sabrina as "showing off."

And Jean Bernard interested Christopher. At first he did n't like him. He did n't seem to have any recognizable boyish qualities; he was neither ingenuous nor boastful, gawky nor fresh — nor had he the grace of young animals, nor was he touching, or shy. He was self-assured but modest, and his manner toward older people was respectful, but indicated a readiness to talk, and an eagerness for discussion. And it was through his talking that Christopher began to like him. He perceived that even as a type he was infinitely better educated than himself, his mind had been drilled to think clearly. It was also full of intelligently assimilated knowledge. The extent of Jean's knowledge, at eighteen, started Christopher thinking about French and American education. (The Americans spelled it with a capital E. The French just worked hard at school.)

And Christopher was also interested by his "moral code." Unlike an American or English boy of his age, Jean could ally beauty and sex with one habit of thought, and identify sex and hygiene with another. (As easily as accepting the fact that water is sometimes just a bath, and sometimes the Italian Lakes.)

Possibly this fixed and dual polarization of the ideal and the necessary gave his entire mind a quality of maturity.

Sabrina also felt that Jean was the most really grown-up person she had ever known. More grown-up than her father, or Christopher, or even the Bishop of Tremayne. She was incapable of analyzing, of course, that Jean's attitude to life was not romantic, but deliberately rational. He talked to her a great deal as they sat on rocks, or wandered about the island, or rowed about the bay; and when he was n't talking fantasy he was apt to embark on philosophical debates, in which he took both sides, for conversation, but always held to the same point of view. Thus he would begin: "One may say that Equality (or Fidelity — or Love — or the music of Wagner) is — this or that — *but* — "

At the end of these deliberations, during which Sabrina watched his brown vivid face with interest, he always summed up on the side of common sense, as demonstrated by precedent. He would say, "In fact, people are like that," or "life is like that."

Mademoiselle Sophie persuaded Christopher that it would be better for him to leave Sabrina with her while he went — with Loo if he liked — to visit Professor Tombwell in Italy. She said — a mysterious phrase to Christopher — "I know that 'world' — that *milieu*. You will find it interesting and amusing. But it is *not* for a young girl."

Christopher was ready to accept her judgment in this matter as in all others. The more he saw of her the more he noticed her common sense; and the more he liked this companionship with a woman who was — as he commented to Herr Fritzl — ruled by her head instead of her heart.

Herr Fritzl's answer to this comment had been: "You do not like 'heart' then in a woman?" — his eyebrows peaked up, an enigmatic twist to his mouth.

"I find a woman like Mademoiselle Sophie more restful!"

"So — "

The evening before Christopher and Loo were to leave, Herr Fritzl came up to the house to dine, and after dinner he played, and persuaded Mademoiselle Sophie to sing.

As she got up and stood by the piano, Christopher thought how delightful she looked: her special sort of fresh, dignified charm emphasized by the plain cut of her dress; her eyes dark and vivacious as she discussed with Herr Fritzl what she should sing. As they spoke together, partly in German, partly in French, as their habit was, Christopher wondered why they had n't married.

Now Herr Fritzl played, and she sang Schubert's "Im Wunderschönen Monat Mai." She had a lovely contralto voice, and as she sang Christopher felt delight and sadness. She also sang "Das Wandern" and "Du Meine Seele." Before she had done he went out and stood in the loggia because he was embarrassed by the intensity of emotions he did not understand, but which made him speechless.

After she had sung she came out on to the verandah and said: —

"Christopher, I have something to propose to you." (She had a little brisk way of saying "I have something to propose to you," and then bringing out some practical little plan.) "I propose that you do not eat your lunch, you and Loo, in the *wagon-restaurant* tomorrow, but permit that Eugénie and I prepare a little *pique-nique* for you — "

The next morning he and Loo embarked in the launch for the mainland; Mademoiselle Sophie and Jean and Sabrina came down to see them off.

Mademoiselle Sophie gave Loo her clean handkerchief as he was starting off with a grubby one. And repeated her special reminder about their "*pique-nique* lunch"; which was that there was mayonnaise to eat with the cold chicken in the little porcelain jar with the screw top.

The train was very hot going to Padua. On the journey Loo was drowsy; and Christopher oppressed by sensations in himself that he had never known before — by a strange mingling of undefined sadness and a vague excitement — unfamiliar nervousness and a new, yet impressive awareness — so that wherever he looked — at the landscape from the train window, at the sky, at Loo's round brown head opposite to him — he saw a different sky, a new range of colors upon the earth, a changed little boy — all of them having a strange beauty and evoking a sadness in his own heart that was somehow its echo.

Mixed up with this sweet-acrid sensitiveness to what he saw were also his thoughts of those last days on the island — and his conversation with Herr Fritzl. . . . He reflected upon the great rich simplicity of Herr Fritzl's heart, on his gentleness freaked with moments of impudent cynicism, on his music, his untidiness, his fits of calm Olympian melancholy; his bawdy stories told with such a saintly gravity in his golden eyes; on his love for Mademoiselle Sophie (on his words, "When there is no love it is more sensible *not* to live — there is no use to remain in a room, however beautiful, when the light is out!").

Christopher thought too that it was natural that Mademoiselle Sophie should feel this devotion to Herr Fritzl — finding his, perhaps more than all other friendships, compensation for the life she had not had.

(Herr Fritzl had told him how her fiancé had been killed in 1918.)

Thinking of them both, and of their manner of living, he reflected that their standard of outward living was simple, but their standard of thinking, and feeling, rich and complex.

He and Loo were met at Padua station by Professor Tombwell, in a neat tussore suit, and a big bald man called Barbizon-Smith.

When they got out of the station into the white sunlight and heat, Professor Tombwell said: —

"This is Zaza's car — she was kindness itself and lent it as mine has been bewitched, or so I like to fancy, ever since the Contessa Ricordo stayed the night. She has, it is well known, the evil eye."

The car was a white Isotta, the inside crimson and buttoned (like the inside of Mummie's workbox, Loo thought).

"P-pure *P-Piranesi!*" said Tombwell, looking back intently at the station waiting room. He took a checked cap out of the car and put it on. "I'll sit in front with the child," he said, "and you at the back, Columin, if you don't mind."

Out in the countryside the vines were like rows of ladies in drapy dark green sleeves endlessly holding hands.

They got into a road that went beside a canal, with

occasional gardens and villas on the other bank. Barbizon-Smith sometimes spoke to Christopher: —

"I thought you were bringing a beautiful girl?"

"No," said Christopher, "she stayed in France."

"What type was she?" asked Barbizon-Smith; his big cherubic face had a worried expression as if he were always thinking and reflecting; but never quite satisfactorily.

"Blonde," said Christopher.

"And old?"

"Sixteen and a half."

The big man shook his head. "Too young —" He leaned forward. "Sixteen is too young, Tombwell."

"S-sixteen?" shouted the Professor backward, loudly because he was driving. "*M-much too young!*" They shot past a lorry. "*V-Venus was forty*," he shouted — "*d-don't you think, Columin, d-don't you?*"

Christopher said he could n't answer such a question offhand.

"Well, what is your personal idea of Venus?" Barbizon-Smith asked him, leaning back again beside Christopher, and turning right round to give him an excited, saddened glance.

Christopher said he did n't think he had any special idea; reflecting that his life had hardly been conducive to the evolution of a personal Venus.

"Of course," said Barbizon-Smith, rolling himself a cigarette between yellow fingertips. "Of course many people admire Zaza. She certainly looked very well last night. She came, you know, because Tombwell happened to mention on the telephone that you were coming . . ."

"I?"

"Yes, you."

"But I don't know anybody called Zaza," said Christopher.

"Zaza de Vouvray?"

"No. I certainly do not."

"But everybody knows her."

"I don't," said Christopher. And, annoyed, he said: "I only know one French lady anyway," and thought of her with a curiously sharp nostalgia.

"But Zaza's not French. She's half Belgian and half American and half Russian. She really looks very well — at night. But she is too thin, and too tall. She has no *volupté*."

At last they reached Villa Cornaro, crossing a bridge to get to it and coming round by its back drive. They got out and Loo was just beginning to feel a little stricken by the gloom of its classical proportions when a tall, marvelously pretty lady in white shorts came out from behind the stone pillars and down the steps; and Loo saw at once that it was the same lady who had come in tall black plumes to meet Sabrina's Beautiful Young Man at the aerodrome at Le Bourget. Now she was n't wearing plumes, but a horse's straw hat on her head, with her hair coming up through it in a sheaf of barley-yellow curls. And then Christopher, when he'd stopped trying to give his luggage to the hostile butler, recognized her also! She was the Ministering Angel at the Hotel des Arènes at Nîmes.

Professor Tombwell said: "I think you know the Duchess."

Christopher took her outstretched hand. Her small high-up face looked quite dazzling under her horse's hat. She gave him a smile that lasted less than a second but had a charm and intimacy that left him startled with pleasure.

Professor Tombwell then introduced the butler as "Signor Bellino — one of Italy's best-known Senators," and Christopher took back his suitcase, and held out his hand.

Then they all went up the wide steps, and between the pillars and indoors into a pale high wall with a dome, whose shape reminded Loo of St. Paul's Cathedral, and Christopher, very slightly, of the Capitol at Washington.

A boy in a white jacket came up and spoke to the Professor, who then said: —

"Lady Charlotte has gone into Venice to buy dog biscuits, but will be back for tea, and says we are not to wait for her." He then led Christopher into a room with a huge four-poster bed and walls painted very prettily with musical instruments, fruits, and ribands. Then he took Loo upstairs to an attic containing a pingpong table, a divan bed, and a carved wooden chest. From the window there was a view of far-away chimneys which the Professor said was Mestre. He also said: "Those cupboards there contain fancy dress, and there is an eighteenth-century miniature theatre in the attic next door."

Lady Charlotte did not return for tea, which was served in a small anteroom with Pompeian designs on the panels of the walls. The Duchesse poured out. She wore no hat now, balanced a plate on her lovely, slender brown knees, and told Christopher with the most ingenuous air that she had read his luggage labels at the Hotel des Arènes the morning he was leaving, to find out his name. Then she added: —

"Please cut me a piece of that lovely crumbly cake, and tell me exactly why you are traveling around? I always like to know why people do things."

"I don't know exactly why," said Christopher.

"That's the best reason," she said. Her eyes were a marvelous uncertain blue. She fixed them on Christopher with affectionate anxiety. He said, embarrassed: —

"I was most — grateful at Nîmes."

"So was I," she said.

He didn't understand and so changed the subject and asked her: "Do you and your husband travel around a great deal?"

"Yes. But he only *used* to be my husband. He's very handsome, isn't he? Did you see him in that picture, *Cinque à Sept?* — The English title was *Cocktail Time*. He was very good in it. Now he's making a new picture, about bullfighting. So he's still at Nîmes . . . I'm going to America to-morrow or next week perhaps. I shall probably get married there or soon after."

"I see," said Christopher. He felt vaguely depressed by this information. He handed her his cup.

"Lemon?" she asked.

"No thanks."

Loo was eating buttery toast and honey and trying to understand the conversation between Professor Tombwell and the big bald Barbizon-Smith. Loo slightly liked the Professor, who, he felt, was silly on top but clever underneath; but felt a vague contempt for Mr. Barbizon-Smith, who seemed always in a flurry, like Giles the Verger at home, and had said Sabrina was too young — who was after all five years older than Loo himself! As for the Italian Senator, he was vying with Loo in eating up the toast and honey, but doing so with a sanctimonious expression, his poached-egg eyes fixed on the two Englishmen.

Much the nicest was the Duchesse called Zaza, Loo thought. He wondered if by any chance she would come up afterwards and examine the theatre with him. Just as he was wondering this one of the boys in white coats rushed in and said "La Principessa Carlotta" was in sight. So they all got up and went out and down to the bank of the Brenta — and there was Lady Charlotte coming towards them, standing and rowing her own gondola and dressed like a gondolier. When she saw Christopher she smiled, showing her white teeth, and shook her oar at him. He waved back, but hoping again that she had forgotten the honorable proposals made to him, via Tombwell, in London.

In fact, though Lady Charlotte was as friendly as possible and tried to teach Christopher how to row a gondola, she made no reference to her past proposal. And Christopher learned from Tombwell that she was now married to a racing motorist; and that her name now was, in fact, Lady Charlotte Pink. Tombwell described how she had met Waldorf Pink in Cairo and married him without a second's hesitation. But when Christopher inquired where Mr. Pink was now, Tombwell said he supposed on Daytona Sands, but he was n't sure.

Meanwhile he discovered that the Duchesse was as friendly to talk to as she was strangely pretty to look upon. Every day of the week she wore a different-colored pair of shorts; her only way, she explained, of knowing one day of the week from another. In the evenings she wore brilliant-colored dresses and painted her eyelids and heels to match them. She played spillikins with Loo every afternoon out in the shadow of the Palladian portico, and told him stories about her childhood in the Caucasian Mountains, and in a haunted château in Belgium; and of the bear, Pushkin, whom she and her brothers had brought up and taught to speak several Russian words, and how their governess had tried to teach him English, but he never would say any English word except "Gomorrah."

Zaza's affection for Loo made Christopher like her. But after a day or two he began to be enchanted by her. For she would come and sit beside him after dinner in the garden and tell him the plot of some gay or funny book she had read; or, if the book had not been either gay or funny, she made it sound so. And on one occasion Christopher was surprised to find that the account she had given him of grotesque creatures, half flowers, half fish, giving poison to a ferocious man who-never-went-to-sleep, was merely a version of the *Times's* account of the British Royal Family entertaining the French Air Minister at luncheon.

The interesting thing about Barbizon-Smith proved to be that he was an inventor, formerly employed by the British Admiralty. And that he had invented recently a diving helmet, of light and luxurious design, to be used, mainly for pleasure, by any private bather. During his visit to the Villa Cornaro he went daily out to the Lido, where he was trying to popularize his "helmet-de-luxe." He had already persuaded a Princess, an heiress, and a well-known artist to buy one; and gave parties every morning, far out on a raft, from which the divers plunged as shallow or as deep as they fancied, to explore the submarine beauties of the Adriatic, to stare at passing fishes — or, as Barbizon-Smith himself did, to shoot them with a type of short light gun he had adapted to the purpose.

Whoever tried one of these helmets returned from their subaqueous plunging with delightful accounts of strangeness and beauty. Lady Charlotte became so converted that she went daily to the Lido, lost interest in her gondola, and was the first to enroll herself for an expedition planned, for September, to shoot shark off Portofino. Zaza, having first sworn she hated uncooked fish, ended by being converted to a helmet because her fellow divers looked so exciting with their big goggly heads and attenuated bodies. She got her maid to sew some green silk fringe she bought in the *Merceria* round the goggly eyes of her helmet, to make eyelashes that could sweep and wave seductively underwater.

Loo of course was eager to dive. But Christopher felt responsible for him and at first would only let him sit on the raft, or splash around it on top of the water under the competent surveying eye of Lady Charlotte's gondolier. Christopher himself, though he had read William Beebe's book and been enthralled by it, had doubts of the apparatus's oxygen supply and imagined himself dying suddenly for want of gills. . . . But like all difficult converts, he became in the end the most impassioned diver of all, stayed longer under the water, talked more than all the others at meals about the length of time he had stayed under, the number of fishes he had seen (though he would never shoot), and the variety of seaweeds, shells, and crabs he had espied. Actually he did n't manage to stay under as long as Barbizon-Smith himself, who, Zaza said, got down for hours among the lowest rocks with the fattest mermaid he could find.

Christopher also gave in about Loo, and ended by buying a helmet for Loo and one for himself (though he would not let Zaza sew him on a long purple fringe for a beard).

The only person in the house party who never tried a helmet was Signor Bellino, giving as his reason that his wife was expecting their fourth child. But he sat on the raft and drank vermouth with the gondolier; and sang "O Sole Mio" (his eyes more pouched than ever when he sang) and "Parlez-moi d'amour" to please Zaza, and "D'ye ken John Peel" to compliment Lady Charlotte. This latter tribute always made Loo laugh so much that the gondolier would not let him bathe while the Senator was singing it. (Secretly in his Palladian attic at night Loo would practise, so as to be perfect for Sabrina, the accent with which the Senator sang the verse with all the dogs' names.)

Professor Tombwell never came to the Lido, as he spent the mornings in his room writing his treatise on "Ornament in Early Baroque Cradles."

The afternoons at the villa were spent in talking, in supine groups in the dry garden, or strolling among the chipped stone statuary and drinking quantities of an iced golden wine, and lapsing into reading or drowsing. Visitors came, in dusty cars, and talked or lunched. And sometimes Professor Tombwell would make them all come in Zaza's car to visit other people in other villas that lay towards the blue dark range of the Alps or westward toward Vicenza and Padua. . . . Sometimes Lady Charlotte would take two or three of them in her gondola out on to the lagoons; or they would all motor into Venice and buy cheese or false pearls or painted chairs or chocolates according to their several tastes. On one of these expeditions Christopher bought two linen bedcovers encrusted with lace to take back as a present to Sophie Lacaze. He got Zaza to help him choose them, but when he answered her question as to whom they were for she opened her marvelous eyes so starred with lashes, and said: "Oh, but that's *very* unlucky for her! There is a Georgian proverb which means 'Give the woman you love a sheet for her bed and it will prove to be her winding sheet.'" Christopher said, greatly embarrassed by such a notion, that she was only a friend. "Then you can't give her lace bedcovers and things, can you?" But by now Christopher had bought them. And Loo had vanished, and there was an anxious half hour before he was found coming out of San Marco, having been up to see the horses again and brood on their no longer being gold — and was now on his way to swap stamps with the man who kept the postcard shop on the *piazzetta*.

Just as they met Loo the man who photographs visitors with pigeons came up and Zaza at once put her arm in Christopher's and said to him: "Quick, is there a smut on my nose?" and while Christopher was peering she signed to the photographer.

When the photographs were fetched two days later, Christopher seemed in them to be looking into her eyes. Zaza laughed about them and gave one to Loo, signed. But Loo saw her put the other photograph in an envelope (and wondered whom she sent it to).

The following evening after dinner, they were all sitting in the loggia in bright moonlight. Zaza gleaming in white like a lovely ghost; the Senator (who had been down to Rome for two days) richly singing "John Peel" to Lady Charlotte; Barbizon-Smith and Tombwell arguing, both a little stumbling in speech, upon the discovery of an Etruscan implement of exquisite design which Tombwell averred to be an instrument of civic punishment while Barbizon-Smith swore it had been used for poaching eggs; and Loo, seated on the landing stage, was fishing — when there was a sharp sudden rattling roar and a flash of headlights on the opposite bank of the canal. Zaza sprang up. Then suddenly a silence. Then a voice calling across the canal with a twanging accent: —

"It 's me, Charlotte!"

"It 's Waldorf! Good going that!" said Lady Charlotte to the Senator. She nodded approval and in the moonlight the jewels sparkled about her grey curls.

Zaza sat down again suddenly. Christopher glanced at her and to his astonishment saw tears on her cheeks as bright as the jewels on Lady Charlotte's wig. He gave an exclamation of concern. She looked so very desolate; for she made no attempt to stop the tears but just sat still letting them stream shimmering off her cheeks on to her dress. They were alone now, left on the steps, for all the others, including Loo, had gone across in the ferry to welcome Waldorf Pink. He said: "My dear Zaza, what's the matter?" But she only shook her head and went on crying. "I wish I could help you, Zaza."

She turned her head and looked at him.

"Perhaps you will . . ."

The next day Zaza made Christopher come sailing with her on the lagoons. (They left Loo teaching the Senator how to play spillikins in the Pompeian room.)

That morning the lagoons, as Zaza pointed out, were blue like blue satin whereas the sky was like blue crêpe de Chine. She did not refer to her tears of the night before, but she told him sad extracts from her married lives. She said she and de Vouvray had fallen in love because he had had a sad childhood also, although he had no Russian blood. His mother, an American of great beauty, had never cared for anything but bridge; and his father, debonair, and a friend of de Maupassant, had ended by taking an overdose of monkey gland which had made him curl up and become a baby, and then vanish with a long startled cry.

But when they were far out she changed the subject and said casually, but with a note of real anxiety in her voice: "You wouldn't like to marry me?" She added, gazing at Venice, which was like a far-off forlorn little wedding cake upon the blue satin lagoon: "It would save me going to America . . ."

Christopher thought: "Do all European women go around proposing to get married?" He was puzzled; because he did not suppose that Zaza, with her chic and her fascination and her gift of friendship, had any difficulty in getting married. Nor did he imagine that she could find him, personally, attractive. She seemed to read his thoughts, for she said: "You see I — like you. It would be nicer with you."

"Yes," said Christopher, "yes — and don't think I'm not — not honored, Zaza, but — "

"Don't say you are n't in love with me. I'm asking you to marry me."

"*Please*, Zaza. . . . If you really want to know I think I am — quite a lot in love with you. . . . Certainly you fascinate me. And . . ."

"Well then, it won't be so bad for you."

"But — I could not hope to make you happy."

"I'm only asking you to marry me."

". . . And — you see, I have practically no money."

"All the more reason for marrying me — I have a great deal."

Christopher looked desperately at her little alabaster profile topped by a black Phrygian cap.

"What are you thinking?" she remarked.

He was thinking that he certainly enjoyed her queerness now that he was used to it; and that there was no denying that several times in the last few days he had felt a desire to kiss her. (A desire which he supposed must have been suggested by the amorous conversations of Barbizon-Smith.) But now that she offered him a situation in which a kiss or two might be included, his puritanical romantic feelings were stirred; and he replied that love and marriage were serious matters. He added: "Why don't you remain married to de Vouvray?"

She went pale under all her sunburn lotions and powders, and said: "For a very good reason." And then looked so desperately miserable that he did n't ask her what the reason was but suddenly felt a pity for her that was as real as his amorous emotion for her was unreal. For he perceived that inside this mixture of flower, bird, and marionette was something as sad as a very small girl lost in a very big forest. He remembered that last night, in the excessively bright moonlight, her much too brilliant and lovely eyes had shed real tears, and that after her tears there had been, not one of her imitation gold silences, which were no more than a temporary caging of twittering and exotic nonsense, but a silence locked and barred upon an Unhappiness.

So he said: "If honestly, Zaza, you think I could help by marrying you — "

"Oh," she said, "oh — darling Christopher! Even if it never gets further than an engagement. . . . *How* that would help!"

On the way back, as the villa loomed up, dark, massive, and decorative as an elephant against the eggshell sky, he said that it had better be "a secret engagement" until both their divorces were complete. . . .

As she stepped out of the boat and across Lady Charlotte's moored gondola to the landing stage, her legs so long and her violet (Friday) shorts so svelte, Christopher could not help reflecting that, compared to his first marriage, and from an æsthetic and elegant point of view, he would do very well.

And though at first — that evening and the next day — the Puritan in him doubted, and the Romantic was uneasy, and the Sentimentalist who had wept over the Schubert in Herr Strelsau's "salon" felt twinges of desire for — something (yet not the fascinating Zaza) — the Optimist in him and the Man of the World (latent in him, but there) coincided in the idea that, after all, Beauty and Wealth may prepare an excellent soil in which to grow Love.

Christopher was flattered, pleased, and yet embarrassed by Zaza's decision to accompany him and Loo back to Hyères. He was troubled, for some reason he could n't explain to himself, by the idea of introducing Zaza to Sophie Lacaze. But when he suggested that Zaza should remain at the villa and meet him in a week or so in Paris or London (by which time his divorce would be through, and she could "really make up her mind about marrying him"), she looked so pathetic that he agreed at once (just as he always had with Alice) that her plan of staying at Hyères was an excellent one.

The Pinks offered to motor two of them as far as Florence. Finally it was decided that Christopher and Loo go with them, and Zaza should go in her Isotta.

Captain Waldorf Pink was small, spare, dapper, black-moustached with polished-looking hair, the only soft-looking things about him being his eyes, which were brown and prominent like those of a Pekingese. His voice twanged like the top of a wire fence; his manner toward his wife and his inferiors was authoritative — something of a military "on parade" inflection in his explanation of plans or giving of orders. To others he was "matey." His marriage to Lady Charlotte had been the result of mutual respect at first sight. Waldorf, meeting her at a dinner party in Cairo, had liked her downrightness, her interest in himself, and the fact of her being the daughter of an Earl. She had liked his spruce appearance, the aggressively masculine flavor (which in England is always found at its strongest in the men of the lower middle classes), and the fact that he could motor 350 miles per hour.

During the journey to Florence Christopher and Loo sat in the back with Button — as the Pinks were in a mood of dalliance, Lady Charlotte keeping her arm about Waldorf's shoulders all the time he was driving, and Waldorf calling her "Kid" — "darling" — and sometimes "little woman"! Their behavior made Christopher feel that his attitude to Button was almost ungallant (though it would have been difficult with Button, even if he had wished it, to be anything but respectful). She sat beside him, gaunt in blue serge, brown fabric gloves, and a smart black toque. She was mysteriously responsive to the least spoken or unspoken need of Lady Charlotte, but passed the last deepening beauty of the Italian summer as if it were someone she did not care to know.

When they got to Florence the Pinks, after hearty exhortations to come and see them in London, went off to have whiskey-and-sodas. Button went into the hotel with the luggage, and Christopher and Loo went to the Uffizi, where among many pictures that he was to forget he saw the Venus of Botticelli, rising from her magic sea.

Later, as he drove to the station, Loo beside him immersed in *Westward Ho!*, he reflected upon the way the idea of Venus occupied men's imaginations. And realized, as he settled into his railway carriage, that the beauty of women had played no part in his life.

As the train moved slowly out through the Florentine suburbs, and Loo continued to read *Westward Ho!*, this realization led him to wonder about happiness in general, and his own in particular.

By the time the train reached Genoa he was wondering at the set of mere chances that had caused him to break out of 181 Maple Street. . . .

One of the customs officials at Ventimiglia had suspicions of his wife; and was in a mood to avenge himself, not only on his suspected rival, but upon every trainful of travelers crossing the frontier.

His jealousy was working violently upon his imagination when the midday train arrived from Genoa. As the passengers entered the *douane* he watched them with hatred. And as they began to fumble and unlock and open their cases and hatboxes and holdalls he watched them with a gleaming eye, waiting, only waiting to suspect . . . to follow up his suspicions, to probe, to look, to discover — and to avenge — !

Christopher opened his leather "Revelation" case. "I shan't declare these bedspreads," he said to Loo in a low tone. "Not worth while. If he sees them I'll show him my American passport and say I'm taking them home."

The idea of smuggling excited Loo as much as it pleased Christopher. He wondered if the man next to them, whose battered case was a gay patchwork of all the labels in the world, was also smuggling. He had a hat with a wide Wild West sort of brim, and was in shirt sleeves; and Loo imagined from his *desperado* appearance that he might have a bomb hidden under that layer of shirts and books and brushes and sponge bag.

The customs officer was now bullying a tall Englishwoman who kept saying: "*Niente! Niente!*"

Loo whispered to Christopher: "Why did n't you put the bedspreads underneath?"

"Better on top," said Christopher. "It's always more deceiving to be simple!"

As he spoke the man in the Wild West hat glanced at him. And then — Loo was too startled to exclaim — with a gesture as swift and inclusive of half a dozen other movements as a conjuror's, he snatched the folded bedspreads at the top of Christopher's case, rolled them into a bundle, pulled out a length of one of them which he draped over the rest of the bundle — and held it in his arms tenderly, rocking it very slightly, and then: —

"Why — *Christopher* — "

Christopher could n't speak at all.

" — just fancy meeting you *here*, Christopher." There was a grin on a brown round face under the hat brim. "You did n't know we 'd had a baby — did you?" He glanced down with pride at the veiled end of the bundle in his arms.

"Why — *Johnny Cotton!* Well — I 'm — "

"Here 's the customs gent. Look sharp, Christopher, and show him all your pretty things!"

With hatred the customs official accused Christopher of having bought his Brigg's umbrella and his suits in Italy. Christopher showed him the name and address in Sackville Street. The man's face showed that he was not to be deceived, but that, in the end, he was not going to lower his violent pride by arguing; and, having surveyed Loo's Brownie camera he distrustfully moved to Johnny Cotton, menacing. But — perhaps the same violent domestic instincts that caused his jealousy of his wife gave him also an irrational adoration for babies. At the sight of the richly clad bundle in Johnny's arms, the man's expression relaxed, mellowed, he fingered the top layer of Johnny's case perfunctorily, his glance resting as gently as a Madonna's on the baby — and moved on.

As they were getting back into the train, Johnny muttered to Christopher out of the corner of his mouth: "A hundred cigars and a set of tortoise-shell brushes. Got off lightly, did n't I? How 'd it be if I bring the baby along to your compartment and we celebrate? As a matter of fact I 'm traveling third, broke as usual, but — "

Christopher said of course he would pay the supplement on Johnny's ticket — and asked him where he was going?

"We-ell — where are you going? You an' this grand kid of yours?" He winked at Loo.

"Well, we 're going as far as Hyères," said Christopher.

"Fine — grand! That 's perfectly O.K. with me. I 'll come along to Hyères too." And he sat down in the corner opposite Christopher and rang the bell and ordered a couple of "Scotch highballs" from the attendant (who somehow understood) and began to ask Christopher one question after another.

Loo could n't have imagined that two grown-up men could be so noisily pleased.

On the way to Hyères Johnny Cotton explained to Christopher his scheme of finding a small but picturesque old house or farm along this coast and running it for Celebrities Only. He said that Celebrities attract each other, even though they don't always respect each other. Once he'd found the right place and a bit of capital too, of course, his wife was coming over from New York and they were going to make a packet of money. (Christopher recognized that "packet," which had always been just around the next corner of Johnny's life.)

Johnny said Hyères was as good a place as any to start investigating in. To Christopher's surprise, when they got out at Hyères, Johnny asked a Cook's man which was the best hotel. But he said to Christopher, who drove him there, that when you were flat broke it was psychologically right to make yourself comfortable because you couldn't pay anyway.

So Christopher lent him twenty pounds. And Johnny said he was going to keep in touch with him and let him know how things were going, and if ever he could do Christopher a good turn, he could be sure . . .

Then Loo and Christopher drove on down to the coast, and caught the four o'clock launch.

When they arrived at the port of the island Jean and Sabrina and Herr Fritzl were there to welcome them. And up at the villa Mademoiselle Sophie had creamy iced coffee waiting for them — this was perfectly delicious after the hot train and the blazing sun on the launch.

Sophie was wearing a white and flowered dress. And Christopher thought how cool she looked.

When they had drunk their iced coffee she said to Christopher that there was a telegram for him.

Marius brought it in.

It was from Zaza saying that she had found rooms for herself and her maid in a fisherman's cottage on Port Cros, the next island.

When Mademoiselle Sophie understood that this friend of Christopher's whom he had met in France was now staying at Port Cros, she insisted, with her usual hospitality, that she should come and stay at the Villa Candide. She sent Marius across in the sailing boat, with a note from herself to Zaza, and she arranged that Jean should sleep down at Herr Fritzl's so that there should be room for Zaza's maid.

The whole situation embarrassed Christopher. It was a situation caused by a certain kindly indecision in his own character. And he tried, as men will when their own weakness has betrayed them, to believe that it was bad luck. (If only he had not been the man that Zaza turned to! If only he had visited the Villa Cornaro earlier, or later. On the other hand, he was attracted by Zaza, and flattered by their romantic-seeming, because secret, alliance.)

Also he expected Mademoiselle Sophie to disapprove of her.

In this fear he misjudged Mademoiselle Sophie; and Zaza. For Sophie did not disapprove of Zaza. Nor did she seem in any way surprised by her quite new, quite unexpected association with Christopher and Loo. In fact Sophie took Zaza so placidly, showing no curiosity as to why she had come, and what she was doing in Port Cros, that Christopher began to wish for some sort of reaction on Sophie's part. He would have liked, somehow, to have had an opportunity either to be a little mysterious about Zaza, or even to hint that there was something more than casual friendship. Interest — or surprise at least — from Sophie would have made him feel better, though he did n't quite know how it was that he felt worse. . . . (Certainly either worse, or different, from his first visit here!)

Sabrina's attitude towards Zaza was that of a very little girl to a new and marvelous doll. Everything that Zaza put on or took off fascinated her. Every sentence that came from between Zaza's (sometimes magenta, sometimes crimson, occasionally orange) lips caused Sabrina's eyes to narrow and beam and her whole person to be possessed by tranquil amused admiration. To Sabrina Zaza was Wit and Sophistication, Glamour and Experience. Fascinated, she watched this creature — who seemed to spin in a coil of her own fantasticness, like a clown in a spiral skipping rope.

And gradually she added to her idea that Zaza was Very Funny a perception that she was also, in the traditional manner of Clowns, Punchinellos, and Whatever-the-Moon-Sees, a little tragic. This notion was strengthened by Loo's little story, confided with embarrassment, that one evening, in the Villa Cornaro, when he was looking for ghosts by himself, he had met Zaza suddenly on a little staircase that led only from the telephone, and she was holding a huge handkerchief to her eyes and crying so much that she did n't notice him. Sabrina commented that she supposed she had a Secret Sorrow, adding: "I expect that's why she clings to Christopher." Loo agreed. He said that he thought there was something very comforting about Christopher the more you knew him. Sabrina said: —

"Mademoiselle Sophie said one day to Herr Fritzl that Christopher has a well-born soul."

"And what did he answer?" asked Loo (who liked to know the whole of a conversation).

"He said that Christopher was 'so *sehr liebenswürdig.*'"

"What does that mean?" asked Loo crossly.

"Worthy to be loved."

Loo looked irritably at his sister: "Sab, when you say anything foreign you have a very conceited expression."

"Oh, *have* I, Loo?" Sabrina smiled at him. A year ago that remark would have provoked her. But now Loo was still a little boy; and she was nearly grown up.

Zaza and Sabrina and Jean lay baking on the rocks, Loo was paddling at a distance in the shallow pools and looking intently for *oursins.*

Zaza and Jean had been playing their usual kind of

fantasy tennis. Sabrina was always a charmed audience. Zaza would make an outrageous or absurd statement and Jean would return from an unexpected angle or in a baffling direction. . . .

But now Zaza said: "I must catch the three o'clock launch to go to the *coiffeur*." She got up.

Jean said: "Last time you came back like Garbo. This time perhaps it will be Claudette Colbert — black — a fringe . . ."

When she had gone Sabrina said: "D' you think she 's going to marry Christopher?"

"One can never tell — with her . . ."

"If Christopher 's divorcing. And I think she must be. She never seems to have a husband."

Jean looked at her, surprised. "Her husband, or rather, the man that *was* her husband, is the cinema star Romano de Vouvray. Did n't you know?"

Sabrina shook her hair. "We 've only been twice to the cinema ever. Mummie believes poetry is better than the cinema."

Jean was amused and yet moved by the girl's limpid quality . . . by a deep, cool, clear childishness in her.

"But, anyway — " Sabrina came back to the problem of Christopher, "d' you think Christopher 's in love with her?"

"Perhaps — a little — with his senses."

"Oh, well, that would n't be enough," said Sabrina briskly. "Think of poor Keats tormented with desire for Fanny Brawne."

Jean glanced at her long, graceful, angel-like body beside him, sunned to amber. "I think of him, Sabrina."

"But of course, he may be *really* in love," she exclaimed. "He certainly seems slightly distraught these days. . . . And he's always reading, which he never used to. And yesterday morning he got up at dawn and went wandering about the island in his dressing gown. What I wonder *more*," she continued, "is if *Zaza* is in love with *him*? Of course I would n't really have thought people over thirty ever did fall in love, but Loo says that when he and Christopher stayed in Italy everybody seemed to be over *forty!* and all absolutely plunged in Romance, so —"

"Christopher has *du* sex appeal," said Jean sententiously. "He also has charm . . . and goodness of heart." He added with that knowledgeable air that always impressed Sabrina: "Many women would find him attractive. . . . As to Zaza . . . ?" His gesture indicated that no one could account for what Zaza might feel. "Come and swim, Sabrina."

She rose too, and they plunged off the rocks.

"Oh —!" gurgled Sabrina, as they swam side by side. "I wish we need never leave here, I wish the summer would never end . . . I wish I was a mermaid and could swish my tail and bathe eternally . . ."

They set out toward the little rowboat that was anchored near the western promontory of the little bay. As they climbed into it Jean said: —

"My grandmother had a receipt for pickling mermaids; and also she preserved a lock of hair of one of the Rhine-maidens that my grandfather gave her when he married her — as a sign that he had renounced the habits of a bachelor."

"What was the lock of hair like?" asked Sabrina. "Was it very beautiful?"

"Not at all, it was like seaweed." As he took the oars he added: "I wish that I could use my grandmother's recipe for you, Sabrina — I would keep you in a big blue glass jar and you would look ravishing. I would put sand at the bottom, and a few charming shells, and you would be like yourself in the poem of Milton."

"It was 'green translucent.'"

"Then a green glass jar . . ."

He started to row.

"Let's row round to the port and go to the *bistro* and drink *sirop*," said Sabrina.

"As Mademoiselle Sabrina wishes — "

The "distraught" air which Sabrina referred to in Christopher was little more than a tendency to be quiet and preoccupied, and to feel sad, now and then, without knowing why.

This vague, hurting melancholy drove him to read. He picked books at random from Herr Fritzl's floor, a novel by Turgenev, a story by Rudyard Kipling, a volume of poetry, a play scanned doubtfully at first.

As he read, and thought, and read again, with the

thoroughness of a person who has n't the habit of reading, he began to perceive that the emotions that had seemed only his were old and communal; that there were no new delights, no special griefs; and that history, recorded by poets, novelists, and playwrights, was only men and women, pleasure and pain, fear and courage. . . .

One afternoon, when he was reading alone on the terrace, he turned back the pages of an edition of Shakespeare thrust upon him, rather than lent, by Herr Fritzl, and glanced at a photograph at the beginning of a bust of the playwright, and recognized his marble friend of the Green Plains Women's Club. He stared, amused, as though it really were a coincidence meeting him here! Noted that same domed brow, slightly protuberant blank eyes, the melancholy carnal mouth, the weak chin — only now the fellow seemed no longer in tacit conspiracy with Christopher, against an alarmingly superior crowd of women indulging volubly in a tea — but to confirm a more explicit friendship. "So it 's you," thought Christopher, "who manage to say the things I feel . . ."

He saw Mademoiselle Sophie now, walking one of the lower terraces with Herr Fritzl. They were evidently engaged in one of those intimate yet desultory conversations which would link on to their endless chain of talks and jokes, and memories and confidences. After a time he saw them stop, and sit on the seat under the arbor of vines. If they were to see him, alone up here, they would feel bound to ask him to join them.

He decided to go down to the bay and bathe. . . . Perhaps Zaza and Jean and the children would be there; and that would be a distraction.

He went down. They were n't there. The bay was deserted and shining dark blue in the afternoon sunshine and so calm that only now and then the waves breathed a long drowsy *ssh*. . . .

Christopher went along to the tent and saw that Loo and Jean had left the Barbizon-Smith helmets down here, after using them that morning.

As he undressed he decided that it would be amusing to swim out and do some diving. As he was pulling on his helmet he caught sight of Loo, right the other side of the bay, standing in the pools, looking intently for *oursins*.

Christopher waded in, then swam. Putting on the helmet reminded him of Lady Charlotte — and the Senator — and those ten days at the Villa Cornaro; yet already they seemed as far off and unreal as if he had closed a book about them. . . . And only Zaza had insisted on staying outside the covers of the book with him — Zaza and these fantastic helmets —

Now he was getting far out. He and Jean had dived just about here yesterday. But the water had n't been so transparent.

Far off, back by the shore, he could see a speck, which was Loo looking for *oursins*. He fixed the straps together now under his arms, and started to sink — going down and down with a practised, almost voluptuous ease. At first, the water was pale and shining, the sun hanging like a gold starfish in the liquid crystal above him; then the starfish blurred, and became a dim golden flower higher and higher above in radiant silver blueness; now the blue, marvelously translucent, was all around him. . . . He felt like a fly, not in amber, but in aquamarine. Now small fishes shot past him gleaming in pale satin — and then — across the spaces of aquamarine, he saw the shape of rocks . . . their great mass looking monumental as he approached them, and rather Gothic in the sombre elaboration of their jutting and arching. . . . Here and there quaint ledges stuck out like gargoyles, and as he approached, the patterns of crimson and orange seaweeds might have been stained glass. . . .

Looking down, he saw that the whole structure descended for an immense distance to what must be the bed of the ocean. And that he was now circling and swerving about, as it were, the roof of a subaqueous Notre-Dame. He thought: "When I tell Zaza she is sure to invent quite an adventure out of this" — and he started to cross the "roof," delighted by the way green streamers of seaweed waved off the turrets, and queer fish dived, jeweled, past the gargoyles. Then, when he was just deciding to ascend again, he caught sight of something white on a ledge beneath a sort of flying buttress of rock. He moved towards it. . . .

Sophie and Herr Fritzl came up from the vine arbor and came indoors.

She ordered some cold drinks. Herr Fritzl said: "I thought Christopher was up here."

She took off her straw hat and laid it on an oak chest.

"Perhaps he has gone up to his room."

Herr Fritzl said: —

"I do not think that he is altogether happy at present."

Marius brought in the tray, ice chinking in the jugs. When he had gone out she said: —

"I think that perhaps Christopher is worried about money affairs. It seems that his wife is remarrying a man — a writer, who has no money."

"*Ach!* And so Christopher pays! *So?*"

"Lemonade?"

"Please, yes, Sophie — *so?* Then he must be either a most excellent writer, or a most filthy-bad one, to make no money. What is his name?"

"Peabody," said Sophie — "a strange name, is it not?"

"*Peabody!*" said Herr Fritzl in a tone that might have struck Sophie as even stranger than the name if Loo had not dashed into the room.

Sophie set down the jug and Herr Fritzl, surprised by the boy's expression out of his usual philosophical repose, rose from his deck chair, knocking over his ash tray.

Sophie stared: "What *is* it, *mon enfant?*"

"Mademoiselle *Sophie!*"
"Well?"
"*Well* . . ."
"*WELL?*"
"Oh — Mademoiselle — Sophie! Christopher — Christopher 's swimming to shore with a bare and dead lady in his arms!"

Jean and Sabrina came in just when they were all starting to follow Loo. Loo repeated his news.

When they all got down to the shore there indeed was Christopher with his helmet off, his brown torso bent over a pallid form. . . .

When they drew near they saw that it was a marble statue of a woman, and that Christopher was so out of breath he could n't speak at all.

They surrounded the prostrate statue as if she were an accident.

" — On the rocks," gasped Christopher — he pointed. " — Under — out there — "

"Gosh!" Sabrina knelt down and smoothed her hand over the statue's dripping marble hair. One tress of it hung down the neck behind the left ear and forward over the shoulder. The nostrils were faintly brown, and there was a pale greyish stain across the forehead, and another down the right thigh; and the big toe of her left foot was chipped. Otherwise she was admirably white and smooth. And her features were a really pretty version of the classic: the forehead low, the eyes set shallow, the upper lip short, the shape of the face oval. Near the corners of the mouth the cheeks had a charming, childish roundness, and the lips themselves curved in an expression too sweet to be quite a smirk.

" — Way down, seeming to be lying there calmly taking a *siesta*," said Christopher. He was getting his breath now.

"I should call *her* Treasure-Trove, would n't you?" Loo said to Fritzl.

"But you must be half dead, Christopher," said Mademoiselle Sophie. "I can't think *how* you got her up."

"She 's not awfully big," said Christopher; but with a sudden secret pride in the unreckoned strength of his own muscles. (His out-of-door life and this swimming all these last weeks must have got him pretty fit!)

"She 's as tall as *I* am!" said Loo, and lay down beside her on the sand to measure.

Then Sabrina said of course they must take her up on a shutter. She and Jean went up and found Marius and got him to take one of the shutters off the kitchen window; and he and Jean brought it down to the shore. Then they laid the statue on it. It was difficult to make her lie steadily on her back, as her behind was so rounded out: and they had to put Herr Fritzl's coat folded under her shoulders and head. Then Jean took the front end of the shutter, Christopher and Loo took each side, and Marius the back. (Marius, who was never surprised but always observant, had only remarked that it was, without doubt, "ancient"; and was without doubt of a certain value.) The others followed.

They took her into the long living room, and Marius fetched a square of red and white linoleum and they stood her on it. Then he fetched a towel and dried her carefully all over, explaining to Sophie that he had brought a soft towel so that there was no risk of spoiling the *patine*. "With ancient things," he said, "one must be as careful as possible — and now" — he stood back — "does not Monsieur Columin think that she has already altogether the air of being at home?"

Christopher had sunk down in a chair. His arms ached worse every minute, and he realized it was sheer excitement that had enabled him to get "her" to shore at all. All the time while he was dragging her to the surface, and all those last staggering, wading steps out of the sea, he had had a kind of superstitious bet with himself that he'd get her there. He'd been possessed by the idea that if he dropped her he'd be dropping his own "luck." . . . (The same lunatic obstinacy had been in him five months ago in Cook's on Fifth Avenue when he might so easily have returned to the Grand Central Station and taken the train home to Green Plains.) Now — exhausted, dazed, facing those gleaming flanks and charming breasts — he felt much as Adam must have when he woke up and noticed Eve.

Also, he got an impression that the lady had already a self-satisfied air upon her face; as if she were here through her own enterprise.

And Sophie remarked: —

"She has an expression of great assurance."

Loo said: "I wish she had n't got that one bit of hair coming down over her shoulder. It looks untidy."

"It has been so for perhaps two thousand years," said Fritzl. "After such a time a habit is not easily cured."

"It's only a 'sweet disorder,'" said Sabrina. "But I wish she had eyelashes. I always *do* wish that statues had eyelashes!"

"She has the most delicious little stomach," said Jean.

Marius, now bringing in a tray of *apéritifs*, said: —

"But yes, Monsieur Jean, how that is true. . . . It is what I have been saying, just now, to Eugénie — in telling her what Monsieur Columin has found in the sea. I said, 'She is without doubt ancient, but she is very well made.'" He set down the tray and turned respectfully to Sophie. "I dare to say, Mademoiselle, that it is Eugénie who has said that without doubt it is a Roman statue. Although," he added, "actually Eugénie has not yet seen the statue."

Sophie accepted the petition: "Let her come in."

"Thank you, Mademoiselle."

Sophie advised Christopher now to change his wet bathing suit, which he still had on under his toweling coat. But he assured her that it had dried in the sun.

Loo said, suddenly noticing: "I wish Zaza had bought you a blue bathing suit and not a yellow one — "

"It reminded her of our first meeting," said Christopher.

He took the brandy Sophie held out to him.

Now Eugénie came and stood in front of the statue, in her white overall, her feet in their felt slippers planted apart on the parquet, and nodded and said that, in effect, she thought that she had reason, and that it was, in effect, a Roman statue; since she could say to Mademoiselle and to these Messieurs that as a little girl she had often visited the Musée at Arles where her family had lived, and there she had often seen statues, "it was chiefly Venuses, I think, who resembled to this one. *But*, Mademoiselle, in an extraordinary fashion — !"

"It is probable that you are right, Eugénie," said Sophie.

"Eugénie is an excellent archæologist," said Fritzl, who was smoking a cigar and walking meditatively around the statue.

Eugénie's brown moon face dimpled. "Monsieur de Strelsau is flattering — " she said, and returned to the kitchen.

At this moment Zaza came in, just returned from Hyères, her hair in golden ringlets pushed back by a black riband. She was accompanied by Johnny Cotton, who had got into conversation with her in the launch. (He was on the way across to visit Christopher, and if possible borrow a thousand francs from him.)

Sabrina and Loo rushed at her: "Christopher's found — he was diving and — Eugénie *sezitsavenus!*"

"A rescued *Venus?*" said Zaza, relieved that once again life was behaving like fiction. . . .

"VENUS!" exclaimed Johnny Cotton, joyfully reassured; for nothing more unusual than an unpayable hotel bill had happened to *him* for three days.

" — We don't know for certain it's a Venus," said Christopher, when Johnny Cotton turned to wring his hand. He introduced Johnny to Mademoiselle Sophie and Herr Fritzl and to Jean and Sabrina; and Johnny exclaimed, "Pleased to meet you," with equal warmth to each of them, and shed on each of them in turn the engaging equivocal charm of the rolling stone. (Later, Christopher discovered Johnny in *Autolycus*.)

"I am sure it *is* a Venus," said Jean. "She has too little muscle to be Diana, she is too *petite* to be Juno, and she looks too stupid to be Minerva. She looks both silly and satisfying, and that, for Venus, is traditional."

"And is that what you admire, Jean?" asked Sabrina.

"No," said Jean curtly.

Mademoiselle Sophie offered Johnny Cotton a drink before he should begin to help himself, and said: "It is an extraordinary find, isn't it?" And glanced with exquisite amusement from Christopher to the statue, and at Christopher again.

"*Very* extraordinary, Mademoiselle Lacaze, *very* extraordinary," Johnny said. "Why, if Christopher 'd been bathing off this coast for years he might n't have struck this — lady! . . . And of course — those helmets — as a matter of fact Christopher was telling me about them when we got talking in the train. . . . That 's pretty extraordinary, too! And the two things together — *why* — !" Johnny broke off and seemed to go into a trance, an excited restless trance. . . . He walked up to the statue, walked round, considering her, considering Christopher.

"How *will* Christopher pack her!" said Loo.

"Or will she stay here?" asked Sabrina.

"I believe that the French Government has a right to her charms," said Jean.

"I am delighted to offer her hospitality meanwhile," said Mademoiselle Sophie.

"Mademoiselle might install her in the garden upon one of the terraces," said Marius; "that would make, a little, the style Versailles!"

Zaza said: "Or we could paint a pink sports belt on her and put a real tennis racket in her hand."

"It really is quite a problem what the best thing *is* to do with her!" said Christopher (feeling now as Adam must have felt when his surprise about Eve had worn off).

"*Do* — with her?" Johnny Cotton seemed to be coming out of his trance, though his stare was still unnaturally bright. "*Do with her, boys?*" His uplifted tone, his zest, his certainty, caught all their attention. They turned to look at him, intrigued if skeptical (as people are to an Evangelist).

"— *Do with her!*" repeated Johnny, now fixing Christopher with a fiery and mystical eye — "*why, boys, what we're going to do with her is* — PUBLICITY!"

He did.
Johnny Cotton did such publicity in the next forty-eight hours that the woman behind the *Télégrammes guichet* at Hyères Post Office got quite bright at sending telegrams, though she continued to snarl and snap at Johnny every time he sent one longer than twenty words, or in English. He got his hotel proprietor (now paid by Christopher and mollified) to translate the ones to Paris papers, and to Tombwell and to Barbizon-Smith, into French, as they seemed more likely to arrive coherent.

Also the Telephone Exchange in Hyères grew quite skillful at getting long-distance calls, and began to know that when the American Monsieur called them from the Grand Hotel it wasn't any use pretending that the lines to Paris were all broken down, or protesting that a call to London — or to New York — would cost Monsieur enormously. Evidently the American knew his way about on the telephone. And on the occasion when they sat in the Exchange and did not reply to the buzzing from the Grand Hotel, within five minutes the American Monsieur himself appeared! — in a wide hat as from the films "*du* Wild West" — and cited the names of certain officials in Paris who, it appeared, were his friends.

After this incident Johnny had no difficulties with long distance, but it remained beyond his power and patience to telephone to Toulon twelve miles away, to get hold of a photographer he'd heard of. So he went himself in a hired car, and fetched the man and his camera back with him, and took them down to the launch and brought them on to the island and up to the villa.

On the journey the photographer listened to Johnny's French without comprehending much except the words "Venus — *publicité* — *vite*" and "200 francs." He was a bulky lazy-seeming *méridional* with an unexpectedly quick sense of humor and a hot temper here and there in his eupeptic disposition, like peppercorns in a rich thick soup. He wore a very small *béret basque* on the back of his head, and kept an extinguished cigarette in the corner of his mouth.

Christopher and the Venus were waiting for them according to instructions. After a few attempts Christopher had given up resisting Johnny's steam-roller tactics. His natural modesty, his mistrust of advertising, his annoyance at having an afternoon's quiet diving developed into such a dead-serious farce, could not stand up against Johnny's force, and noise, and persistent mystical enthusiasm.

He informed Johnny that Professor Tombwell had arrived this morning, by the early launch — and had already made a learned diagnosis.

"What's he say?" To the photographer: "Listen now. This is significant!"

"He believes," said Christopher — "that she's Greek."

"Greek? Why, that's fine — the Greeks had a word for her! — Eh!"

"Late Greek — debased Greek," said Christopher.

"Debased? No, no! I don't like that so well. . . . We won't have that. . . . What else?"

"Well, his theory is that the Venus is a part of some spoils that must have been on a ship that got wrecked sometime early in the last century. There was a war between Turkey and Greece about then, it seems, — that was when Lord Byron was killed, Sabrina says, — and Lord Elgin, and quite a lot of other Englishmen, took to stealing all the antiques they could that happened to be lying around in Greece just then. The Professor's idea is that one of these society Englishmen had probably gotten his yacht full of this kind of junk and was taking it home to England, and of course they had to sail around by Gibraltar in those days, and then his boat got wrecked off this island."

Johnny took all this in. Then he pronounced: —

"Of course a wreck a hundred years back is n't exactly *news!* Just the same it makes a background. It might be worked up somehow. The only thing that really gets me about that piece is the notion that maybe the Venus belonged to Lord Byron."

"But she did n't — " began Christopher.

"What's the difference? Anyways, we'd best fix these photographs now." To the photographer: "Come on, *monsieur*. Now, here's the lady — after all, Chris old boy, the main thing to concentrate on is, you pulled this dame out of the ocean, and you were wearing one of Inventor Barbizon-Smith's grand new diving helmets. (I've been telephoning to Italy to Barbizon-Smith all about that — he's getting on to an agent that's going to advertise the thing properly for him, just at this psychological moment, and of course he's tickled to death! Incidentally, I can't get a picture of him. He says he does n't have any; and the best I've been able to do's to cable his mother. I got her address from him just on the chance.) Now come on, Chris — you stand over there right beside the dame — come on, *monsieur* — get the idea? *This monsieur* and *cette dame* — eh?"

The photographer anyway got the idea that he had to pose his subjects and motioned to Christopher to stand nearer to his Venus. (Christopher had put on a white linen suit, as Sabrina had thought it would look nicer if they were "both in white.")

Johnny shouted at Mademoiselle Sophie, who had just come in to watch. "Excuse us, ma'am — many thanks for letting us use your parlor — now Chris, you got to look kind of *triumphant* — "

The photographer, casting aside his coat and his beret, got his camera fixed and then approached Christopher and indicated that he might perhaps adopt a pose in which he put his hand on Venus's shoulder . . .

Johnny cut him short: "No, no — that won't do — stand away from her, Chris, stand away — we wanta keep this thing clean. . . . You gotta have a sort of philosophical attitude — d' you get it? You fished her up but she ain't the likeness of a woman to you, she 's just kinda — *abstract*. An abstract chunk of Beauty." He turned to the photographer and repeated this idea in French. The man nodded, blank and flustered, but got back behind his camera.

"Now then — "

The man took several photographs of Christopher standing stiffly beside the Venus, his head averted from her, looking into the camera.

This satisfied Johnny as far as Christopher was concerned. But he got a fresh idea that he 'd like to have some pictures of the Venus herself. Because he was getting in touch now with the illustrated magazines, and some of the highbrow ones would n't want the human element. (Here Johnny dug Christopher in the ribs.) *His idea was* (he now turned to Sophie) to try and get something really out of the ordinary! Something really lovely! Now why could n't they take a few of her down on the shore? Get her all beautiful and white with the *real sea as her background*? (Sabrina and Loo had come in; and he saw an answering gleam in Sabrina's imagination.) ". . . Stand her up somewhere — near the edge of the waves? . . . Why, I believe I 've seen a picture posed something like that. . . . A kind of a Venus — and the sea — and waves. Only she 's standing on some sort of little raft, I should say."

"A shell?" suggested Sophie.

"A shell? Why, *so* it is! — Thank you, ma'am. Now why could n't we fix up a *shell* for the lady?"

Sophie suggested that it was hard work to get Venus down to the shore. Her firm manner convinced Johnny at once. "Then we 'll just have to fake up the background — see?" He began in French again, telling the photographer that he was to take some "straight pictures" of the statue, and afterwards to put in a background of sea and a shell under her feet. When Johnny had done, the photographer, perspiring with the effort to comprehend, was enlightened by a few sentences from Sophie. His face lit up at once: —

"*Ah! — Le genre Botticelli —* "

Sophie nodded quickly.

"*Bien, bien, mademoiselle,*" and genuinely inspired by such a conceit he dropped a new plate into the camera and put his head under the black cloth.

"You see, ma'am," said Johnny to Mademoiselle Sophie the next morning, "we got to get to Paris while this business is still hot." He was alone with Mademoiselle Sophie on the terrace. Christopher and the children were packing, and Zaza was down at the Villa Cunégonde saying good-bye to Herr Fritzl. "I quite understand that," said Sophie, "especially now that the Director of the Louvre himself has telegraphed."

"Inventor Barbizon-Smith's agent is meeting me in Paris.... That's why I'm going ahead by plane this morning. I've been trying to persuade Professor Tombwell to come with me to Paris, but he seems set on staying here."

"He has very charmingly said he would stay two or three days."

"I know, I know.... Still, he's probably missing a chance of having his name in the news for several days!"

"What! As well as Christopher, Mr. Cotton?" She looked gravely from under her white parasol.

"Not a star turn of course, naturally. But Tombwell's got that story about the Venus really bein' stolen by Lord Byron because she resembled one of his mistresses."

"Has he?" said Sophie gently.

"Why, yes — he could 've cashed in on that . . ."

At this moment Professor Tombwell appeared, very neatly dressed, in tussore. Johnny got up and wrung his hand.

"I've just been sayin' to Miss Lacaze that it's a shame you are n't coming with us all to Paris . . ."

Professor Tombwell began a little smile, but was in too abstracted a mood to finish it. "I do-on't like

P-Paris to-day — very much. Haussmann did such ab-bominations — d-don't you think, *mademoiselle?*"

She nodded and indicated that he should come and sit down beside her. And they fell into a conversation which Johnny did not hear; though he remained beside them, smoking, until it was time for him to go.

Six hours later it was time for Zaza and Christopher and the children to leave also.

Herr Fritzl had come up for the farewell occasion. Healths had been drunk, and Venus had been toasted and then taken away by Marius and Jean, and swathed in sheets and packed into a crate in straw.

And at the last, when the others had gone on down to the port with Venus's crate in the back of the Ford, Christopher went to find Mademoiselle Sophie, to say good-bye to her, and thank her.

She was in the long salon, having come in from waving farewell to the others. He suddenly thought of that evening when she had sung the Schubert songs. The echo of the songs seemed to be now in this shuttered light.

He thanked her. In his stilted thank-yous he meant that she had given him a kind of hospitality which he had never known, letting him stay among the tranquil and gay and lovely qualities of her character.

He said: "Good-bye, Sophie."

She said: "Good-bye — my cousin." And then: "I'm so happy that you have had such a success — there are few men of the Old World or New who have been able to bring Venus herself out of the sea." She smiled as she spoke. But he felt an ache right through him that was like an unresolved chord. And not knowing what the chord was that should resolve it, he decided to say good-bye and go at once.

Then he saw that she was holding out her hand. He took it, and bent and kissed it. And having said, "Thank you, Sophie," he turned and went, very quickly.

And Sophie stood watching the doorway where he had gone.

He went down the hill on foot, down the sandy road under the pines, and found the others already waiting by the launch.

Zaza was superintending the crate with Venus in it, which was being lowered into the stern. She did n't speak to Christopher when he came, or look at him. And on the way across she spoke to him once in a businesslike way about the crate, but otherwise kept out of his way and kept Loo with her, while Jean talked to Sabrina.

Jean was to come to Hyères station with them. He was very gay and voluble in the launch, and played "fantasy tennis" with Zaza. And at the station he bought papers and got porters and joked with Madame at the bookstall.

But when the train came in and he had to say good-bye to Sabrina his gayety failed him. And so did his philosophy — which, like most philosophies, could give him a little courage but no consolation. None of his acceptances, none of his "life is like this," made Sabrina's going easy to endure. And her going so cheerfully, only a little troubled that he seemed to mind, made him realize that she was still a child (in a cool, shining way that Loo had never been a child) — and that though Love often occupied her fancy, it had never touched her heart. And as they all got into the train it was Zaza who put her arm through Jean's for a second and said: "Jean, don't show her you mind — it's unlucky." And added when they were all leaning down out of the windows and the train was moving: "Write to me, Jean — if I can do anything for you."

"*Merci* — Zaza!" he said. But he was looking at Sabrina. She was smiling at him, waving to him: "*Au revoir, Jean — au revoir.*" And the train was moving out.

A suite had been reserved for them, by Johnny, in Paris.

Loo thought that although the Ritz was bigger, the decorations were not so pretty as at the little hotel they had stayed in before. But Sabrina reveled in the luxury of her bathroom, the soft, deep carpets, and having a telephone beside her bed; and the hot melting deliciousness of the *croissants* on her morning tray. And she enjoyed the view from Christopher's sitting room down on to the Place Vendôme.

Johnny, who was waiting to welcome them, had engaged a room for Zaza in the hotel, but not in the suite.

He explained to Christopher, as soon as the two of them were alone, that that would keep everybody guessing about Zaza, but not too much; that the main thing at present was to keep the Christopher-Venus situation in Big Type! And when interest in her started to get less, *then* you could use the human lady in the case, i.e., Zaza, by working one in with the other; Christopher — turning from Antique Beauty to Flesh and Blood Duchess — something of that sort, eh? There was nothing better than a Romance for keeping a man in the public eye, and if that romance could have a scandalous flavor about it, all the better: and though titles were n't big news, "Romano de Vouvray the Movie Star" certainly was, and once his name was in it, and you gave 'em the idea about a divorce coming and Columin being cited, you 'd got a story! And if you were to work that up a bit, pull out the pathetic stop and give 'em the Pagliacci idea, fr'instance — poor Romano making that picture, smiling and debonair the way he had to be and yet his heart . . . See? There was n't any reason why that should n't make quite a big story following *on* — that was the point . . . keep it back right now, use the Venus for all she was worth — was n't she doing fine? Eighteen reporters waiting in the lobby of the Ritz, cameramen up in the suite all ready to shoot the very minute she comes out of her crate; a special newspaper woman come along to take her measures . . . a fellow from *Vogue* to get a fancy photograph of her an' Christopher. . . . The only pity of it was, said Johnny, turning on Christopher with that blend of bullying and affection he always had for him, the *foolish* thing was not to make a better story out of the children — yes — certainly, one or two of the paragraphs had *mentioned* them *in spite* of Christopher's trying to hush 'em up. But who was going to get any kick out of the situation of Christopher traveling around for his summer holiday with a couple of English kids that were related to him? Not even pathos in it! Now if the girl had been ill, and Christopher had come upon her just in the nick of time and taken her south, to the eternal gratitude of her family? Or — see here now — s'posin' this boy Loo — had been saving up an' saving up every cent he got so as to take his sister to a climate that would make her *well* . . . ?

Christopher said: "You 'd better save your imagination, Johnny. The children are *not* in this racket. If I can make a little money by getting myself talked about with this darned chunk of old marble, well and good. I need the money. . . . Incidentally because I 'd like to be able to help with the education of these two children. . . . So, all this is — rather an opportunity." Christopher took off his coat, glanced irritably at all the telegrams on the desk, and settled down in his shirt sleeves to have a cigarette.

"Opportunity!" said Johnny. "I should say it was! My! Christopher Columin, if you don't make big money out of this frigid female you fished up . . . why — there's a book in it (I'll get that written for you — do it myself prob'ly) — as well as all the feature stuff, weeklies, magazines. I've been phoning up this last two days since I got here. . . . And if there's a book, there's a movie, too. . . . Of course they'd alter it a bit; maybe they'd work in a kind of Pygmalion idea — getting your Venus coming alive or something. . . . Anyways, can't you see the possibilities? . . . Under the ocean — people like that (it's a grand change from the air). And there's an intellectual side to it — educational — archæology — people like that, too! And now what about a couple of Scotch highballs?"

Christopher agreed with this last suggestion. While Johnny was ordering them, he began to read some of the telegrams. Among the usual enthusiastic but confusing invitations or suggestions from unknown professors, editors, stockbrokers, learned societies, curators of museums — there was a telegram of congratulation from Alice. He noticed that it was signed, still, Alice Columin. And had been sent off in Paris itself.

Alice walked into the Ritz wearing her new Lanvin suit, and told the porter she wished to see Mr. Columin.

The man's immediate reaction was defensive, though deferential.

"*Madame*, Mr. Columin is very busy — "

Alice guessed, rightly, that Christopher was besieged by every kind of caller.

" — as a matter of fact, *madame*, I think that Mr. Columin is out at present."

"Call up and ask."

"You — could not leave a card or a message, *madame?*"

"Certainly not." The man was a fool and probably took her for a common autograph hunter!

"Very well, *madame*."

While he took up a receiver Alice looked in her pocket mirror and prinked. In Paris her Roman features were more made-up than in Green Plains.

"I am sorry, *madame*. 'E is not in."

"Who is then?" she snapped. "Who answered you?"

"I — I think it was Mademoiselle Columin."

Alice withheld any comment. (As she said to Hamnet at Amiens, if Christopher chose to . . . Christopher famous had a kind of right to . . . do things . . .) "I will go up and see Miss Columin."

The porter gave in; he disliked scenes. Alice, going up in the elevator, reflected that probably a little firm dealing would fix that girl — or — maybe — a check (Alice had read of such situations) . . . As for the rumors in the gossip columns, about Christopher and the notorious Duchesse de Vouvray, Alice just did n't believe a word of it. For what could a woman like that see in Christopher? The rumors had begun before his celebrity; so that there could have been no possible attraction. . . . Either, as she'd told Hamnet, the rumor had no foundation at all, or, as Hamnet had suggested, the Duchesse had chosen to use Christopher as a "blind" for some other *affaire;* a piece of duplicity that Christopher characteristically had been too simple to realize! . . .

As Alice followed the *chasseur* along the corridor to Christopher's suite, she wondered if Christopher had yet received, as she had, the news of their divorce. The idea of seeing him again — not as his wife but as a free woman — excited Alice, and appealed to her liking for situations with a sentimental-exasperating flavor. She had been anticipating the little twinges of pain it would give Christopher to see her, and realize how completely he had lost her. . . . She had also in her imagination rehearsed little tantalizing sentences: " — Of course, Christopher — there have been cases of remarriage — " She had foreseen herself rousing, a little painfully, a beautiful hope in him — and then, very, very sadly, destroying his hope again — and yet not destroying it so completely that she would n't leave him guessing. (For, after all . . . Hamnet was certainly a great genius, but there was n't any doubt that lately he *had* been . . . selfish . . . queer — and that secretary Duval always around — and Christopher, now famous as well as submissive, had — advantages . . .)

Outside Christopher's suite two young reporters and a woman in green tweeds were waiting. The woman asked if she might have Alice's name. But Alice, quickly deciding in her mind to "time" her interview with the press, said she was sorry, but her visit was "incognito," and passed into a vestibule, where she was met by "the girl" she'd seen with Christopher at Avignon.

"I'm sorry," said the girl, "but Christopher's out. Didn't the porter tell you?"

"Yes," said Alice, "he did. But I'll wait." She walked through an open door into a sitting room carpeted pale pink and with its marble chimneypiece and white tables stacked with vases of expensive flowers. She wondered who sent Christopher all these. "I'll wait until he comes in," she said, and sat down on a sofa. She saw that the writing table was littered with press cuttings, cables, telegrams and photographs and gardenias and orchids in tooth glasses. The place looked like an actress's stateroom!

The girl (dressed ridiculously, like a child, in a pink-and-white-striped cotton) said: —

"I s'pose I can't give Christopher any message for you?"

"No thank you."

"Would you like a book or a paper? I don't think he'll be back for an hour or two."

"No thank you . . . I have certain personal and intimate matters I wish to discuss with Christopher . . ."

"He's awfully busy, you know. Whenever they are n't being asked out to meals they 're being photographed or interviewed and whenever they are n't being interviewed or photographed they 're being asked out to meals."

"They?" demanded Alice.

Her tone seemed to startle the girl; for she hesitated quite a while before she answered: —

"Y — yes."

"Who d' you mean by *they?*"

"Just — *them*," said the girl (very oddly, Alice thought).

Alice snapped: "What d' you mean?" (She was n't going to give the idea that *she* believed any gossip.) "You mean Christopher and — "

The girl's sly-looking long eyes had a curious look. Then she said: —

"Christopher and his *bride*, of course."

Alice took in the word. And it seemed to her that the girl was watching how she took it. ("Relax! Relax!" thought Alice.)

"His — bride?"

"Yes," said the girl coolly. Yet Alice had an infuriated sense that the girl was mocking at her.

"Bride?"

"Yes, Mrs. Peabody."

" — My name 's — *not* Peabody."

"I'm so sorry. . . . You see we thought it must be, by now."

"You mean Christopher is — married?"

"Y-yes."

"Then — and — *who* is his — his wife?"

"Well — just his wife."

"Where is she?"

"In — Paris."

"*Where?* Please tell me. I must know. Is she — *here?* He can't have been married long! The divorce was only fixed up a week ago."

"He married yesterday," said the girl.

There was a sound like a cat sneezing. The girl turned sharply and stared at the door.

"*Yesterday!*" exclaimed Alice.

"Yes."

"And *where*, I should like to know?"

"In — in Notre-Dame — very quietly though — they had a very quiet service, hardly any music at all — "

Alice said: "I'd — heard she was a Roman Catholic. And where is she now?"

The girl looked embarrassed. Evidently Christopher was trying to keep his marriage a secret and the girl was realizing now that she had given it away!

"You'd best tell me!" said Alice, bullying at the first sight of weakness.

"She's — lying down."

"Lying down — at eleven in the morning?"

"Yes," said the girl — still speaking in that irritatingly doubting and self-excusing manner — "you see, she's tired — after the wedding — "

Alice's nerves and temper made it difficult for her to appear sane.

"I *must* see her."

And when the girl, flushed and defensive, protested, Alice went on: "I *will* see her! I *insist* upon seeing her! Does she imagine that just because she's a French Duchess she can treat me this way — !"

With a gasped, "Just one minute — I'll ask her," the girl was out of the room. Alice thought she heard that little boy's voice in the vestibule outside. Then another door banged opposite.

Alice waited. Maddened by the realization that Christopher, suddenly desirable, had been snatched from her, she was determined at least to insult her successor.

When the girl came back she said: —

"I'm afraid she's still asleep."

The little boy was behind her. He said: —

"We've just been in to see."

Even in her state of temper Alice realized that there was something queer in both their expressions; and her imagination darted to the conclusion that, in fact, Christopher was not out at all: but there, in that room opposite, *with* that notorious woman.

Alice looked from the girl to the boy. "It's no use trying to deceive me," she said, and walked straight past them, and into the vestibule, opened that door opposite, and went in.

The room was dimmed, the blinds being drawn down so that only narrow bright troughs of light lay just below each window. And in that first quick-breathing moment, Alice, staring at the shadowed pale shapes of the furniture, thought that the room was empty.

Certainly, there was no sign of Christopher, lounging (as her maddened fancy had foreseen him), with the farmyard pride of the newly mated, in a sybaritic silk dressing gown; nor of any *chic*, shameless, and seductive young Frenchwoman. . . .

Across an armchair lay a man's overcoat. Another chair, primly against the wall, supported what was evidently a pair of folded evening trousers. Two ivory brushes (Christopher's) lay on an otherwise deserted dressing table; and several pairs of men's shoes were ranged below it. The bed was unruffled, and pristine, in a counterpane . . .

But then Alice perceived at right angles to the fireplace the shape of the chaise longue (the children were by now just behind her on tiptoe) and on it, resting among a quantity of little pillows lightly covered by a satin quilt, was a woman. . . .

In the half-light Alice saw that her eyes were shut; and her cheeks flushed with sleep. . . . About her shoulders was a softness of swansdown and round her head some kind of satin turban fastened in front with a brooch that glinted. . . . There was a quality of "houri" about her, of supine insolent luxury. . . .

Alice made a move forward; and felt a hand on her arm. "Please don't wake her," in an urgent whisper, "she — she took something — "

"Ah!" said Alice. Then she stopped and turned and let herself be led to the doorway intent on her own next question: —

"*What* did she take?"

"I — something to make her sleep — "

"Ah!" said Alice again. (The girl shut the door behind her.) "And I suppose Christopher *took something*, also?"

"Oh — *no!*" said the girl, with what seemed a kind of false ingenuousness. "I told you. He's gone out."

Alice gave her a last stare. Then said: —

"Thank you . . . I shall *write* to Christopher" — and went.

When she had gone they went into Christopher's bedroom and drew up the blinds again, and took Zaza's swansdown bedjacket and little pillows back to her room. Then Sabrina washed Venus's face very carefully with cotton wool, and managed to stand her up once more in the corner, ready for the Director of the Louvre, who was coming back with Christopher and Professor Tombwell after their luncheon at Larue's.

Just after Alice had left Zaza came in from the *coiffeur* with her hair made into gold astrakhan above her forehead, her face shrimp-colored from the dryer. She felt too plain to go down to the restaurant, so she ordered *foie gras* and a salad, and orange juice, for herself and the children in the sitting room. She seemed very nervous every time the telephone rang, though each time it was only an archæologist, or newspaper, or a French hostess speaking English, or an American hostess speaking French, demanding Christopher. After luncheon Zaza smoked several cigarettes, asked questions and did n't hear the answers, and went up to the glass several times to see if her face was recovering its pallor, and finally went out again, telling Sabrina that "if anyone telephoned" she was to say that "*Madame la Duchesse est à Newcastle.*"

"But — " Loo began, as Zaza's long slim-in-black figure was going out of the door. "Because Newcastle sounds like the other end of the world to French people," said Zaza. They heard her shut the outer door of the suite, and her voice telling something to the press. (They knew that she always told them the same thing — "that she was n't able to make any statement yet.")

"But — " said Loo, "*what* French people does she want to think that she 's gone to Newcastle?" He was feeling peevish. *Foie gras* and orange juice did n't agree with him.

"Zaza's life is dark with mystery," said Sabrina, going to the window to look down into the Place Vendôme. As she spoke the telephone rang and she rushed to the receiver. A man's voice demanded the Duchesse de Vouvray. "*Madame la Duchesse est à Newcastle,*" said Sabrina.

There was a pause. Then the voice said, with a French accent: "I'll bet my bottom dollar she's in Paris," and the speaker rang off.

"I wonder —" began Sabrina.

But now Christopher came in, accompanied by Professor Tombwell and the Director of the Louvre.

Loo went away to his room to go on reading *Westward Ho!* . . .

Sabrina saw at once that they had lunched well. (She had begun to know at a glance the look of men who have fed well from men who have merely eaten. She recognized the air of heightened complacency.) She went with them into Christopher's bedroom, where the Directeur, a round, clever, hedonistic little man, on seeing the Venus said: "Ah, ha. . . . Ah-ha!" in a deep, rather gloating tone. He walked round her, and touching her here and there with an expert finger, peering close at her left ear, and then at her lock of hair, and then at the dimple in her chin, murmured: "Ha — h — ha . . . ha-hm," to himself. Then he said: "She is ravishing — she is delicious! She is charming!" Then he stood back several paces and, nodding his head with expert and sensuous pleasure, said: "But she is exquisite . . . *exquise* . . . *exquise*" . . . so rapt and yet so expressive in his admiration that Sabrina (in whom Jean had roused the first instincts of coquetry) said: —

"Yes — isn't she lovely?" — simply so that the Directeur might notice that she, also, was in the room.

He did. And reacted in the most reassuring manner, turning and exclaiming to Christopher: "But, my friend, you have not presented me! What is this — a Nymph? — A *sylphide?* — Another goddess?"

Sabrina responded at once. She smiled, flushed, bridled, and looked through her eyelashes (Loo would have been deeply ashamed of her), and so distracted the admiration of the Directeur that no reasonable discussion about the Venus had yet taken place when Johnny Cotton came in with the information that the wife of the American Ambassador wished to give a tea, early in October, "to meet Mr. Christopher Columin. What d' you think of that, Chris?" At the same time Johnny pulled out of his pocket a cable which he handed to Christopher. "How are we doing, Chris? How are we *doing?*"

Christopher read it: —

HAVING SEEN ANNOUNCEMENT OF YOUR LECTURES AT COLUMBIA AND HARVARD IN NOVEMBER THE MEMBERS OF THE GREEN PLAINS WOMEN'S CLUB ARE EXTREMELY ANXIOUS TO FIX DATE FOR A LECTURE FROM YOU WHICH WOULD PRECEDE THESE OTHER DATES STOP SUGGESTED HONORARIUM TWO HUNDRED DOLLARS STOP ALL MEMBERS OF THE CLUB JOIN HEARTFELT CONGRATULATIONS E. PECKETT PRESIDENT

"Well," said Johnny, "how about it?" (The Directeur was now in a corner talking to Sabrina.)

Christopher did not immediately reply. He reread the cable. He looked at Johnny. He turned and looked at Venus, who returned his glance of exasperation with that oversweet marble smirk. Then he said: "It seems a matter of choosing between the Women's Club there, and the Embassy here. I shall certainly choose Green Plains."

"But why?"

"Because," said Christopher, "when I have to choose between two evils I prefer the paid one."

He grinned at Johnny, gave him back the cable to answer, and turned to call the Directeur back into the realms of art.

When the Directeur had gone Sabrina stopped behaving so vivaciously, and Christopher, now a little dry in the mouth from his luncheon, ordered tea.

"Where's Loo?" he asked.

"In his room reading."

"Dearie me. . . . He ought n't to be in on this lovely day — " He'd been feeling worried about the children ever since they'd arrived in Paris. He knew this whole atmosphere was wrong for them . . . yet he could n't seem to escape himself. And when he'd suggested sending them home right away, they had been desperate with disappointment.

"And where's Zaza?" Among the feelings he had for Zaza, and they were many, there was definitely the same feeling he had for the children: a desire to protect and benefit her, combined with doubts as to whether he was n't doing her more harm than good. "Where is she?" he repeated, a little harassed — for of the three of his charges Zaza was the most incalculable.

"*Madame la Duchesse est à Newcastle*," said Sabrina. Tea was wheeled in by a waiter.

Christopher felt tired enough to be a little irritable. "What *are* you saying, Sabrina?"

"I 'm saying what Zaza said! She said if anyone — "

At this moment the telephone rang. Sabrina answered it. She said: "No, *monsieur, Madame la Duchesse est à Newcastle.*"

"Have you gone crazy?"

Christopher stared at her, really troubled. It would n't do for Sabrina to get her mind playing tricks like Zaza's. For though he knew that deep down Zaza was, rather desolately, sane, Sabrina could n't realize this. "You know she has n't gone to Newcastle!" said Christopher wearily, thinking of Benjamin and Fanny and conscientiously determined that Sabrina must be kept to facing facts. "You know very well that is not so."

This pedagogic tone coming after the Directeur of the Louvre's sycophantic references to Nereids, Dianas, and the Loves of Ronsard — and coming, of all people, from Christopher — startled Sabrina into a violent sense of injustice. She started; and every line of her face changed to goblinesque resentful curves. She shrugged her shoulders, raised and dropped her long arms, and was just stalking out of the room when Zaza came in, her face swathed in a rose-pink veil.

Christopher said, "Sit down and have some tea, dear," and started to pour it out for her.

She sat on the edge of a chair, not yet taking off her rose-pink gloves, and said to Sabrina: —

"Did anyone call up?"

"Yes."

"Who?"

"A man — he did n't give his name."

Zaza drew off one glove, and asked in a tone of brittle indifference: —

"What was his voice like?"

"Nice," said Sabrina. "Slightly French — but slightly American too." (It had reminded her of the voice of the Lovely Young Man; and therefore given her a pain of rather petulant sentimentality. She had still an unconscious grudge against Christopher for having debunked her Ideal.)

"What did you tell him?"

Sabrina gave Christopher a defiant glance. "I told him you were at Newcastle."

Zaza took off her second glove and stared at it.

"D' you think he believed it?"

"Oh yes!" said Sabrina, always an optimist in the cause of friendship, and partly to do credit to her own powers on the telephone (an instrument she had rarely used until this last week, for the call box in St. Tad's outside the post office was never used by children).

Zaza demanded nervously: "D' you *really* think he believed it? Was he in Paris? Or was he calling from a distance? D' you suppose he'll call up again?"

"Oh *no*," said Sabrina. Once more serene, and feeling she had done well, and that Christopher must now be aware that he'd misjudged her, she helped herself to a chocolate éclair off the tea table.

"Of course," Zaza broke out — "if he *believed* it!"

She looked suddenly miserable, her face as small as a button behind her pink veil.

When Zaza's face got small like this Christopher was always moved to acute and angry pity. Why could n't that fellow leave her alone? Driving her to most foolish lying! He felt suddenly convinced that she really did need him; and his conviction came as a kind of relief to his own vague depression. Whenever he got the idea that it was his duty to marry Zaza, he found himself half in love with her (of such are the Puritans). And in this moment he foresaw her — perhaps for the first time quite certainly — as his wife.

He said: "Zaza dear, I wish you 'd try and drink some tea!" And he added, as he perceived her eyes piteously bright and her lips vividly tremulous behind their filmy pink prison: "I think the sooner we leave Europe, dear, the better — "

She nodded. Loo came in, reading *Westward Ho!* as he walked, and fell over one of the many little tables. It tipped on to Sabrina's foot. And Sabrina, less serene than usual, — having been a Dryad, a telephonist, heard a nostalgic voice, and read *Three Weeks* in Tauchnitz all morning, and had *foie gras* for lunch and no fresh air for two days, — screamed "Little beast!" at Loo and burst into tears. And Loo, bewildered by such an attack and at the sight of Sabrina in tears, and his own knee hurting, and his reading interrupted in the middle of a paragraph, gave a little furious cry that changed into a sob — and ran out of the room.

"Evidently," said Christopher, getting up and going to Sabrina and handing her his handkerchief, "Paris is getting on everybody's nerves."

Three days later there appeared in the Paris edition of the *New York Herald* the announcement that Mrs. Alice Columin and Mr. Hamnet Peabody, of Green Plains, Massachusetts, had been married in Paris by special licence, and sailed from Cherbourg on the *Queen Mary* the same evening.

They got on the *Normandie* at last. But Christopher was tired out with digesting too many courteously offered lunches; Zaza was depressed and quiet; and Loo was noisy one minute, because the ship itself excited him so much, and truculent the next because he and Sabrina were getting off at Plymouth, and the marvelous holiday was at an end. And Sabrina was in a state of dreamy melancholy, only half really sad. Only Johnny Cotton was vital and optimistic, opening

Christopher's telegrams, and tipping stewards in advance.

They all went up to the grill for luncheon (and it "seemed to be the Ritz *all* over again," sulked Loo, secretly near tears, and suddenly feeling it would be a relief to have a normal meal at home again, with everything on the table at a time, and the animals sitting round!).

When the headwaiter showed them to their table they were roused out of their several moods by finding Fritzl sitting there, his napkin already tucked in his waistcoat, eating cantaloup!

To their many exclamations and questions he replied tranquilly: "I have long wished to go to America. And now I have decided to do so . . ." He added later that he had left Professor Tombwell to keep Sophie company.

The tender out from Plymouth approached the *Normandie*. Benjamin was on it, in spite of every blessed thing having gone wrong since early this morning: Kitty lame; having to borrow Mrs. Dovey's pony; nearly missing the train at Tremayne, getting delayed in Plymouth itself; all that fuss getting his permit to go on this blessed "tender," as they called it . . .

He reread a telegram in his hand several times. It was a telegram they'd got on Wednesday from Christopher, sent off from Paris, asking Benjamin to meet the children at Plymouth this Saturday, and saying that Christopher had to go on to New York.

Fanny had thought how wonderful it was for the children to have that last bit of their trip on a liner. But Benjamin had shaken his head over what that telegram must have cost Christopher! And what all the rush and confusion of meeting them, in this way, would mean.

And so far Benjamin's fears had been justified! Just supposing he *had* missed the train and never got to Plymouth! What then? Sabrina and Loo being turned loose in a crowded place like Plymouth!

However, here he was! And there was the *Normandie*, my goodness! Ten times as big as that cruiser Benjamin had been on in the war. But not more seaworthy, he'd bet . . . Benjamin said this to a man standing beside him. Then he said to a woman on his other side that he'd think some of these great colossal vessels were n't half so safe as they were made out to be! . . . And no ship was ever meant to be the size of that one! The woman, who was chill from waiting, and hostile by character to talkative strangers, gave in inevitably to the parson's absolutely unquestioning goodfellowship — and the blue twinkle of his eyes, and the cheerful rosy melancholy of his whole face. She even heard with amusement that Benjamin's two children were on the ship, and that he had with him, in the papier-mâché case he carried, some roast-beef sandwiches and some plums from the Rectory garden —

THE ADVENTURE OF CHRISTOPHER COLUMIN

"because you never know what they'd have offered them to eat on that French boat!"

But now they were getting near and Benjamin began to scan the people up on the decks, small figures shoulder to shoulder against the rails. "What a crowd! . . . Fancy having to take all these people on board for every voyage. . . . Cater for 'em too. . . . And sleep the lot of them. Well, I s'pose it's what a great stout vessel like that is built for. All the same — I would n't be the captain — not for a fortune. . . . You never know who you'd get traveling — " He stopped, and then beamed and started shouting and waving madly — "There they are! Both of 'em! Hello! HELLO!" And it actually was — Sabrina! Loo! Christopher too! They were all there, waving back!

But on board Benjamin was once more distraught, anxious, and ready to renounce all hope of finding them. He hurried and banged to and fro up and down the corridors, his face red and perspiring, his mackintosh flying. The telegram had said, "Meet us smoke room," but it was as easy looking for smoke rooms as for one flea in a stable.

But Sabrina found him, by rushing from steward to steward asking if they had seen "a Monsieur Priest, *anglais*, with a despairing expression." (She knew the state he would be in.)

She led him to Christopher and Loo in the smoke room. Loo rushed to him. Benjamin, between his greeting of Christopher and his thanking of him, and his panic that now he'd found the children he'd never get 'em off on to the tender again, hardly observed Zaza or Fritzl, to whom he was introduced. Also he was deeply impressed by the unhealthiness of those corridors down there. . . . "Like traveling in the crypt of a cathedral!" he said, and advised Christopher to get his steward to make up some kind of bed on deck. "Better get some air up there than be stifled in a bunk downstairs."

Nor did Loo's insistence that they were "*beds*, not bunks, Daddy," impress Benjamin's mind at all.

When they did have to go off the children made Christopher promise to come to the Rectory *as soon as* he got back to Europe. And Benjamin added his own and Fanny's assurance that there was always a home for him when he'd done "trapesing round."

Just as they were off Benjamin said: "By the *way*, Christopher, what's this Mrs. Dovey's got out of her paper, about your getting photographed with the Venus de Milo or something? I never seem to have time to read anything except the news myself."

"*Come*, Daddy," — urged Loo, — "or we really shan't get off!"

"Not de Milo, I'm afraid," said Christopher.

"Come, Daddy," said Sabrina, "we'll tell you *all* about it on the way home."

Christopher went up on deck and watched the tender go off, Fritzl with him.

The children waved and waved.

As they got smaller and far away Christopher felt desolate, as if they had been his own children.

"You're a bit of an enigma, Fritzl," said Christopher as they sat in the Winter Garden of the *Normandie*, exotic birds in cages all about them and cocktail glasses in their hands.

Fritzl said: "How so . . . ?" His surf-like voice was the only sound about them suggesting the proximity of the sea.

"Well — just why are you coming to America?"

"For a most excellent reason." Fritzl could present a genial simplicity more baffling than any air of mystery. He drank down his cocktail and wiped his beard. (Christopher noticed that already since he had left Sophie's jurisdiction he'd begun to forget to send his handkerchiefs to the laundry.)

"But you also, Christopher, you are an enigma!"

"I?"

"Certainly. You and that sweet, foolish Zaza." Now, behind his geniality, his glance was wary, and Christopher got a sense of being under an extremely benign microscope. "Of course, dear Christopher, at your age to fall in love with a so young woman is most natural. It is — " he murmured now as gently as a summer evening's tide — "it is most natural."

Christopher said obstinately: "Zaza and I have a good deal in common" — and realized that he couldn't have made a more unconvincing statement. In fact he felt more and more like a man who, with a falcon attached to his wrist, would have preferred a wrist watch. "She is extremely charming" — he said this so often to himself.

"And also she is in love with *you* . . ." said Fritzl soothingly.

Christopher was glad Johnny Cotton came along at this moment, followed by Zaza, who had been up to the wireless office again. She held a marconigram in her hand and looked in better spirits than she had since they sailed. Johnny took Fritzl off to make sure of the same table they had all four had in the grill yesterday.

Zaza handed the wire to Christopher. It read: —

SUGGEST YOU PROCEED RENO AS SOON AS POSSIBLE STOP COMMUNICATE YOUR DECISION TO ELSTREE ROMANO

Christopher said: "And what *did* you communicate?"

"I communicated that I would proceed to Reno after Green Plains."

"I — I s'pose you are certain, Zaza, that this is a good idea?"

She sat down, crossed her knees, lit a cigarette, and said: "I could n't be more sure. It ought to be an ideal marriage. We are n't in love; so we won't ever hurt each other. We like different kinds of lives. So we won't ever bore each other — "

"Zaza — "

"Yes. What is it?"

"You 're — you 're *sure* you are n't really in love with Romano all the time?"

"What a darned stupid question."

Alice Peabody sat alone at breakfast.

As she drank her coffee she glanced at the front page of the *Herald*. At the head of the right-hand column she read: "*FAMOUS DISCOVERER OF VENUS RETURNS TO GREEN PLAINS: Welcome at South Station by Members of Women's Club.*"

There was a photograph of Christopher in an extremely sophisticated black Homburg hat. Below it a long paragraph beginning: —

Mr. Christopher Columin, whose famous deep-sea dive rescued a Grecian statue of remarkable pulchritude, arrived off the *Normandie* yesterday. He was accompanied by the Duchesse de Vouvray (now, it is rumored, divorcing her husband Romano de Vouvray, movie-starred descendant of famous ducal family), and an Austrian friend, Herr Schmidt, who are both over here on a visit. Mr. Columin and his two friends arrived at the South Station at 4.45, where they were met by Mrs. Philip Van Zoon, Mrs. Ellsworth Kimmins, Mrs. Nantucket Lee, and Mrs. Angela Dane, who drove him to the Lincoln-Plaza Hotel. Many cables, telegrams, and letters and flowers were awaiting him.

Mr. Columin did not say how long he intends to remain in the States. He admitted to having two lecture engagements, one at Columbia, one at Cambridge, as well as the lecture he will deliver at the Women's Club this afternoon.

Interrogated on the subject of the Venus, Mr. Columin said that the statue is now in the possession of the French Government and will shortly be transferred to the Louvre Museum, Paris. Asked if he intended to continue diving, after his remarkably lucky discovery, he said, with a twinkle in his eyes, that having found Beauty last time, maybe on his next lucky dip he would discover Wisdom! Mr. Columin looked brown and fit, and, interrogated, admitted that the habit of completely submerged sea bathing, as made possible by the Barbizon-Smith Patent Helmet, is extremely invigorating.

The Duchesse de Vouvray, who is a lovely blonde, dressed in the latest Paris styles, on being interrogated would not admit she had any special plans. On the subject of Mr. Columin she denied the statements of several gossip columns and affirmed that her relations with Mr. Columin were "absolutely platonic." She also said that Mr. Cholly Knickerbocker had got her mixed up in his mind with her cousin, Zélide de Valois. On being interrogated about Herr Schmidt, the white-bearded handsome Austrian, who retired immediately to his room, she replied: "He is my uncle. He is here to chaperon us. . . ."

Alice turned to the social page: "*Women's Club will Honor Returned Celebrity at Tea following Lecture this Afternoon:* The Lecture Season of the Club will open therefore with an Especially Notable and Interesting Talk by *Christopher Columin* — when he will give an account of his discovery of — "

Ericson came in.

"Please, ma'am, Mr. Peabody says he will be using the car to-day as he is going up to the country for the week-end. And taking Mr. Duval," Ericson added, referring to the secretary.

"Very well, Ericson. . . . Have Mr. Peabody and Mr. Duval both had their breakfasts?"

"Yes, ma'am."

Alice asked nervously: "Did Coral remember about Mr. Duval not liking the pink tray cloth?"

"Yes, ma'am."

Alice realized Ericson's glance had strayed down to the newspaper. She folded it quickly.

"Very well, then, Ericson. And you'll see I have a taxi — in time this afternoon?"

"Surely, ma'am." Ericson was at the door when his profound stolidity gave way for a moment, and he said: —

"When Mr. Peabody read his noospaper this morning, ma'am, he threw it right across the bed on to the floor."

Mrs. Peckett parked her car on the side of the drive, then she tripped through the dignified portico of the Club across the hall beneath the Zorn portrait of Mrs. Cary Kimmins, went across the lecture hall, which was already filling, into the library, where Sally and Robert were helping the waiter from Schmidt's set the cups and saucers, the plates of sandwiches and cakes, on the buffet.

Sally's white smile flashed in her dark face. "Yess, Mrs. Peckett," in answer to Mrs. Peckett's question, "de flowers yo' sent is come — and Miz Hamnet Peabody has been in and she fixed them. She thought they looked best on de platform in dere."

"Where's Mrs. Peabody now?"

Robert said: "She told us she was goin' right along to the Lincoln-Plaza, ma'am."

"To — call upon Mr. Columin, I suppose?"

"I should 'magine so, ma'am."

"De lady reporter from de *Evenin' Tel'gr'm* was here, Mrs. Peckett," said Sally. "She was hopin' to get an interview befo' de lecture. But Miz Peabody said to her, Mr. Columin would n't have no time for her — "

Mrs. Peckett went back in the lecture hall. Most of the members had now arrived. Among those still arriving she saw two strangers: one a very tall, narrow blonde in black with a small pale pink face and big startling eyes; the other a magnificent-looking man with a white beard. Mrs. Peckett guessed they must be the Duchesse de Vouvray and the Austrian referred to in the *Herald*. So she went up and introduced herself, and escorted them to seats in the front row. She asked them if they had come with Mr. Columin. But the Austrian said: "No! A most *busy* woman came when we were finishing our lunch at the hotel, and told to Christopher that she will occupy herself with him and that we, the Duchess and I, must go together separately." He added slowly: "She seemed much excited, poor woman." Then he looked round the hall and asked Mrs. Peckett: "This is all the members of your Club?"

"Nearly everybody's here this afternoon. It's a great occasion, you know!"

The Duchesse did n't look up while this conversation was going on; she sat absorbed in a copy of the *Evening Telegram.*

It was now three o'clock and Mrs. Peckett decided that Alice and the lecturer must have arrived, and went through the side door by the platform to the waiting room, where she found Alice and Christopher.

Now in the hall the noise and buzz of talk subsided and there was a hush — a scraping of chairs and leaning forward of bosoms. And then the side door opened and Mrs. Jabish Peckett came out again and she and the lecturer walked on to the platform.

Mrs. Hamnet Peabody, the secretary, took her chair at the end of the front row.

Immediately clapping broke out. And murmurs and quick whispers from one to another: "Of all things!" — "Why — does n't he look wonderful?" ...

Christopher sat down while Mrs. Peckett stood by the desk, and hushed the applause and made her little introductory speech. She said that they all knew enough about Mr. Columin's famous and remarkable exploit to want to hear every possible detail as to how it *really* took place! She ended by saying that she was sure she spoke for all of them when she told Mr.

Columin, before he began, that however much they were "set up about him" now as a celebrated citizen of Green Plains, they wanted him to realize they had *always* been just as proud of him, when he was a private individual!

This statement caused an outburst of whole-hearted clapping. Mrs. Peckett saw Alice's kid-gloved hands beat together with pathetic zeal.

Christopher rose to his feet.

During the next forty-five minutes Christopher gave a detailed, candid, humorous account of his finding of "his Venus," from the moment when he became a Barbizon-Smith-helmet enthusiast on the Lido, to the moment when the Director of the Louvre Museum fetched her away from the Ritz Hotel.

The details had, of course, been blessedly provided by Fate; but the candor was Christopher's own. So was his humor: a quiet humor on the whole, yet, from time to time, ironic — and then perfectly gentle and benevolent again.

During his talk Mrs. Peckett sat in her high-backed chair, like a delighted robin, and watched him.

At first she was preoccupied by the improvement in his looks; and by the quite obvious change in his manner, which amounted to his having gone away timid, and come back with poise. His personal charm, formerly a hidden quality, was now clear to everybody. Here, in a minute you saw, was a really *likable* man.

Likable . . . Mrs. Peckett watched him. She listened to what he was saying; and how he said it. She watched poor Alice listening, fascinated by something in the lecture (or the lecturer?) that she could n't in the least explain! And the others! Mrs. Peckett glanced at Mrs. Lilian Van Zoon, at Angela Dane and dear old Mrs. Cockspur (for once not asleep at a lecture) — all of them reacting the same way — fascinated.

He was more than "likable," decided Mrs. Peckett. He was interesting. Also she got the impression that, while he had in some ways grown deeper, he had managed, in other ways, to remain most beautifully clear.

And yet she felt toward the end of the lecture — "There's something wrong, not *with* him, but *for* him. What is it?"

He sat down. The applause broke out. He turned and smiled at Mrs. Peckett.

She rose. And thanked him. And announced that Mr. Columin "is looking forward to meeting you all, now, in the library."

Then, as she and Christopher lingered for a moment on the platform, he muttered: "How long d' you think I need stay?"

"Talk plenty, show them those photographs you promised them — and then slip away and come up to tea with me at my house . . ."

"*Christopher!*" He turned. "Christopher dear, you were just *wonderful.*"

"Thank you, Alice." For now Alice, foremost, and

a dozen others, began to encircle him and to lead him towards the library, in the manner of Bacchantes leading Bacchus to a Bacchanal.

"Wonderful — Interesting — Fascinating — " they chanted around him, pressing against him and hanging on, and enchaining him with the heavy garlands of their admiration.

He looked about for Fritzl, for Zaza? . . . But they seemed to have disappeared.

"Just to *imagine* — " they chanted. "Extraordinary!" . . . "Thrilling" . . . "Miraculous" — their voices intoned.

Over their crowding hats he had a glimpse of Mr. William Shakespeare in enviable isolation in his corner.

Now he started handing out the draped photographs. They seized them like goblets — draughts of the warm south.

"Typically Greek" . . . "Archaic beauty" . . . "Such classical lines," they intoned.

"She must be really lovely, Mr. Columin," mewed Mrs. Van Zoon, coming up in a surge of mink.

Christopher was glancing furtively at his wrist watch.

"She has a delicious little stomach," he said.

As Christopher came out of the portico of the Club a young woman darted forward.

"Mr. Columin . . ."

He stopped, annoyed. A slim dark young woman —

"Mr. Columin, don't you remember me?"

(Where *had* he seen her before?)

"You once sent me champagne, and the children — Mrs. Green — ! I do some reporting."

"But of course! It's — " He smiled and shook hands with her. "Diana Devonshire."

She smiled too. She said, rather diffident: "As a matter of fact, I've been trying to get hold of you. I'm afraid you can guess exactly why." She colored.

"Listen here," he said. "I'm going up to Mrs. Peckett's now for tea. But if you like I'll give you a really grand batch of stuff to write up after. I'll see you get enough to fill a full-page interview."

She started to thank him.

"I'll tell you what I'll do. If you'll permit me I'll come around to your place afterwards, and then I can inspect those famous kids of yours."

"The cowboy outfits — " she began.

He cut her short.

"Husband fit again?"

"Yes, thanks. He's working now. But you bet he'll be in when you come. I'll call him up, and he'll have some old-fashioneds ready — "

"See you later then." He took her hand, to say good-bye, in a manner that struck her as somehow, just a little, wonderfully foreign . . . And leaped in a taxi. . . .

Mrs. Peckett's yellow curtains were as delightful as ever, the room as genially disordered, her armchair as comfortable; and Bridget brought in again an excellent tea.

"And now, Christopher," she said, "now I can congratulate you in private, on your success."

"Thank you," said Christopher.

"Make yourself a piece of toast, Christopher."

He said: "I've become quite an expert at toast making — " While he made her a slice he boasted to her of his corn muffins.

Mrs. Peckett poured out his tea. "When you are married to your French Duchess, will you continue to make corn muffins?"

"I should say not." (Christopher decided there were few things Mrs. Peckett did n't observe.)

"She has great chic," said Mrs. Peckett. "She made every other woman at the lecture look like less than two cents." She added: "Mary Peabody need n't have bothered to stay home."

"Then why did she?"

"She had n't a new dress. . . . Half the women of Green Plains went to New York to get their autumn clothes early on your account, Christopher . . ."

Bridget came in. "Please'm, Miss Peabody." And Mary Peabody came, flustered yet eager, wearing indeed her old black dress, but with a new creamy frilling sewn in the neck, and new white gloves. She was troubled yet excited by this impulse of hers — coming over because she "just *had* to welcome Mr. Columin." Mrs. Peckett jumped up.

"Why, Mary, how delightful — "

Christopher took her hand. It was trembling a little. The habit of small anxieties had made her nervous, so that small pleasures, when they came, were difficult to take with equanimity.

"My dear Miss Peabody — how pleased I am to see you!"

Christopher made her sit down in the big chair, drew another chair up beside her, and asked if he might have the honor of making her a piece of toast.

Mrs. Peckett said: "Two lumps and cream, is n't it, Mary?"

Mary nodded to all these amenities, and threw out little fluttering smiles and looked and looked at Christopher.

"Christopher looks well, does n't he?"

Mary Peabody was too flustered to do more than agree. But when she 'd taken off her gloves she got out: —

"Oh, Mr. Columin — I want to congratulate you — I only wish I 'd been able to be present this afternoon. . . . But — "

"Mary does n't like to leave her kitten, who 's been sick," said Mrs. Peckett, "and her maid goes out afternoons."

"Dear me," said Christopher, "I do hope he 's recovering."

"Yes — oh yes, *thank you* . . ."

"Christopher made an excellent speech," said Mrs. Peckett, "and I imagine that at this moment the other members of our Club, Mary, are still looking at the photographs."

"Photographs?" asked Miss Peabody.

"Of the Venus," said Mrs. Peckett. "Draped, of course. Several members stipulated that." (The draped photographs of some other Venus had been got by Johnny.)

Bridget came in, bulky and excited.

"*Please, ma'am?*"

Mrs. Peckett asked: "What is it, Bridget?"

"Please, ma'am, there's the van of Zeiss the Florist's right opposite at Miss Peabody's house and the man knocking at the door, and there's no one there — !"

"*My* door, Bridget?" exclaimed Mary Peabody.

"Sure, Miss Peabody."

"*Zeiss's* van, Bridget?" she insisted. (Zeiss was the luxury florist of Green Plains.) "Why, I'm sure there must be a mistake — "

Mrs. Peckett said: "Hurry over the street, Bridget, and make sure."

"Yes, ma'am."

As Bridget lumbered rapidly out, Mrs. Peckett teased: "It isn't your birthday, Mary?"

"Oh dear no — I gave up birthdays many years ago."

"Maybe," suggested Christopher, "the flowers are for the convalescent kitten!"

"Of course," said Mrs. Peckett, "that must be the explanation."

Miss Peabody was just beginning to try and adjust her mind to the pleasure of nonsense (a pleasure so rare to her that she felt quite apprehensive) when Bridget returned carrying an immense long white box, tied up in bright green riband and with a gold-and-white label attached to the bow. "Miss Peabody an' no mistake!" Bridget, beaming and breathing hard from her hustle, set the box down across Miss Peabody's knees.

"*Me!*" Mary Peabody stared down rather as if her lap were unexpectedly accommodating a strange baby. "For *me!* . . ." After another second of staring, and her nervously transparent features glowing a startled pink, she touched the label with the finger and thumb of her right hand. Then she looked up at Christopher as if for some kind of reassurance.

"That certainly is addressed to you, Miss Peabody."

And Mrs. Peckett chirruped: "Undo it, Mary. Undo the beautiful green ribbon. I'm dying to see what's inside!"

Between them they got the ribbon off, the lid off, the paper folded back —

"American Beauties!"

"Oh — but — but *who?*" was all Mary could say. Then she bent and sniffed them, but very gingerly, as if they might at any moment stop being superb pink roses and become snakes, or go off suddenly like alarm clocks.

Then Mrs. Peckett perked her head down into the box, like a bird about to drink.

But now Bridget came in again, this time her fat countenance agog.

"*Please, ma'am!*"

Mrs. Peckett lifted her head from the roses.

"Yes, Bridget?"

"*Please, ma'am* — there's a *gentleman* over the street now, knockin' and ringin' away at Miss Peabody's door!"

"A *gentleman*, Bridget?" chirped Mrs. Peckett.

"A — gentleman, Bridget?" said Mary Peabody.

"Yes, ma'am. Yes, Miss Peabody."

"I — think — " began Mary Peabody, really beyond being flustered now, and beginning to deal with her own amazement as if it were a traffic situation in which the best thing to do (however alarmed you felt) was to stay still.

"Go and look again, Bridget," said Mrs. Peckett, "and see if he's still there."

Bridget lumbered rapidly away. In a half minute she was back.

"*Sure* an' he's still there and — "

Mrs. Peckett asked: "What does he look like, Bridget?"

"Well, ma'am, he — "

"Go across the street, Bridget, and tell him Miss Peabody's here, and ask him if he won't come in — "

Bridget was gone before the sentence was done.

They heard the front door opened as Bridget went out.

"*Golly!*" murmured Christopher. He was beginning to stare at Mary Peabody; Mary was keeping still, holding on to the box on her lap. "Who*ever* — " she murmured.

Then the door opened. Christopher got up. Mrs. Peckett got up.

"*Fritzl!*" said Christopher.

There was a long minute's silence. And Christopher realized that Fritzl was n't speaking because he could n't. Mrs. Peckett's glance darted from one face to another. Mary Peabody stayed quite still, her shell-tinted face blank and stoical as though she were in a crisis of invisible traffic, converging upon her from all directions.

Then at last Fritzl spoke, his deep tones extraordinarily uncertain. He came a step further into the room; his usually sure step extraordinarily unsure. He said: —

"Mary — when we were at Vevey, you used not be such a chatterbox!"

Still, for a moment, Mary's blank look remained. Then a first fragile tremor of expression came into her face; then another, and another; then her eyes opened wide, her color came, her nostrils dilated, her hands clutched on to the box, and the frilling round her neck began to tremble.

"Fritzl!"

He came right across the room towards her now.

Still with an unsure step, but holding out his two hands.

"*So!*" he said. Murmured: "*So?* — Mary!" He stopped. He looked down at the box lying across her lap.

Mrs. Peckett made a sign to Christopher. He followed her out of the room. And they went into Jabish's study. (Jabish was out golfing.)

As for Fritzl . . .

It was the first time in his life he had not said "how do you do" to his hostess on entering the room.

When he left Mrs. Peckett's Christopher left a message for Fritzl that he would meet him at seven o'clock at the drugstore at the corner of Maple Street (Fritzl's hobby since they arrived had been the drugstores). Mrs. Peckett had promised to deliver the message when she could to the couple still behind the door of the room with the yellow curtains.

So when he had said his many cordial good-byes to the Green family he drove back to the drugstore, where he found Fritzl and Mary Peabody sitting up at the soda counter both eating Virginia-ham-and-fried-eggs-on-rye. It seemed to Christopher that Mary had started to get less anæmic and thin even on her first few mouthfuls. Christopher sat up on Mary's other side, and they asked him to eat something. But he did n't feel he wanted anything except a small orange juice.

Then Fritzl announced: "My dear Christopher, I have to tell you that since we have met I am once more ennobled!" He turned, chuckling, to Mary, who was blushing. He put down his coffee cup and caught her hand. She looked at him. (Christopher marveled at that look — in "poor Mary Peabody's" eyes.) And then she said to Christopher: —

"Maybe — I *know* it's silly and — and terribly snobbish of me — and I happened to say to — Fritzl, that he ought to have his title, because it seems sort of romantic, and — " she broke off.

Fritzl said slowly: "I have told to Mary: 'There is nothing in the world I will not do for you.' Then she asks me: 'Be once more a nobleman — ' And so — if she likes all such nonsenses — !"

Now Fritzl and Mary Peabody ate hot chocolate-fudge sundaes, and coffee cake with that, and followed that up with two coffees each. They seemed to want exactly the same things; and this obviously delighted them both. Evidently Fritzl had already made a great friendship with both the boys behind the soda counter and with the druggist himself, who happened to have started off as a Hungarian, and they were swapping boyhood reminiscences about mountain places with sneezy and guttural names; and finally the druggist ordered another round of coffees and coffee cake "on the store"! . . . And if it hadn't been for several customers coming in, Christopher thought they would have remained at the counter all night, celebrating;

the druggist and those two boys and the negro in the white apron were very near being told (what they must certainly have suspected by now!) that Fritzl and Mary Peabody were engaged.

Finally, when they had escorted Mary back to her little house and Fritzl had asked her how early he might call the next morning, Christopher and Fritzl walked back to the Plaza.

On the way back Christopher stopped to buy a newspaper. As he took it he glanced at it and gave an exclamation.

"What is it?" Fritzl asked.

Christopher pointed to a photograph halfway down the page, and the caption: "Famous French Screen Star Injured on Set" . . .

"*Ach* — who?"

He read: "Screen hero Romano de Vouvray, now starring in *Zuleika Dobson*, the picture being made at Elstree, England, by British Films, Ltd., had a fall yesterday and sustained several injuries and had to be taken to hospital . . . It is not known yet . . ."

"*Zaza!*" exclaimed Fritzl.

"She may be rather worried," said Christopher, "even though — " Zaza had told him so often how Romano had ceased to exist for her.

"I do not suppose it is serious," said Fritzl, who was in a mood to believe that nothing could be unpleasantly serious.

"I hope not."

They walked on in silence. Then, abruptly, Christopher became aware of Fritzl's deep tones questioning him: —

"Beloved Christopher, why *do* you marry her?"

Perhaps the abruptness of the question startled him into making a frank reply. He turned and looked at Fritzl and said "Chivalry!" — and then lapsed into gloom, now recognizing openly that that mediæval ideal (injected into the American male in infancy) was about to wreck his life (for a second time!).

"Does she in fact love you?"

"No."

"Then why did she not remain with a most excellent and sweet, handsome husband that she already has and whose photograph I have seen fall out of her cigarette case?"

Christopher, remembering Zaza's words on the lagoon, said: "For some very good reason, I imagine . . . some terrible reason."

Now Fritzl's eyebrows went up and up. "A — *terrible* reason? So? . . ." Down came the eyebrows again, and a detached gleaming amusement woke in the eyes. "*So?*" he repeated. "Sweet Christopher — this is a full nonsense!"

They were back at the Plaza now. And though Fritzl in the fullness of his heart suggested that Christopher should come into the bar and "drink wine with him," Christopher preferred to go up to his room.

When he got into his room he found a box of lilies-of-the-valley with a card enclosed. On it "Mrs. Hamnet Peabody" was crossed out, and "from Alice" was written. Also, neatly, on the other side of the card: "Your talk was wonderful, dear. I'd like an opportunity to tell you what it made me feel — "

Christopher tore up the card. As he was dropping the pieces into the scrap basket he saw among the inevitable litter of press cuttings on the dressing table — a pincushion. It had a homemade and even improvised look (and the stuff of which it was made was a silk printed with little pink hearts). On it was pinned a note addressed "Christopher."

He opened it and read — there were only a few lines — in a large hurried writing: —

Madame la Duchesse has gone to Elstree.
P.S. — Mr. John Cotton has accompanied her.

After several moments' thought he took the note along to Fritzl's room. It was quite difficult to attract Fritzl's attention, for he was standing at the window, looking at the new moon.

But when Fritzl had read it he said: —
"So-o-o-o!"
"What d' you make of it?" said Christopher.
"Make of it?"
"Well — d' you think she's gone off with Johnny?"
"With *Johnny*? My *dear* Christopher! Naturally she has gone — to Elstree — because her husband is there. For Johnny — he goes, naturally, to get the story!" He shook his head thoughtfully and then

added with his heavenly smile: "This is a most *excellent* thing! — Most excellent — !"

Fritzl and Mary Peabody were to be married in Green Plains as quietly as could be managed, considering the excitement that was caused by the announcement of their engagement. The dramatic reappearance of a long-faithful lover, the sentimental touch about the Attar of Roses, the remarkable fact of the lover's having reappeared through his connection with the famous Christopher Columin, preoccupied even Mary's most distant acquaintances and made bridge their secondary occupation. They discussed her endlessly, including the change in her appearance! For she not only had six new dresses, purchased on a trip to Boston, but her face seemed to have been subjected to some unnamed beauty specialist. And then there was the extraordinary, fascinating, exasperating fact that, of all things! — Mary — Mary Peabody (of all people!) was to be a Countess. The Gräfin von Strelsau.

Mary's telephone, which had so long been a taciturn companion, now shrieked at her all day, until she had really to take refuge at Mrs. Peckett's opposite. And she spent quite a lot of time refusing, very politely (but not without secret humor), invitations to dine with Mrs. Dane and Mrs. Kimmins and Mrs. Van Zoon.

Fritzl arranged that their wedding should be the

day before Christopher's departure for Europe. And that when he and Mary had seen him off they should proceed on their trip to the Grand Canyon. ("It must be altogether too big, that canyon, and altogether useless! Nevertheless, I *wish* to see it . . .") And to Mary each of Fritzl's wishes seemed wittier and more charming than the last.

Christopher got on board, surrounded by friends, as well as reporters. And when Mrs. Green was pouring whiskey into tooth glasses, and Mary von Strelsau was starting to arrange his flowers, and Fritzl was delightedly examining the adjoining shower bath, Christopher was conscious that of all the people so kindly and gayly seeing him off, Mrs. Peckett was the only one who understood that he was sad; and that though he might be going to Paris to be fêted by professors and directors, and to London to a public banquet, and in fact his feet seemed set (by an admirable freak of chance and deep-sea diving) in such a path of distinction — that "things," real things, were about as bad as they could be.

Yet — what things exactly? When Fritzl had reproved him for canceling his other two lectures "on grounds of health," Christopher had replied that he was, in fact, in bad spiritual health.

"You are a child too long at a party," Fritzl had said. Maybe he was. He took the glass of whiskey from Mrs. Green (who'd certainly made a wonderful write-up out of the material he gave her that night at her home). Mrs. Peckett said: "When are you coming back to America, Christopher?"

"Not yet."

She looked up at him and said after a second: "Don't come back alone. Solitude is n't good all the time."

She shook hands with him, and so did Mary, and Fritzl and Mrs. Green; and all wished him a grand voyage, and as they were going off the ship Christopher remembered he had n't posted a letter on the dock.

So he gave it to Mrs. Peckett. (It was a formal letter to Alice containing a check for her to get herself a new fur coat for the winter.)

Now they were off — on the deck — Fritzl waving and smiling and shouting: "My love to Sophie!"

"To Sophie," thought Christopher a little bitterly. He 'd written twice to Sophie and had n't had a word from her. . . .

As he waved good-bye he could n't help thinking that they all belonged somewhere. They all had a person, a home, to go back to . . .

(Did Christopher, in that moment, have a very faint, yet curiously nostalgic remembrance of 181 Maple Street?)

Now the ship was moving down the river. Christopher leaned against the rail. He thought that it was only eight months since he left New York, feeling like a joyful stowaway on a ship that seemed to embody "adventure." That stowaway seemed very much younger than the self he could feel inside him now. But his common sense told him this was because he had been certain then, and now he was uncertain.

But, uncertain of what?

The things that he had set out to find then were still there in the world to be enjoyed. New places, different people, various forms of freedom. He was, if anything, freer now than ever. He had begun to know his way about leisure. He had just begun to have definite ideas about what he wanted to read — to see, to learn.

He went down to luncheon. Seated alone at a small table he thought: "Uncertain about what, then?"

Was he going to be beaten by his own leisure? Beaten back into business? Be driven to keep himself sane by making money he did n't want?

He ordered a sole *meunière*, a bottle of Chablis iced, then cheese and a *tarte aux abricots* to follow.

Maybe he was just the spoiled child after too many parties! Maybe he'd got used to being a celebrity without realizing it? . . . Or else his conscience was acting up and he was in for an attack of the urge-to-service?

Or did he miss Zaza after all? Life was certainly a good deal less decorative without Zaza around!

He spent most of the trip on deck, for the weather was good; late autumn sun and an indigo sea. He paced around the decks by himself; or sat in his deck chair reading and thinking . . . remembering . . . looking forward. Of course, in Paris he'd have to fulfill the surprising amount of social obligations that Venus had let him in for. Then he'd go over to the Rectory for a time. . . .

And then, he decided, he would go to Rome. He imagined that your own individual problems would get to seem transitory in Rome.

But before he went to Rome he'd go and see Mademoiselle Sophie; for Fritzl had said she was back in Paris now for the winter. He wondered if Professor Tombwell was in Paris, too. And if he was seeing her all the time.

The weather changed as the boat entered the English Channel. The sea got rougher and the rain began.

As they were getting into Le Havre the rain hung in crystal curtains across the harbor; and as the ship docked the passengers waited about on the covered decks, turning up their coat collars against the damp chill air.

Christopher walked to and fro, impatient for no special reason. The weather, as it does, became symbolic of his own state of mind; this chill air and grey rain said that winter was coming; that after all there was winter in Europe the same as everywhere else. . . .

The gangplanks were down. The crowd began to move towards them, blue embarkation cards in their gloved hands. Christopher went down the gangway and on to the concrete, which was France. A belted official was droning like a hornet about the *douane — à la douane* . . . Christopher moved with the crowd, getting out his passport as he went.

During the push and struggle at the customs he felt so depressed he decided to go and have a drink before he got on the train. The porter shut his cases. "*Le train pour Paris, m'sieur?*"

"*Oui.*"

While Christopher locked his dressing bag, the customs official watched him, as if he wished he had not chalked his absolution upon it. Christopher put his keys back in his pocket and turned to go, the porter following. More hornet voices blared: "*Le train pour Paris — le train pour Paris* . . ."

"*Christopher!* So *here* you are!"

". . . So*phie?*"

" — I must have gone to the wrong gangplank — "

"Sophie . . . ?"

"Fritzl cabled to me you were coming — "

He held her hand now. "Why — But . . ."

"So stupid of me to miss you," she said, and she smiled and withdrew her hand.

"You have finished with the customs already?"

"Yes." Then he noticed she looked pale: and his first coherent sentence was: "You have n't been ill?"

"*Ill?*" (Something in her tone suggested the reproof that, after all, even if one had been, all admission of illness is a little vulgar.) "No, indeed . . . *mon* cousin." Then lightly: "I thought it would be amusing to come and meet you. Also I could not wait to hear *all* news of Fritzl's romance! . . . But *what* a romance. . . . Imagine he did not even *hint* to *me*! But quick! Recall your porter — tell him not to take your luggage away. Also, it seemed so amusing to come and meet you in the very town of our mutual ancestors! Is n't it? . . . And did n't you write to 'Monsieur Lacaze' here? But quick — recall your porter!"

"But what about the Paris train? Is there another after this?"

She drew herself up and said with her charming impatience (that might have been temper when she was a child) : —

"The train for Paris is of no importance. I have the car here. Let us visit the house of our ancestors . . . I have already made inquiries and discovered it."

A black Renault was driven up — by Marius, in a black uniform. Marius touched the shiny peak of his cap. Mademoiselle Sophie got into the car and motioned to Christopher to sit beside her. Marius placed a rug over their knees.

"Now to that house I showed you, Marius."

"*Très bien, Mademoiselle.*"

The precision and the comfort of the whole arrangement (however odd in its purpose) were characteristic of Sophie. Christopher glanced at her as they drove. He had never seen her in a motorcar before. This one, discreet, elegantly out of date, suited her. So did the fur cap that she was wearing. So did her pallor. She was looking beautiful. And it struck him that when she did so she did n't look so much like "a beautiful woman" as like "a romantic story about a woman who was beautiful."

The house was less than five minutes' drive. Sophie leaned forward and pointed it out to him. A narrow, tall, shabby house, in a cobbled side street, and with a tobacconist's shop on the ground floor. The rain made the façade, with its grey narrow shutters, seem especially drab. But Sophie gazed at it, her face lit by æsthetic as well as tender pleasure.

"It is so *much* the eighteenth century!" she exclaimed. " — So much!"

Even at this moment, when Christopher's reaction to the house was complicated by his poignant sense of Sophie's nearness, and of his sweet hurting delight in everything about her, in her voice, her gesture, the violets pinned in her furs, still he thought "Their darned eighteenth century again!" Curious obsession.

She turned her head, and caught his expression. She said, half laughing: "My poor Christopher. . . . To me the eighteenth century seems a period of such taste and enjoyment! . . . One has an inevitable nostalgia — !"

"What? With starvation everywhere? And society women having fleas in their hair!"

She looked at him. Then she murmured: "There is always something lacking." But he could n't make out if she was serious — or if she smiled. Then she said in a thoughtful small voice like a little girl saying her thoughts: "All the same, it is strange to think that in that house (that *I* find *charming*, Christopher!) our great-great-grandfather, a little *bonhomme* in buckled shoes, came in after an exasperating day in his little office down by the Port — over there" (she pointed) — "and perhaps he said to his wife: 'My dear — what wouldst thou say if I had to go to New York?' . . . Perhaps she was delighted by such a prospect — or perhaps she cried! Or perhaps she was too excited about the first tooth of the first baby (our great-grandfather!) to trouble herself about such schemes. . . . Or perhaps she said: 'It 's been raining, dear . . . go and change your coat!' . . ."

As she talked Christopher began to see those two — the solid little merchant, coming up this cobbled street, in rain like this, in at that door — two yards off. (Was Time just a gigantic Barnum and Bailey Circus, with innumerable turns going on in innumerable different rings — only blinded to one another by their own limelight?) He realized Sophie again beside him.

And whatever Time was, the present hours were niggardly, quick-going. . . .

She was beside him now. To-morrow he would be alone . . .

He asked, matter-of-factly: "And now, Sophie?" — knowing that he could leave it to her to arrange that they should now do whatever was most proper, or most comfortable, or most charming.

"Now — ?"

He waited; thinking indeed how little he cared *what* they did (and that he was prepared to look at a dozen battered old houses in the rain), if it was in her company.

"Now, Christopher," she said. And then she hesitated. . . . "I have something to propose to you."

He smiled; but could have sighed, at the familiar phrase. "Very well — " (If it was luncheon, out of that efficient-looking little basket at their feet, it might be delicious enough to overcome his lack of appetite. . . . If it was a series of exact arrangements for his entertainment in Paris this evening, or the recommendation of a cleaner who would most efficiently and reasonably deal with the overcoat he was wearing — in any case, it was her idea — and perfect.)

"What is it?" he asked. "What do you propose, Sophie?"

For another moment she did n't answer. Then she said: —

"It is — marriage, Christopher." And, taking out

her exquisite handkerchief from her bag, she burst into tears.

Following his own telegram, Christopher arrived late on a Sunday afternoon. (Hiring the old Daimler at Tremayne, as he could not be met.)

As he drove up he saw Sabrina and Loo rushing to meet him, and shouting and screaming and jumping on the running board; pulling the door open, Sabrina flinging her arms round his neck.

"Christopher *darling* — "

A fervent handclasp, a most ecstatic smile from Loo . . .

So the children had n't changed.

And the Rectory was most wonderfully, endearingly the same. The same cool "dairy" smell; the cats; the Scottie; and Milly; and the red-moustached man. . . . All just the same — and Fanny in the kitchen getting the tea; quite flustered with pleasure at the sight of him, and walking around stiffly because she had on her Sunday shoes. . . . Sabrina said: —

"Well, and we *are* glad about Mademoiselle Sophie!" She admitted, her mouth full of scone: "Loo *always* said it would be *her!*"

Loo colored and smiled, and helped himself to cream. He had no words to congratulate Christopher; but his heart was full of benevolence.

"And," said Sabrina, "I *do* think you and Zaza would have been rather 'ill-mated.'"

"Extremely," said Christopher smiling, able to think of Zaza now with delight.

"Is Zaza that French Duchess?" asked Fanny, taking Christopher's cup to give him more tea. "I get so muddled with all their names — and all the places and the hotels!"

"Of *course*," said Sabrina patiently. She and Loo had almost given up trying to make Mummie remember the difference between Zaza and Nicolette, and Nîmes and Hyères, and Herr Fritzl and Professor Tombwell. (And it was irritating, somehow, to perceive how little Mummie really cared.)

"Zaza is the *tall* lady married to the *film actor*, and returned to him again," said Loo, patiently. "Also the film actor is the *same* as the Lovely Young Man that Sab was soppy about at Nîmes."

"Only one sugar in the second cup, is n't it, Christopher?" said Fanny. "Of course, I see, dear," she said to Loo. "How stupid I am. And then Mademoiselle Nicotine is the French lady that Christopher is going to marry?"

"OH, MUMMIE!" exclaimed the children together.

"It 's Mademoiselle Sophie — Mademoiselle *Lacaze*," said Sabrina.

"And it 's *Mrs. Nicolette*, anyway," said Loo.

"Black-currant jam, Christopher?" asked Fanny. "And who is her husband then? I s'pose that Father Christmas Austrian?"

"*NO, MUMMIE* — oh, Mummie, you never — !"

"What delicious black-currant jam!" said Christopher firmly. "Who made this lot?"

Christopher went up to meet Benjamin, who had been taking the evening service. And when they had greeted each other warmly they stood in the churchyard, Benjamin lighting his pipe and Christopher watching the rooks circling against the pale green evening sky above the elm trees.

Then Christopher said: "There's something I want to ask you, Cousin Benjamin."

The parson blew a contented puff of smoke into the evening air. "Go ahead, old boy."

"I — ugh — should very much like you to marry us, Benjamin." He added: "Mademoiselle Lacaze is a Protestant, you know."

The parson hesitated. Then he said: "Yes, yes, I know that. And I'd have been very sorry to hear you got mixed up with a Papist, Christopher . . ." Then hesitated again; glanced sideways at Christopher, and said: "There's no objection of that sort . . ."

Christopher saw he was troubled. "Is there any other objection then?"

Christopher thought Benjamin's color deepened. "Well, perhaps you did n't know, Cousin Christopher, but our — Church — the Church of England, does n't recognize divorce."

"Oh . . . dear me . . ."

They fell into step, crunching down the path toward the churchyard gate, Christopher feeling very deeply disappointed. For in his imagination he had planned out an English wedding, here, in his cousin's church, and with Benjamin to wed them. . . . And this plan had been full of simplicity and poetry and delight.

Benjamin unlatched the gate and held it open for him. It clicked after them. They crossed the road. In the drive of the Rectory, Benjamin took his pipe from between his lips and said, perplexed: —

"Y' see, Cousin Christopher, the Church, out there in America, married you forever in the sight of the Lord."

"But — " said Christopher, "but we did n't get married in church! Alice and I, we only had a civil ceremony. . . . Because Alice is an agnostic, you see — "

As Christopher spoke the parson stopped. They were in sight of the house now. (From the open windows of the drawing-room came the sound of "Chopsticks" being played by Loo.)

"Agnostic, you say? . . . You say you were n't married in a church out there?"

"No," said Christopher.

"Well, *well!* — " said the parson. "Well, well, well!" Then: "I s'pose you realize what I should have to say about that, Cousin Christopher? — As a

parson, of course, and speaking for my Church — "
His eyes twinkled.

"No," said Christopher, puzzled.

"*Well?* Well, well — "

Benjamin laid a heavy and friendly arm on Christopher's shoulder. "Well, my boy, as far as I'm concerned you've never been married at all! In fact you have been — been — living in — er — with — what did you say her name was? — "

"Alice," said Christopher.

"In fact — "

"I see!" said Christopher.

They turned and went toward the house, Benjamin keeping his friendly arm across Christopher's shoulder. "But," said Benjamin as they entered the hall, "on the other hand, Cousin Christopher, whatever you did with — er — "

"Alice?"

"Yes, yes — with Alice — is none of my business! None at all. And the fact remains that there's no conceivable reason then why I shouldn't marry you — "

Fanny's voice from the dining room called out: "Come in and have some supper, Benjamin."

They went in. And Benjamin, beaming and twinkling, announced that Christopher's wedding was to be celebrated here in the church — that he himself would be the "officiating clergy." . . .

And the next day, after a telephone call to Paris (during which the call box outside the post office was surrounded and almost mobbed), it was decided that the wedding should take place in the late spring.

The preparations for the wedding were stupendous. The scrubbing and polishing that went on up and down the parsonage! The repainting of the stair treads by Loo! The upholstering of the drawing-room sofa by Fanny with yards of tulip-patterned chintz bought recklessly in Tremayne! The revarnishing of both the coal boxes, in the dining room and drawing-room, by the parson himself; and the purchase, by common consent, of a strip of crimson Wilton carpet to lay in the hall across the tiled floor (now washed daily with buttermilk!). A hip bath was bought specially for the spare room. For it had been settled that the bridal couple should remain for a week at the Rectory. A set of new coat pegs was put up by the front door. And even the red-moustached man, infected by the zest of prenuptial furbishing, and with a white cloth draped over his bowler hat, whitewashed the ceiling and walls of Kitty's stable, polished up her harness and her rump until they gleamed like a new-peeled horse chestnut. He was also to be seen, late and early, weeding the drive, scarcely pausing to answer Mrs. Dovey, who, with her man's cap drawn well down over her hair (chronically in curlers — also "in preparation"), would come and lean over the gate, throwing out shrewd conjectures as to the number of guests expected, their income and rank and the likely elegance of their attire.

As for the two days preceding the wedding, the baking and boiling never ceased in the kitchen; the oven door was opened and shut by Fanny as often as the portals of a fashionable restaurant; the larder shelves filled up with cakes and biscuits, creams and jellies, trifles, syllabubs, junkets, meat pies and pasties, and bedroom jugs of lemonade.

On the morning before, Fanny made meringues, her cheeks flushed, her wisps of gold hair streaking down her white neck, her smock snowed with icing sugar; but her mind quoting Spenser's *Epithalamion:* —

> Never had man more joyful day than this,
> Whom heaven would heap with bliss.
> Make feast therefore now all this live-long day.

Benjamin trimmed every lamp in the house, muttering and exclaiming that he would never, on his dear life, get his sermon written; and Sabrina washed every animal in sight (including Milly, the ferret — whom she also sprayed, desperately, with "Chypre"), and Loo painted "WELCOME! A HAPPY MARRIAGE" in scarlet paint round the new hip bath.

Even the weather seemed to have caught the gay, golden, and bustling atmosphere of the Columin family. For early May was behaving like June; and while the grape-hyacinths and primulas lingered late and refused to show the least signs of fatigue, every rose in the garden seemed determined to bloom in time for the wedding, and to be, if possible, in the church itself.

Most of them were.

For Fanny and Sabrina spent the afternoon decorating the altar, the chancel, the pulpit, and even the choir stalls. Sabrina made garlands of white roses and honeysuckle and hung them across the screen, and Fanny banked the sides of the altar steps with white lilac in (invisible) jam jars. Sabrina — hindered by Mrs. Dovey, who had insisted upon "coming up to help with the church" — wound yellow climbing roses around the lectern, and made the vestry itself gaudy with tulips of all colors. "For in the church the flowers must be gorgeous and celebrating," Sabrina said.

In the house the decorations, also according to Sabrina's scheme, were chosen more for scent, and less for color — "for *after* the service everybody will be thinking about food and pleasure — their eyes will be tired of looking, but they will enjoy smells."

Only in the spare bedroom — the "bridal chamber" as she called it — Sabrina lavished the first red roses, but modifying their intoxicating and luxuriant crimson with little bowls of violas "mauve here and there, Loo, because Christopher and Sophie are both slightly old." But she also made a heart out of picture wire

THE ADVENTURE OF CHRISTOPHER COLUMIN

and wound it about with jasmine (not yet in flower, "but that's a symbol," she said to Loo) and hung it above the chimneypiece, and pierced it with a fleur-de-lis (from her own garden) — as an arrow.

"Also a symbol," she said. "For the heart is Christopher's and the lily is France!"

"But *her* heart is pierced just as much," said Loo.

Loo's own contribution to the bridal chamber, as well as inscribing the hip bath, was a turkey's egg — blown, and painted gold by himself, which he considered looked glorious lying on a strip of purple satin riband on the window sill. As he was putting it there it reminded him of the room he and Sabrina had had in that hotel in Paris. And as they were going out he glanced at the white counterpane and thought, regretfully, that it would have been too expensive to buy a purple velvet cover and gold-tasseled bolsters. He said to Sabrina, as they went down to the kitchen to help Mummie fill the meringue cases: "I wonder what became of Mrs. Nicolette?"

"Whatever made you think of her?"

But Benjamin's voice was shouting up to his daughter.

"Sabrina? *Sabrina?*"

"What is it, Daddy?" She leaned over the banister.

"A telegram from Christopher to say that he'll be here at seven to-night, and that Miss Lekayzer and all those visitors will be staying at the Lamb's Head in Tremayne."

"Yes, Daddy, but that's just what we expected! Is n't it, Daddy?" she cooed soothingly.

"Yes, but, my goodness! Somehow telegraphing makes it seem twice the trouble. . . . And how we shall any of us get through to-morrow I don't *know*. . . . There's your mother still filling meringues and here am I without an idea of what I'm going to say to Those Two to-morrow! And what the Bishop'll think *I don't know*. As for how we're going to find *room* for all these foreigners . . ."

Sabrina came downstairs and took a feather brush out of one of his hands, and a tin of paraffin out of the other. "Loo has had an inspired idea, darling," she said, her manner calm and cajoling. "He has persuaded Mummie to put little tables out on the lawn, like she does for the Mothers' Outing. And Loo bicycled into Tremayne by himself yesterday to go to Gill's and try and buy a striped awning and he met the Bishop, who knew of bits of an old striped circus tent somewhere and sent it out this morning — "

" — *Yes* — *and*," said Loo, breaking in, "and you *see*, Daddy — old Dovey is fixing up two posts to hold up the awning that we're going to stretch out from the top of the dining-room windows so that then it'll be like a café in Paris, and then the foreign visitors will feel at home — "

Sabrina tilted her head and smiled up through her

lashes. "We were all going to break it to you to-night, after supper — "

"*Café?* On the drive? What next? What next, I wonder? Fanny? *Fanny?*"

"She can't hear you anyway, darling," said Sabrina. "Listen to the egg whisk!"

"A French café on the drive of the Rectory! My dear l— "

"But," urged Loo, desperate, eager, on tiptoe. "But Daddy, as the Bishop *gave* the awning — "

"Yes," said Sabrina, "then it must be a blessed café. . . . Must n't it?"

Benjamin stared at them. Stared, anyway, at Loo — frowned, in exasperation, at Sabrina. And then, suddenly, his rosy agitated face smoothed, rounded, and creased into an irresistible smile, and an immense chuckle rolled upward from his stomach and set light to his blue eyes.

"A . . . blessed café! I should think it will be a blessed café! Well, well, well! What a wedding it's goin' to be! My goodness — what a wedding! Why, St. Tad's won't ever have seen the like of it — Gracious — " he broke off — to stare through the open door of the hall at a large grey car slowing up the drive — "not Christopher already! — Why, it's not five o'clock yet."

A man leapt out of the car. *Not* Christopher. A young, spruce man in a brown suit. He said: "Excuse me — but are you the Reverend Benjamin Columin? I'm from the Associated Press and I want to know if we might take a few advance photographs of the church — and — "

Benjamin moved slowly, staring, towards the door. "Daddy, it's only the press!" whispered Loo.

"*Photograph — the church?*" Benjamin repeated.

"Yes sir — if you'll allow us, sir — you see we shall only be taking our actual news flashes to-morrow — "

"The *church?*" repeated Benjamin, slowly. And then somehow, suddenly, his great chuckling humor returned, yet with it, now, a sensation of topsy-turvy, of madness, as if the whole of life, including the Rectory and its French café and the Bishop and his awning and the Young Man from the Associated Press, were all revolving together up and down as well as on and on, on an immense, gay-colored merry-go-round. . . .

"Photograph the church?" he repeated. "Why, certainly, my boy — run along — photograph the tool shed and the cow stalls too, if you like — and the lawn mower, and the rabbits — and when you've done come back here and we'll give you a glass of ale! That is to say — if we've got any to spare! With the whole of the Tower of Babel expected here to-morrow morning!"

The next morning Loo took Christopher his tea (in one of the small bedrooms, as the bridal chamber was being kept ready for the bride).

"Good morning," said Loo, "and . . . many happy returns."

"Thank you, son."

"I put three sugars this morning!"

"Thanks a lot."

"Mummie says how d' you feel about breakfast? Would you rather *not* have ham this morning?"

"Perhaps best not."

"She always gives us a 'light diet' before a party."

"She's quite right."

"Now I must go. . . . I'm going to put on my new suit — the trousers are long ones."

"Grand. . . . So are mine."

"Good-bye then for just now. I'll tell Mummie you don't want ham."

"Thank you!"

As Loo went back to his room he reflected that to-morrow morning he had better take the bigger tray. Unless of course Mademoiselle Sophie didn't take early tea.

He dressed with unusual care. He put on a clean shirt, the new grey suit, and the blue tie Sabrina had bought him at Christmas. He cleaned his nails, and borrowed some of his father's brilliantine to smooth down his hair.

Then he went to Sabrina's room. She was in a petticoat brushing her hair like mad. She said: "Oh, Loo! You *do* look magnificent!"

He asked: "Where's your new dress, Sab?"

She pointed to a scarlet dress lying across a chair. She pointed with a certain triumph, because the dress had been a subject of controversy. Mademoiselle Sophie had sent her ten pounds to have it made, and Mummie had wanted her to have white net over pink silk, and carry pink roses, and have a white net mob-cap — because "that looked so fresh-like and bridesmaidy." But Sabrina, during those unreal days in Paris, had been taken to the Louvre by the Director and had been delighted by the Italian pictures, and especially by the clothes of the young men. So what Sabrina, cajoling with her mother, obstinate with the astonished "little dressmaker," had conjured into being — and what she put on now, before her entranced little brother — was a dress of fine scarlet cloth, long-sleeved, tight and plain in the bodice to her narrow hips, with a swing-out skirt reaching just below her knees.

"And scarlet hose!" she said — and Loo watched her draw the stockings over her long legs. "I had them dyed specially."

"But what *will* Daddy say, Sab? Won't you look awfully — fancy-dress in *church*?"

Sabrina stood before the glass in the wardrobe door. "Oh, he'll just say: 'My dear life, what next!' Anyway, bridesmaids often look fancy-dress — only my fancy is different . . ."

Loo left her posing happily.

Downstairs Daddy was rushing to and fro, still in

his dressing gown, his slippers shuffling and slapping the stone floors. Mummie, a smock over her best silk slip, was urging him to "sit down for ten minutes, Benjamin, and have a cup of cocoa or *something*, dear — you'll be fagged out."

Mummie's head alone signified that a supremely Grand Occasion was impending. (Loo could not remember its looking like this since the morning of Sabrina's Confirmation two years ago.) For her hair was in curlers, and she looked as if she were wearing a wreath of silky gold snails. But these, as Loo remembered, would undo into fuzzy gold waves above her white forehead; and make her look *very* pretty, though different.

"What about *you*, Fanny dear?" Benjamin was fussing angrily and tenderly. "You've been up since six and you haven't touched a thing except that tea I brought you — "

Loo went out into the drive. The sun was bright and the air cool. The weather couldn't be better; and the sky was clear above the elm trees. Both the cats were sitting on the dining-room window sill, their eyes like slits of chrysoprase in the sun.

Loo felt rather at a loose end and decided to go down and see Mrs. Dovey. He thought he might pass the time by entertaining her with his imitation of Signor Bellino singing the second verse of "John Peel." (Twice already he had had a singular success singing this for her, making her screech with amusement, and scratch behind her ears. He was quite unaware that if he had sung any song to her in a plummy gurgle, and made poached-egg eyes, she would have been just as loud in rustic joy.)

But this morning Mrs. Dovey was in no state to receive Comic Entertainers. Indeed, she was in no state to receive anybody — as Mr. Dovey explained to Loo. For she was "a-cleanin' of herself"; and as Loo paused in the yard he heard stamping and splashing and the ring of tin behind the closed kitchen door — Then, just as he was turning away, and wondering if Giles would still be at his cottage, or how early vergers had to be in vestries on wedding mornings, Mrs. Dovey screeched out of the kitchen window that he was to wait and in two minutes he should come in.

So while he waited he had a staring match with one of the turkeys. (He had always really been afraid of turkeys, and when they gobbled and gave their fierce stare at him from red rims they made him think, with sweet malice, of next Christmas.)

It was actually more than twenty minutes before Mrs. Dovey unbolted the kitchen door and came out into the yard. Mr. Dovey, who was seated on a bench plucking a chicken, gave a cackle, partly of admiration, partly of what he considered to be wholesome derision.

Her wooden-soldier figure (Mrs. Dovey's "best corsets" were of twenty years' standing) showed to advantage the wide black-and-white stripes of her "costume," which was relieved on the lapel by a buttonhole of artificial pansies — yellow and freaked with purple. Her toque was made of the same pansies and set well forward upon the crowning frizz of her hair, just allowing her fringe to peep between the pansy leaves and her sparse eyebrows, and over the whole hat was a white veil through which shone her scrubbed red cheeks and sheeplike pale eyes. She had several rows of pearls round her neck, a purple handkerchief in her breast pocket, sunburn stockings and white-and-black patent strap shoes. She was in process of buttoning her white cotton gloves and carried her red silk parasol tucked under her arm.

She looked almost as fine to Loo as she had just now, to herself, up in her bedroom glass.

"I think your hat is lovely," said Loo, as she seemed to be waiting for comment.

She raised her gloved hand and touched it gingerly. "I bought it in Tremayne only last Market Day. . . . Hats like these is all the 'eight in London, they say . . ." Having buttoned the other glove, she put up her parasol and her head and shoulders were bathed in a red radiance. Loo thought it made her look quite mysterious.

Flattered by his gaze, she asked him if he would like a gingersnap before she was to go up to the Rectory. She said she would just run in there before going up to the church, since she had promised Mrs. Columin she would help with the "breakfast" after an' she 'ad best see everything was ready. And was it true, she asked Loo, what they were saying, that the bride — Madamaselle Cayzer her name was, was n't it? — was to be given away by a German Baron?

"An Austrian Count," said Loo. He said this rather crossly. He did not agree with Sabrina that it was lovely, Fritzl's being a Count again. He thought it silly; and likely to attract the attention of the press.

At half-past eleven the antique Daimler from Tremayne with the Mickey Mouse on the radiator cap came up the drive. In it were the de Vouvrays, Johnny Cotton, and Mary von Strelsau. They all looked so elegant — Johnny Cotton in a hired morning suit, Mary dressed by Lanvin, and Zaza and Romano so really dazzling (Zaza in her feather hat, as she had promised Sabrina, in response to an urgent postcard; and Romano the apotheosis of all male smartness for weddings, his hat and waistcoat so pearly grey, his gloves, his carnation, his tie, his spats, so chalky white) that poor Fanny, in a sudden fluster, could not help exclaiming: "Goodness me — I s'pose they all imagine they've come to Paris!"

But Christopher, beside her, said: "My dear Fanny, however smartly they may have fixed themselves, they can't beat Milly!" Nor could they. For as they got out of the car Milly bounded out of the dining-room window, a white satin bow about her thin orange-colored neck, and her person, as she flashed on to Christopher's shoulder and off again, redolent of chypre. (Inwardly, Christopher was relieved to see that de Vouvray was dressed like himself — It did n't seem so absurd if *two* of them looked like Fred Astaire.)

Zaza came up to Christopher and said that Sophie was going straight to the church with Fritzl. Then Christopher introduced Zaza to Fanny; who looked at her hat with imperfectly hidden amazement.

Then Lady Charlotte and Waldorf Pink and Button arrived in a new open Bugatti, having started from London after supper last night and done the 275 miles to Tremayne in five hours. Lady Charlotte looked very wind-blown, her grey hair in wisps and streaks, but seemed in wild good humor. She asked Sabrina to take her upstairs to tidy. Button followed them carrying a hatbox and a dressing bag. When Lady Charlotte came out of Sabrina's room she had lavender kid gloves on (she never wore a pair twice), a mauve feather boa, and curled hair surmounted by a black straw hat with white tulle and white violets upon it. She looked superbly Edwardian.

Button as usual wore blue serge. (It was to the credit of Button's judgment that she had observed Fanny Columin's real distinction at a glance. So, as soon as she had dressed Lady Charlotte, she went to Fanny, who had had to run off to the kitchen, and respectfully offered to help. And she was invaluable all the afternoon — showing Mrs. Dovey and the three village women what service could be. . . .)

Meanwhile, Waldorf Pink began snooping round the house to find Christopher, with the idea of getting him to come down and have a good stiff whiskey in the study. (In Waldorf's mind there did not exist houses without "studies.") But Christopher was actually having his whiskey, not very stiff, with Benjamin, up in the "bathroom," above the kitchen, where they could be sure of five minutes' respite before leaving for the church.

So Waldorf did not find them. And as they looked down furtively into the drive, they saw him rejoin the group of people, and single out the Bishop's wife, who had just arrived, and talk to her, jutting one knee as he stood and holding one coat lapel. They also saw Loo and Mrs. Dovey come up the drive. Even in his nervous state Christopher could enjoy her clothes. "'All the 'eight,' eh, Benjamin?" The Bishop was being led away by Sabrina round the corner of the house, presumably to see the successful use of his circus awning on the lawn the other side. Johnny Cotton was standing at the side of the drive, about him a group of young men with cameras whom he seemed to have conjured out of the air. And the other guests, friends and neighbors, kept arriving and mingling with the others like supers among the chief characters. (Among them was Benjamin's old friend Samuel Quince, and his wife, and their twenty-year-old son, Edward Quince, who was studying at Sandhurst.)

Now, up in the bathroom, Benjamin looked at his watch; and gave what he meant to be a cheering grin at Christopher. "I s'pose you and I had better be getting along, up to the church? If we slip out at the back door we can get there in peace — eh?"

"And maybe without being photographed," said Christopher. That momentary bitterness in his tone may be accounted for by the fact that he was in an acute state of nerves.

Once Christopher was in the church his nervousness left him and everything took on a lyric quality: the flower-filled church; the penguin choirboys; the ingenuous solemn music . . . and Sophie, in white, serene, and Sabrina following her in lovely scarlet . . . Benjamin rosy in his fresh-laundered surplice, yet with a mystic benediction in his very homeliness (and those curiously impressive English words — "for better for worse, for richer for poorer, in sickness and in health . . .").

And then the vestry — the riotous signing, and embracing, and slappings on the back (and Sophie's hand in his suddenly). And then the procession, Sabrina drifting and smiling down the aisle after them; and, after Sabrina, all those delightful little penguins — and even the cameramen outside the porch seemed delightfully friendly.

And then —

And then the "party."

"The café," Christopher assured Loo several times over their clinking glasses of champagne — "the café *is* a *riot!*"

The café, the Bishop assured Loo (modestly disclaiming any credit for its festive firmament of red and white), "was indeed an inspired thought!" The little tables set under it "had imported," said the Bishop to Loo, "a most delightful Continental atmosphere. . . . And the victuals," said the Bishop to Fanny, "are of a *rare* deliciousness, Mrs. Columin! . . ."

The cameraman from the Associated Press got a picture, just at this moment, of the Bishop of Tremayne, soberly and quietly splendid, in his gaiters, and that silk apron of the highest service, bending across one of the tables toward Fanny. But Fanny had sat down only for a moment, for as the camera clicked she was up and on again, on to the next table, where Professor Tombwell had been elated by the offer of a "syllabub" and was stammering happily to the Gräfin von Strelsau on the subject of eighteenth-century recipes; to Lady Charlotte, breezily describing the killing of elephant in Ceylon; to the Bishop's wife . . .

Mrs. Dovey also went among the tables. . . . She would come out from the kitchen side door, a veiled zebra bringing a tray across the sunlit grass, and offer the dishes in the order of a social hierarchy worked out in her own mind. Thus His Grace the Bishop took precedence of His Grace the French Duke (that somebody had told her was an actor, but she did n't believe such a thing! A Duke to demean himself!). Then, having pressed a meat pie or a chocolate whip upon Romano, Mrs. Dovey was distracted by her wondering admiration of Her Grace the French Duchess's plumed hat. Then, having urged Zaza to try a "pasty," she proceeded to the Austrian Count and Countess. The Count (such a laughin' kind of gentleman) was quite gallant with Mrs. Dovey, and congratulated her upon the beauty of her toque; and he said to "the Bride Herself, who he was setting with, and they was both of 'em 'eatin 'merrangs': '*Mrs. Dovey also looks like a Bride!*'" But her proudest moment was when the reporter from the *Western Mail*, who had been dancing up and down for a catch like a zealous wicket keeper, mistook her for Lady Charlotte Pink — !

The delightful "breakfast" proceeded.

The glasses were filled and refilled (the glasses themselves were of a slender beauty that enchanted the fastidious soul of Mary von Strelsau) — and Waldorf Pink rose up to help dispense this champagne (the mysterious case of Veuve Clicquot 1928 was discovered to be from Fritzl). The Bishop proposed the health of the Bride and Bridegroom, and made a benevolent erudite little speech, in the course of which he was allusive (as a "First" in *Litterae Humaniores* may be) on the subject of the Bridegroom's renunciation of Aphrodite for Sophie — "might he also dare to pronounce that name Σοφῶς?"

Mrs. Dovey was heard to clap the loudest of all at this final learned quip. Then Christopher replied, in a short speech informed by gratitude and affection. . . . He ended by saying that "as to the Lady in his past," whom the Bishop had unkindly referred to, he would prefer to have her looked upon as a kind of wild oat that had blossomed into a quite respectable harvest — whose profits enabled him to offer, very humbly, a small check for restoration of the tower of his cousin's church —

As he sat down, Benjamin sprang to his feet in astonished delight, and then thanked him with a most comical endearing mixture of his pulpit and his domestic manner — and followed up with a couple of jovial jokes about "matrimony."

There was more applause. And Lady Charlotte was heard to repeat loudly that there was "nothing like marriage for keeping you fit."

Then there was more champagne, and more pasties and more meringues for those who could still eat. . . . Zaza, who had been sitting blissfully with Romano, decided it was time she seemed a little wayward again, and came over and sat with the Bishop. She delighted him, immediately, for as a connoisseur of souls he perceived at once that hers had a courage and a curious recondite honesty. At Zaza's suggestion, she and the Bishop walked and talked together under the trees, and in their wandering came upon the rabbit hutches; of which one contained a pale pink rabbit. This delighted Zaza and deeply interested the Bishop (neither of them knowing that Loo had wished his favorite rabbit to look festive, and dyed it with red ink mixed with water). Zaza gave the pink rabbit a fragment of meringue that she was carrying. As they walked away they met a red-moustached man, in a bowler hat, looking very hot (he had just been helping get the piano out on to the lawn). He touched his bowler and said "Your Grace," and stared superstitiously at Zaza's black plumes.

Meanwhile, Fanny Columin had struck up a quiet friendship with Romano, as they discovered a common passion for herb gardens. She took him to see hers; and he told her about the one his aunt had had in Normandy. . . . Fritzl found them by the camellia hedge. He was now in a mad mood and made Fanny waltz round the sundial with him. And then they went back to the upper lawn, which had the house and the café on one end, and the hedge of pale pink rhododendrons at the other. And since the piano had been brought out (Sabrina's idea), Fritzl sat down and began to play the "Blue Danube" — his sheer high spirits evoking something of that waltz's sentimental magic from that piano (which was tinkly with damp).

Immediately Benjamin opened the ball with the

Bishop's wife; Romano waltzed gracefully with Fanny (she'd decided now he was "a dear," and she really *would* find time to see him at the Tremayne cinema); Waldorf and Lady Charlotte swung round and round, their intense vitality spinning them into a kind of human top; Professor Tombwell absently revolved with Button, saying, to make conversation, that he hoped her husband the Bishop didn't object to her dancing? Loo, after a little hesitation, asked Mary von Strelsau if she would dance with him. (And Christopher, watching, thought that it was impossible to imagine that that laughing whirling creature had ever been Hamnet Peabody's "poor aunt.") Since she and Fritzl returned from the Grand Canyon she had grown quite plump; and seemed to have caught some of Fritzl's own airs of golden folly. . . .

Christopher himself did not dance, because he could not. (Alice had never allowed him to.) But he strolled around, talking to everyone in turn, and vaguely conducting that lilting waltz with his hands. Sabrina, pirouetting by herself, called to him to dance with her. But he refused, and she laughed, shook back her shining hair, and went twirling and spinning away on the tips of her toes, her scarlet skirts fluting out stiff against the dark green leaves and pale pink clusters of the rhododendrons, the Angel without Tobias. . . .

Zaza and the Bishop did not dance either, but came and sat down with Sophie. And during the animated course of their talk the Bishop said he would like to demand the privilege of paying the Bride a personal compliment. Sophie, betraying an unexpected dimple, granted him the privilege. So he said that it was many years since he had wished to offer a lady the adjective "stately," but that, if he might say so, Mrs. Christopher Columin had impressed him as a "most discreet and stately bride!"

Sophie thanked him. And said that as she was inclined to be plump, it was appropriate she *should* be a little stately!

The Bishop nodded, faintly amused. He did not say that he also approved of her type of figure, one secular compliment being all he allowed himself in one day.

Then Zaza engaged him in conversation again. She asked him whether he thought it would have a bad effect on the village of St. Tad's if she were to give her hat to the "zebra woman" who had served them, and who had told Sabrina that if ever she were to put on that hat she would "die happy"?

While they were talking Sophie's mind became detached, and she gave herself up to a sense of her own happiness; and to contemplating the *Fête Champêtre* before her eyes. Fritzl was now playing the *Rosenkavalier* waltz, and its interpretation by the rustic tinkling piano seemed to accord exactly with the scene.

Sophie, in her pearly stiff satin, sat looking calm,

and feeling deeply moved. She thought how curious were the chances by which this distant American cousin had come into her life. And she remembered how in that first meeting she had been amused by his simplicity yet surprised by his charm.

She watched him now, as he posed, courteously, for the little photographer from Tremayne. And her ironical humor, and her tender heart, were satisfied.

The wedding continued to fill the verbal gossip columns of St. Tad's for more than the summer and winter after it took place. And when Sophie and Christopher had long settled down to a happiness which fulfilled their expectation, the cottagers still talked of that unprecedented mating of the parson's cousin (the Owner of Twenty Ranches!) with the French lady (who possessed an island on the way to India and who had given Miss Sabrina a necklace of real pearls). Over again the red-moustached man would tell how he had come upon the Bishop and that Foreign Duchess giving meringues to the young rabbits; and how Mrs. — our Mrs. — Columin had picked a bunch of camellias off the hedge and how the Austrian Count had taken two and set one above his ear and bit another between his beard and moustache, and seized our Mrs. Columin about the waist and waltzed her round. And Giles the verger had stories on end: about the goings-on in the vestry when they were all signing the register, and how Parson had kissed the French bride and the bridegroom had embraced Mrs. — *our* — Mrs. Columin and Miss Sabrina too, and they was all laughing one moment and near crying the next, and Master Loo looked a real young gentleman in his long trousers.

And the three chosen matrons who had "helped," with Mrs. Dovey, had enough information to beguile the evenings of two winters. About the "breakfast" itself — the quantity and quality of the food — the wine, the flower decorations, the silver and linen upon the tables, the lace-edged table napkins, the crystal jugs and glasses, the gold-and-white best china cups (and how the Bishop's wife herself had said to one of them: "You don't see china like this often nowadays"). And about Miss Button — all the way from Egypt — and then the bride's "things" upstairs! (Mrs. Dovey had led that furtive expedition up to the bridal chamber.) With nods, and exclamations, and reminiscent sighs of respect (and in whispers when the men were about), it was told, and retold, that the French lady's petticoats were some of pink satin, and some of blue, and others of pure white! . . . And there was lace — real lace and wonderfully fine, here! and there! — trimming, and inset. . . . Everything she had — this — and them! — dainty beyond imagining. . . . And as for her nightgowns, and what, Mrs. Dovey had explained, must be her *négligé*. Such gleaming softness! Such rosy ruffling! Also it was affirmed that the French lady washed herself in pure bridges of the Seine and pausing on the bridge in the summer dusk, and going on again — or, when the voice of one of the Charming Women says "Jean — " and he does not hear, he thinks of Sabrina; and sees her with his heart; and desperately wants her beside him, on a rock — sweet and laughing and utterly indifferent, her eyes narrowed against the sun, and the wind blowing back her hair.